Sarah Starts Living

GINA MEDVEDZ

BALBOA.
PRESS

A DIVISION OF HAY HOUSE

Balboa Press books may be ordered through booksellers or by contacting:

Balboa Press
A Division of Hay House
1663 Liberty Drive
Bloomington, IN 47403
www.balboapress.com
1 (877) 407-4847

Print information available on the last page.

ISBN: 978-1-5043-2986-6 (sc)
ISBN: 978-1-5043-2988-0 (hc)
ISBN: 978-1-5043-2987-3 (e)

Library of Congress Control Number: 2015904089

Balboa Press rev. date: 07/31/2015

In memory of Sr. M. Doretta Logoyda,
S.S.N.D., beloved aunt and beautiful soul.
For my parents, Gene and Gail Ginda, who
always thought I would write a book.

Transition

SARAH'S STOMACH DROPS AS THEY enter her daughter's assigned room. There, lying on the bottom bunk is Bethany's roommate, Lexi. Although the girls have chatted on the phone about the logistics of everything, such as who would bring the TV or the refrigerator, Sarah could never have pictured the girl who leaps up and pulls Bethany into a bear hug.

"Roomie! You made it!" Lexi cries. They seem happy in that moment, a perfect study in contradiction: Bethany, with her flowing hippie-skirt and tie-dyed t-shirt, and Lexi, in her leather mini-skirt, black and white striped leggings, and combat boots. After listening for a while to Lexi's endless chatter, Sarah's husband Jeff starts eyeing the door.

"Ready?" he asks Sarah in a low voice. She scans the room. There isn't much else she can do here, and it seems as though she and Jeff are intruding on the girls' private time.

1

"Is there anything else you need?" Sarah asks Bethany.

"No, Mom. We're great."

We. They are already "we." Sarah knows Bethany will do well. On the day the acceptance letter arrived from Boston University, her daughter ran in circles with a silly grin stretching from ear to ear. High school was never a challenge for Bethany. Boston is a top-rated research school and this is her grand opportunity to excel.

Still, Sarah will miss her. She loves the sound of Bethany's guitar echoing down the hall from upstairs and her excitement when she bounds through the front door after school. Sarah is the kind of mother who loves to have her kid around. The kind that celebrates school holidays and hates when summer ends. Bethany is a joy in her life. Her only joy, if she's honest. Jeff's great, but their relationship is comfortable, predictable. It lacks the enthusiasm that Bethany brings every day with her new ideas and interests to explore. Sarah and Jeff wanted her to experience as much as possible, so they went on road trips, travelled throughout Europe, and visited exotic locations as often as their budget allowed. Their efforts were worth it; Bethany loved England and wants to study abroad there.

Jeff hugs his daughter goodbye and tears come fast to Sarah's eyes. She's amazed how quickly Bethany has grown into a young adult before her eyes. Her little girl isn't crying, though. She's energized and ready, and she'll be fine. Now, if only Sarah could feel so confident.

The ride home is quiet. After a discussion of Lexi's piercings and a disagreement over what to call the electric blue color of her hair, Sarah falls asleep. She dreams that she's sitting in a waiting room when the doctor suddenly appears in his white coat, lifts a hatchet, and chops off her left arm. She awakens to find drool flowing out of the left side of her mouth and her arm tingling with pins and needles.

Sarah spends the next morning raking leaves and cleaning out the flowerbeds. Later as she showers, the warm water feels wonderful coursing over her sore muscles. The dirt under her fingernails will still be there next week, but she can make herself presentable enough for the bowling alley. Jeff has a tournament with his team, the Bay City Rollers. Allentown Pennsylvania is hardly a bay city, but Jeff's best friend Donny thought it was the coolest name, and the rest of the guys didn't have the heart to shoot it down.

Sarah doesn't mind the tournaments. She likes the other wives well enough, and they've built relationships over time. The conversation is light, usually about the kids or the latest episodes of their favorite shows. Donny's wife Amy is sweet. They can't have kids, and Amy has taken an interest in Bethany's life. Donny and Jeff lived next door to each other growing up. As the wives of such close childhood friends, Sarah and Amy formed a sisterly relationship. They might not have chosen each other, but fate has pushed them together. Shared experiences have paved a rich history, and Sarah is grateful to have Amy in her life.

When Sarah arrives at the bowling alley, she walks around the table, exchanging air-kisses with the other wives.

"Who are you talking about?" she asks, after catching the tail-end of Allison's whining.

"My brother's in town," explains Allison. "His kids make a mess and never clean up, and it's driving me crazy. I can't wait for them to leave. Why does this always happen to me?"

"You think you have problems?" asks Kate. "I have a pain in my side that won't go away. It feels like butterflies most of the time, but then suddenly, it's like someone is thrusting a pencil through my ribs from the inside out."

"You should go to the doctor, Kate," offers Amy, "that doesn't sound right."

"I know!" says Kate. "What do you think it is?"

Everyone ventures a diagnosis, and Kate's mysterious illness seems to subside from a dose of opinions. Sarah considers her hypochondriac symptoms to be a cry for attention, and Kate's banter flows in one ear and out the other.

After what feels like hours, Jeff's hooting and hollering mercifully interrupts their conversation. Another strike lands the Rollers in first place. After high-fives all around, Jeff goes off to the bar for a drink. Sarah is hoping they can leave soon. She has had her share of bowling alley fun. She's looking forward to climbing into bed with her novel. Forty-five minutes later, Jeff looks like he's been celebrating a little too much at the bar, so Sarah offers to drive. On the drive home, she wonders what tomorrow will be like, her first Monday without Bethany. On Mondays, she does laundry and grocery shopping, but really, there isn't that much laundry now that Bethany is gone. Cooking for two people will be strange too. What is she supposed to do with that third chicken breast in the package? She could devise a system of freezing every third breast, until she has two frozen ones, which could then be thawed for a meal. *Wow.* Is this what her life decisions will be like from now on, and if so, will she die of boredom?

The bed looks appealing. After a quick shower to remove the cigarette smell, Sarah dries her shoulder-length, chestnut-colored hair, grabs her book and reading glasses, and climbs into their king-sized haven. Jeff is already in bed snoring quietly. She gazes at his gray stubble and his salt and pepper hair, and she feels blessed. She leans over and kisses him lightly on the lips. Jeff is a great husband and father. His work in sanitation brings in a decent income, and they've been smart about putting money away. Their parents are generous too, and she's grateful. There hasn't been a time when she wished for more. Tonight though, something feels different, and it goes beyond the new reality of Bethany living in Boston. An awareness dawns of a newly formed space in her heart that needs to be filled. Tomorrow she'll call Desiree. Des always knows how to make her feel better.

———◦◦◦❦◦◦◦———

When Sarah awakens, Jeff is already gone. She brushes her teeth, washes up, and throws on her favorite jeans and a gray, long sleeved t-shirt. Jeff has made coffee, she pours herself a cup and snuggles on the couch with their labradoodle, Click. He rests his big head on her thigh, and she runs her fingers through his silky, beige curls, wondering why she still can't shake this strange feeling of emptiness. She dials Des, thankful that her friend has a flexible work schedule. Des deals in high-end accessories, which she buys in New York and sells at home parties here in the Lehigh Valley. Women clamor for the name-brand purses, shoes, and costume jewelry that she sells at prices so low it seems illegal.

Des picks up on the third ring. "Hey Baby! How are you?" she asks.

"I'm alright. Actually no, I'm not alright- I suck. Something is wrong with me." Sarah sounds pathetic, even to herself. In fact, she is reminding herself of Kate, which is definitely *not* okay.

"Tell me everything. What happened?"

"Nothing really happened," replies Sarah, "it's just that I feel like something is wrong. I feel like there's a hole in my heart."

"A real hole, creating physical pain, or does it just hurt your heart in the hypothetical sense?"

"Yes, that one," replies Sarah. She proceeds to tell Des about the day before, at the bowling alley, when she had such an odd feeling of separation. She almost felt guilty for wanting to get out of there so desperately.

"You and Jeff should go on vacation."

"What?" Sarah questions. "How is that going to help anything?"

"Look, baby," Des responds, "This Bethany thing is a big deal for you! Let's face it, who are you if you're not Bethany's mother? You chauffeured her around for seventeen years. You cooked, cleaned, shopped for her, and carted her all over the universe; all so she wouldn't grow up to be an ignorant fool like me. This is your time now. You're going to have to sit with all of your pains and holes, and figure out what you need to fill them. This isn't something I can fix for you, because you have to do it yourself. If it were me, I would get a massage, or have wild and noisy sex with Bob. You have options now, and you need to take advantage of that!"

Sarah hangs up after they promise to get together soon. She knows Des is right. In truth, she's always right. Des jokes about her ignorance and the fact that she never went to college, but when it comes to common sense, this girl has it. Sarah knows needs to make some decisions about her life, but how can she go about that? She doesn't even know what her passion is, or if she's ever felt any, outside of her role as a wife and mother. Sarah walks over to the mirror in the entryway. It's been so long since Sarah focused on herself, she doesn't recognize the woman staring back. *Who is that woman? What does she want?*

———◦◦◦❯❮◦◦◦———

At ten minutes after four, Jeff walks in the door and heads upstairs. Sarah is in the kitchen trying to decide what to make for dinner. It's only been one day, and already she's struggling with her perplexing indecisiveness about what to cook for two people. The water in the shower patters like rain above her head. Jeff comes downstairs, pours himself a scotch, and wanders into the kitchen wearing faded jeans and a clean, white t-shirt. He looks like a catalogue model, one of the more distinguished ones for sure, but he looks pretty good for his forty-eight years. He slides into the booth and watches her as she throws together western omelets and a salad.

"How was your day?" she asks.

"It was pretty much the same. We had to pick up leaves after the trash run, so that's why I'm late. You?"

"My day was okay, I guess. I talked with Des this morning. I'm going to go into the city with her tomorrow to help her shop for inventory. I don't know if we'll be back in time for dinner, so you might have to fend for yourself." She places the plates on the table and seats herself across from him.

Sarah looks up at Jeff to find him staring at her with a strange expression. "Is that okay?" she asks, nodding toward his plate.

"What?" he looks startled. Glancing at the eggs, he says, "It's fine. Sarah, we need to talk."

"Okay, what's up?" She notices that he seems nervous. *Perhaps Jeff has a plan.* She hasn't even thought of that. She and Bethany are the ones who usually organize things. Maybe Des is right, and she and Jeff could use a vacation to get to know each other again, and set some goals.

"I can't do this anymore." Her neck nearly snaps, as his words yank her from her thoughts. *What is it that he said? He can't do what anymore?* She stares into his eyes, suddenly noticing his fear, or is it concern? She waits for him to continue, thinking that nothing will come out of her mouth if she tries to speak.

"You know as well as I do that this isn't working." His eyes fall to his food, as Sarah's eyebrows shoot up.

"I do?" she squeeks, shocked. "I know this? This is weird, because I don't feel like I know this!" She shakes her head, trying to rid herself of the words that are stuck in her ears like burrs.

"We don't have to make a big deal out of this."

"We don't?" She laughs instinctively, because this is such an understatement. *Isn't this the biggest deal possible? What's a bigger deal than this, death? No, death is not such a big deal, because then one of us will get the insurance money and life will continue. How does this work? Will I have to move? Can we afford college and two residences? Oh my God. What will Bethany say? Where will she go for Christmas?* It seems trivial and Sarah knows it, but for some reason, this is an issue. *Maybe we will still be living together by Thanksgiving. Thanksgiving isn't that far off. Do divorces happen in less than a month?* She doesn't think so.

"Look, Sarah, we've grown apart. It happens. We'll both be happier this way." He seems convinced, and a sickening feeling in the pit of her stomach confirms that he has given this much thought.

"I don't understand why you keep including me in this, as if I've ever even considered it!" She can feel herself getting angered by his assumptions. "Do you have any idea how much I love you? Don't you know that I would do anything for you?" Tears squeeze from her clenched eyelids and burn down her cheeks. "How can you do this to us, to our family? How can you think that I want this?" She chokes out the last word on a sob. Her body is shaking with a bone-deep cold, that won't release her from its grip. Sarah doesn't think she will ever be warm again.

Her mind is racing. *How did this happen? How stupid am I, that I didn't even see this coming? My God, have I been living under a rock?* Sarah reviews the past few weeks and months in her mind. Nothing stands out as unusual. Dinners out with Des and Bob, bowling nights, and family time with Bethany- all process through her memory. Jeff never seemed uncomfortable, or unhappy. *Did I do something to upset him?* Again, Sarah strains her brain, trying desperately to recall their previous conversations. They don't have sex a lot, but it still happens. Just last week after bowling, they were laughing in the kitchen, playing with the can of whipped cream. Was he thinking of leaving her then? Nothing is making sense to her right now, and she can feel herself shutting down.

Unable to speak, Sarah drags herself up to her room. Click follows along, watching her with big, brown eyes full of concern. It is only five-thirty, but with her head throbbing, and her heart filled with a pain she has never known, Sarah climbs into her bed fully dressed, and pulls the covers over her head. She hears the door open a short while later, and the unzipping noise has her imagining Jeff taking his things out of his drawers, and placing them in the suitcase. *Is he leaving? Where will he go?* A part of her realizes she is in shock, and that she is thinking he is packing for a trip, from which he will return. *He will have to come back eventually, won't he? He has no place to go.* At that thought, she hears his footsteps at the edge of the bed.

"I'm going to Donny's. Call me when you're ready to talk." Jeff stands there for a few moments in silence. When she doesn't respond, he walks out and closes the door.

—∘∘◦⟩◉⟨◦∘∘—

Sarah wakes up to the sound of her mother's voice on the answering machine. "Hi Honey. Listen, Gladys and I are heading down to A.C. I have comps at Caesars, so we'll be back on Wednesday. It won't kill you to stop by and see Sal. Make sure he eats something. You know how he is, and the last thing I need is to come home to a dead husband. Thanks, Honey. Toodles!"

Louise spends her spare time in Atlantic City with her best friend Gladys. She arranges bus trips, so that she and Gladys can go for free, and they use the profits to gamble. It isn't a bad set-up, as it keeps Louise busy, and gives her something to talk about. Occasionally, Sal will go along, but he says that it's crazy to throw your money away on those one-armed bandits. Louise always argues that it's other people's money, but Sal isn't buying that. "Once they give the money to you, it's yours. You have choices, you know." Deep down, though, Sal is a teddy bear. He is Louise's second husband, and he treats her like a queen.

Sarah rubs her face with her hands, and inhales deeply, surprised that she hasn't died of a broken heart during the night. She rises, throws on her pink terry-cloth robe, and makes her way to the coffee pot, which stands as an empty reminder that Jeff is gone. Last night, she didn't really want him to go, but now, she feels too embarrassed to face him. *Why doesn't he love me anymore? What did I do?* She squeezes the small roll of fat around her middle. She knows she should have kept up with those yoga classes. But surely, Jeff wouldn't leave her because she gained a few pounds, would he?

Sarah adds a sugar cube to her cup, and carries her coffee out to the sun porch, Click close on her heels. She settles in the padded, wicker rocker, and he flops down at her feet. It's chilly out here in September, but the sun's rays feel warm, and even though it doesn't seem to make her heart feel any better, she knows she shouldn't shut herself up in the dark.

Her cell phone buzzes with a text from Des, offering to pick her up at nine fifteen. Sarah groans. She loves these shopping jaunts in the city, but it can't happen today. She quickly texts back that she's sorry to miss it, but that she'll talk to her later. Des must accept it, because the phone remains silent.

Sarah wonders what she should do, and for the first time in her adult life, she feels lost. There's always been an unwritten timeline: go to college, get married, have children, and then raise them. The last part, after she raises her children, suddenly seems like a huge oversight, although she imagines that it ends with selling the house, and retiring to someplace warm.

She gazes down at the steam rising from her coffee, smelling its rich aroma, and feeling the warmth on her chin. Suddenly, she's overcome with the knowledge that everything is going to be okay. It is so peaceful, loving, and fleeting, that as soon as she acknowledges how wonderful it feels, it is gone. Sarah tries to rekindle the sensation. She closes her eyes and notices her mind frantically searching for that peaceful place, but the moment is gone, leaving Sarah bereft. She wonders if that feeling was God. She hasn't thought about God for a while now, and ponders whether or not he really exists. After all, if God drew her and Jeff together, then what kind of sick joke is this turn of events? What kind of God would do this to her, or to Bethany? She needs to call Bethany, but worries that it's too soon. Maybe after a few days, Jeff will come to his senses, and none of this will matter.

———◦◦◦❦◦◦◦———

Tuesday is karaoke night at Wannabee's Pub. It's not a big deal in the lives of most people, but Desiree Phillips is not like most people. Aside from being *The Accessory Maven*, Des is a karaoke queen, and quite good. Along with her husband Bob, Sarah and Jeff are her two biggest fans. When Sarah's phone rings on Tuesday around four o'clock, she knows it's Des calling to confirm the plans for the evening. Will they have dinner at the pub, or do they want to go somewhere else before heading over to Wannabee's? Sarah knows that if she drops this bomb on Des right now, she will insist on coming over and hearing everything. The decision is too much, and she lets the call go to voicemail. The phone immediately starts to ring again, and Sarah groans. "Please just hang up. Please." She is relieved by the silence.

Forty minutes later the doorbell rings. Sarah can't help but smile. Des isn't one to give up, and besides, who doesn't want her best friend there while her world is crashing down? Still wearing her robe, Sarah cracks open the door, half-heartedly smiles at Des, and says, "Hi."

Des looks her up and down, notices the dark circles under her eyes, the puffy redness of her face, and the rat's nest on her head. "What the hell? Are you hung over?"

"No, come on in." Click gives Des his typical jolly welcome, and they all move together into the kitchen.

"Do you want anything?" Sarah asks.

"No, thanks, are you sick? Oh God, you don't have cancer or something, do you? That would be terrible. I mean, we'll get through it if you do. I don't think I would go to Lehigh Valley for oncology, but the University of Penn isn't too far of a drive, and I could take you. I would definitely be able to drive you there."

Sarah stares at Des. *Do I look that bad? I probably should've thrown on some clothes this morning and maybe brushed my teeth.* "That's a really nice offer for a girl like me, but I don't have cancer. I'm almost sorry that I don't, because you're so supportive. Thanks for that." She shoots Des a half-smile, and pours herself another cup of coffee.

"Oh, you're funny. That's great. I am trying to be a friend here, and you are mocking me. So what's up then? Spill, because I want details." She grabs Sarah's cup of coffee and pulls it toward herself. Taking a sip, she scrunches up her face, before spitting it back into the mug.

"Hey! I was drinking that!" Sarah laughs.

"Well then I saved you, and you should be thankful. That was one of the worst things to ever cross my lips!"

"I know. Jeff usually makes the coffee." Her eyes fill with unexpected tears. Sarah is just now realizing the full implications of Jeff's leaving. She can't imagine this being any worse.

"What on earth? Come sit down." Des leads her over to the sofa. "Tell me everything."

After revealing the whole story, and using a third of a box of tissues, Sarah finally looks up at Des. "Can you believe this?" Des stares at her friend. She always liked Jeff well enough. He's funny and a great bartender. Des thinks that she and Sarah could use one of his Saturday night special martinis right about now. At the same time, Des always felt a little bad for Sarah. Sarah and Jeff just don't have the intimate relationship that she has with Bob. Jeff doesn't dance, he isn't spontaneous, and if Sarah and Jeff have plans for something fun, it's Sarah's proposition. Des always wished that Sarah had a more supportive partner. She needs someone who'll boost her self-esteem and encourage her to follow her dreams. Sarah wants to do some acting, and she could be a fantastic writer if she would just give it a shot. As much as she feels sad for her friend, Des can't help but feel a tad bit of optimism about the opportunities that Jeff's absence might provide.

"No. I can't believe this," Des answers; because sometimes, you just have to lie. Let's face it, just like Sarah, Des never saw this coming. In fact, this is the last thing she would have expected from Jeff, although she could never understand how he could be content with his mundane life.

"He must have just been waiting for Bethany to leave so he could get away from me. I keep replaying everything over the past two weeks, looking for signs or signals. Honestly, everything seemed fine! In fact, I think he has been happier lately. My God, do you think he is just so elated to be rid of me? Am I that bad?" Sarah grabs another tissue.

"Honey, I am not going to begin to guess at what Jeff is thinking. We need to focus on the facts here. First, you have been the best damn wife to that man. You cook for him, clean up after him, and basically add some interest to his otherwise tedious life. If it were up to Jeff, he would go to work, come home, and watch marathons of reality shows with those people who have no teeth and brew alcohol illegally in the woods. Oh, and he would bowl. Let's not forget that! Sarah, you're an angel to sit through those bowling nights and tournaments with him. This isn't all bad, honey. You're going to be fine."

"I'm not!" Sarah counters. "I'm never going to be fine again. I can't even believe this is happening. How am I going to tell Bethany? I can't even think! I have all these questions and it's so scary! Des, where am I going to live? I can't afford this house, I don't even work! My God, I haven't worked since I was twenty-seven years old! What will I do? I don't even have a car!" The realization makes Sarah nauseous.

"What are you talking about? Your car is parked in the driveway."

"No! It's not mine," Sarah sobs again. "I told him to put it in his name. I always hate making big purchases. Spending money like that is such a commitment and makes me feel sick, so I just told him to buy it himself."

"Well, honey, you're going to get to keep the car. You need to stop worrying about that stuff right now. Tomorrow we will get you a lawyer, and put your mind at ease. My friend Lauren is a great divorce lawyer, a real shark. I'm sure she would be happy to represent you. In the meantime, why don't you go jump in the shower, and come out with Bob and me tonight? You can't just sit here and make yourself crazy. Go. I'll call Bob and tell him we'll pick him up in an hour, and I'll wait here and watch some TV."

Sarah stares at Des. *Does she really expect me to go out tonight? Clearly, she hasn't heard a word I've said. My heart is broken. You don't just go out and watch karaoke after your husband leaves you, do you? Is there a protocol for this?* Whatever it is, it just doesn't feel right to Sarah. *What if I see people there and they ask me about Jeff? What will I say? God, this is so awful. The weird thing is that this major thing has happened in my life and nobody knows. My mom is in some casino, eating more than she should at some buffet, completely clueless to the fact that she has a soon-to-be divorced daughter. And Bethany, poor Bethany, has no idea that her father is sleeping on his best friend's couch, with no intention of coming home again.* At least, Sarah doesn't think he is ever coming home again. *But, he didn't say that, did he?* She can't remember what he said. Now that she's thinking about it, they didn't actually talk. *What if this is just a temporary thing? What if he is planning to come back, and we're just separated? Some people get separated and then they get back together, after they work things out. Yes! I need to talk to Jeff, now.*

"Look, I know you are trying to help," offers Sarah. "There is just no way I can sit in Wannabee's and pretend to have a good time while all of this is happening. You go, and I'll be fine." Des looks at her as if she has two heads.

"Honestly," Sarah pleads, "I didn't sleep very well last night, and I'm just going to take a long bath and then watch a little TV before I pass out. I'll call you tomorrow. Good luck tonight. I hope you kick Hairy Andy's butt."

"Oh, please," Des laughs, "I always kick Hairy Andy's butt. That boy has nothing over me! Seriously, though, are you sure? I don't feel right leaving you here, alone."

"I'm not alone, I have Click. We'll be fine, you go."

"Alright, then, but are you hungry? Do you want me to order a pizza? I can make you eggs."

"Des, I didn't forget how to cook. Go. I'll be fine." Sarah hugs Des, and holds on for a few moments longer than usual. "I love you. I'm sorry about all this." Des pulls away.

"Don't you dare apologize! This isn't your fault. We're going to get you through this, and you're going to be better than ever, I promise."

Sarah is hopeful. She can barely wait for Des to close the door behind her, before she runs to the kitchen for her cell phone and hits the text bubble. Jeff just needs time, she's sure of it. If they can talk, she knows he'll agree. Maybe she isn't the best wife, but she can do better. All he needs to do is tell her what he wants from her, and she'll do it. The keyboard pops up and she types her message. "We need to talk." His text comes right back. "Can I come over?" *Yes.* That is the answer she wants to see.

———∘∘∘⟨◉⟩∘∘∘———

Jeff taps lightly on the door. It feels strange knocking at his own house, but he isn't sure that he should just walk in either. Sarah, after trading her robe for jeans and a sweatshirt, is at the door in a flash, and she motions for him to come inside. Click does his typical happy dance, acting as if Jeff has been gone for years. Jeff notices that Sarah doesn't look too upset, and he's grateful. He knew she would see it his way, once the shock wore off.

"So, I was thinking," Sarah interrupts his thoughts, "and you're right. We need some time to reevaluate things. If I haven't seemed happy to you, please know I've just been frazzled with Bethany leaving. We just need to talk about what we expect from each other, and it'll be fine. It's smart. Bethany's gone, everything is different. We need to figure out what our life is going to look like now. A separation could be good for us, but I don't even think it's necessary if we both work on making this right. So, I just want you to know that it's fine with me if you want to stay here. You could sleep in the guest room if you want, although I don't think that's going to help us. What do you think?"

Holy crap. Now, Jeff is in shock. Looking at the hopeful expression on Sarah's face, he realizes that she has no idea that their marriage is over. She's thinking she can fix it by changing, or, worse, by changing him. He feels like an ass. Sarah is such a good person, and such a good mother. The same question that's been plaguing him for the past year is back. *How can I do this to her?* He must, though. He's come this far, and he can't let her drag this out any further.

"Sarah," he begins, "I don't know what to say."

"It's okay, I get it. We don't normally talk about deep things, so it's weird, but we can…"

"No, Baby, you don't get it." *Shit, I called her Baby.* "Look, I know you want to fix this, and…"

"I do!" she declares.

"Please, just let me finish." Jeff takes a deep breath and continues, "That's not what I want. My reasons for leaving don't have anything to do with you." She looks confused. "I know it sounds ridiculous, and I'm sorry. I just can't do this anymore."

"Do what, Jeff?" Sarah is getting annoyed now. "You said that the other day, too. I just don't understand what it is that you can't do anymore. Is it me? Can't you stand me anymore? Is it the responsibility of a family?

What? How can it have nothing to do with me? If you're leaving me, then *why*? You have to tell me why. I can't just keep wondering what happened to you. What did I do?" Sarah starts to cry. "I mean, what the hell...what's happening here?"

Jeff sits down on the couch, and runs his hands roughly through his hair and over his face. He'd do anything to teleport himself anywhere else. "Look, Sarah, I'm sorry." There doesn't seem to be anything else he can say that will make this okay for her. His therapist would tell him to speak in sentences that use the word "I." He gives it a try. "For a while now, I haven't been happy. I go to work every day, I bowl, and I come home. I feel like something's missing, and while I wish that you could complete the picture for me..." *Shit. There doesn't seem to be a good way to end this sentence.*

"I don't." She finishes it for him.

Jeff hangs his head. He can't look into her sad brown eyes. How he loves her eyes. It's torture to sit here while she cries, and not put his arms around her. But he knows that she will take it the wrong way. People don't just stop loving each other, and Jeff still loves Sarah. He just doesn't want to spend the rest of his life with her. She's a great friend and the perfect mother for his daughter just not the perfect partner for him. If there was something he could do to change the way he feels, he would've done it years ago. Jeff spent his whole adult life trying to get to that comfortable place, with a constant companion, kids, a nice home, and true friends. What he found was that once he had all the things he thought he wanted, it still wasn't enough. Two winters ago, he went skiing with a couple of guys from work for a weekend, and it changed everything for him. It was like a switch had clicked in his brain, and he realized that he was too young to stop trying new things. Life isn't about getting to a certain point and being happy, but about stretching limits, and experiencing new things, and creating. Jeff isn't doing any of those things in his marriage. He just doesn't see the possibility of changing inside the constraints of his relationship with Sarah. How many more nights can he waste sitting in Wannabee's, watching her friend Des sing, while he makes small talk with Bob?

"Sarah, don't cry, please." He hands her the tissues from the coffee table. "Honestly, I never wanted to hurt you, or Bethany. I just don't want this for us, because we deserve better. All of us deserve better. We need to show Bethany that life should be something that makes you want to wake up excited to start every day. We're her examples, and I don't want to teach her that this is enough."

"Is this some kind of mid-life crisis? Are you going to buy yourself a red convertible?" Behind her tears she looks truly curious.

"No, I mean, *no*, I'm not going to buy a convertible. Is it a mid-life crisis? Maybe it is, but only in the sense that it's a difficult time, and something has to change to make it better. Sarah, you have been such a great mother..."

"...just not such a great wife." Her eyes fill with fresh tears.

"No, I was going to say that you've been a great wife. I don't have any regrets about the time we had together."

"Ha! You just don't want any more of it! Nice. This is so unbelievable. It would be easier if you just tell me that you hate me, and I'm fat, and I disgust you, and then leave. I can't listen to this." Her shoulders shake, and she has these weird hiccup things happening, or perhaps she is just gasping for breath. She does feel as though she can't breathe.

Jeff crosses from the other sofa, sits next to her and puts his arm around her. "Sarah, I can't tell you that I hate you. I would do anything to make this easier for you, but I can't lie to you. I have to do this for myself."

"What about Bethany? Where will she live?" She starts sobbing again, when softly she adds, "Where will I live?"

"What?" Ugh, Jeff feels like an idiot. *No wonder she's so upset. Does she think I'm going to kick her out of the house?* "You'll stay here. Bethany is in school, and when she finishes we can sell the house. In the meantime, you'll stay here and I'll get an apartment."

"I have no job, Jeff! I can't afford this house. What am I going to do? Oh my God, I can't believe you think this is so simple."

"It'll work out, you'll see. We'll make it work."

"We're not 'we' anymore." She can't believe she has said it, but it feels good to throw it in his face.

He frowns. "I'm still me, and you're still you, and together we'll always be Bethany's parents. I don't want you to worry about that stuff."

"My car is in your name." She figures that she may as well put that out there.

"What? Oh, the title? We can change that, it's not a big deal."

"Okay." Her eyes fill up again. He was being so nice. "You should go."

"Yeah, okay. Are you alright?"

"Jeff..." she rolls her eyes at him, pretty sure she's never going to be alright again, and positive that she doesn't want to be around him while he looks so concerned and caring. Right now she wants to hate him, but he's so damn cute, and he smells so good. He needs to leave. She gets up and walks toward the door, and then she has a thought. Turning around to face him, she asks, "About Bethany, what should I tell her?"

"Um..." He's thought about the conversation with Bethany, but it always included both of them. "Can we tell her together?"

"How will that work, a three way phone call?"

She has a point. That might be awkward. "Can we wait until Thanksgiving break?" he asks.

"So, we say, 'Happy Thanksgiving! Your parents are getting divorced?'"

He smirks a little because he can't help it. Sarah always did have a sense of humor, although she probably isn't trying to be funny right now. "Yeah, we might want to word it a little differently."

"I don't know. It'll be awkward talking to her before then. I don't think I can lie to her." Sarah can't even imagine how she'll be able to speak about anything else. She wants to call Bethany right now, and hear her voice. They have a great relationship, and she knows Bethany will be upset if they wait to tell her. "It just doesn't feel right."

Jeff doesn't know what to say. *God knows what Sarah will tell Bethany if I'm not there.* "I would prefer to tell her together. Also, I don't think we should burden her with this during her first few weeks of school, you know?" He sees her face lighten as he hits the mark.

"Okay. We'll tell her at Thanksgiving. I still think it's cruel, but I guess there's never going to be a good time."

Their eyes meet and he quickly glances away. Guilt can eat a person alive, and that isn't going to happen to him. He needs to leave. "I have to go. I'll see you."

"Okay, bye." Sarah shuts the door. She feels better than she had this morning; better, and yet infinitely worse at the same time.

No sooner has Sarah closed the door, than her cell phone begins to ring. Thinking it's Des, she grabs it, and is caught off guard by the sight of Bethany's cheerful face on the screen. *"Shit! What do I do?"* She looks at Click and his eyebrows rise. His head tilts as if she has asked if he wants a snack. She presses the answer button and brings the phone to her ear. "Hi honey!" Sarah forces enthusiasm in her greeting.

"Hi, Mom, I feel like I haven't talked to you in forever! I can't believe you haven't called me yet. You and Dad must be having a great time without me, huh?" She laughs, and Sarah starts to shake from nerves. This is going to be even harder than she imagined. Sarah sits down on the kitchen barstool, and fiddles with her necklace.

"So, tell me everything. How is it?"

"Oh my God, Mom," Sarah can tell she's smiling, "It's so freaking amazing! Lexi is great, and there are six of us on our hall that hang out together. Abby and Kristin live next door, and Liza and Audrey are across the hall. Our resident advisor is really cool and she organizes all these activities for our hall, so we get to know each other better. We had this scavenger hunt, and it was so funny! One of the things that we needed to find was a condom, and none of us had one, so I said, 'Hey, let's go down to the health center.' So, we all walk down there, and there is this old guy at the desk, and everybody just looks at me. I couldn't stop laughing when he asked if he could help me, so then he looks at Abby and says, 'Is she drunk?' And then, Mom," at this point Bethany is laughing so hard she can barely finish, "Abby says, 'No. She just needs a condom.' Can you believe it? So then, he brings out a bowl and asks, 'What color would she like?' I almost died laughing. It was so hilarious!"

"Well, that certainly sounds like an adventure! At least now you know where you can get colorful condoms if you need them." Sarah takes some comfort in that, although she can imagine Bethany turning red on the other end of the line.

"I guess. So how's Click?" Bethany is an expert at changing the subject.

"He's great, honey, and he's right here. Do you want to talk to him?" At Bethany's enthused response, Sarah places the phone near Click's ear. Bethany begins speaking in her doggie voice and Click lifts his brows and tilts his head.

"Who's that, Click? Is that Bethany? Yeah, you miss her, right?" Sarah puts the phone back to her own ear and says, "He misses you, honey."

"Oh, I miss him, too. I miss you, Mom."

"I know. I miss you, too. But it will be Thanksgiving before you know it and you'll be home again. And, you can call me anytime, you know that."

"True. Hey, is Dad around?" Bethany asks.

"No, no he's not. Um, I believe he's out with Donny. I'm sure he'll be so sorry he missed your call."

"Oh well, just tell him I said hi." Bethany sounds disappointed.

"I'll do that. I love you, honey."

"I love you, too, Mom. Bye."

"Bye, baby," Sarah hangs up the phone and lets out a huge sigh of relief. Living a lie is exhausting.

That night in her bed, with Click curled up next to her, Sarah thinks about her moment on the sun porch. She desperately wants to experience that peaceful feeling again, but she isn't sure how it had happened, so she doesn't know how to recreate it. She closes her eyes and thinks about the color black. The girl who cuts her hair is into meditation and she mentioned that she thinks about the color black when she's meditating, because it keeps her brain from having a monkey in it. Or was it from having a monkey mind? It was something like that. So, Sarah pictures the blackness. After a moment or so, she thinks about Jeff, and wonders if there are any bills she needs to pay. I must get back to black, she thinks, and before she knows it, she is humming an AC/DC song that she listened to as a kid. She sings the chorus in her mind. Wow, black does not seem to be working for her. Sarah imagines clouds. She supposes that if God were anywhere, he would be in the clouds, so she watches the swirling shapes move in her mind. It feels comfortable and safe, and before she knows it, Sarah is fast asleep.

—ooo◦)◉(◦ooo—

Sarah's eyes pop open at the sound of the doorbell. *What time is it?* The clock says ten sixteen as Sarah peeks through the blinds and spots Louise's yellow Camaro parked in the driveway. She throws on the pink robe and her fuzzy, leopard-patterned slippers and heads downstairs to open the door. Louise has her hands up on the glass to block the glare as she peers inside. Apparently, she can't see Sarah coming because she nearly falls in as the door swings open.

"Well good morning! I didn't wake you did I?" Louise kisses Sarah on the cheek and heads right to the kitchen to put down her bags. "I brought you some head-cheese and liverwurst from the Polish guy." Louise always stops at Joe's Meat Market on the way back from Atlantic City. She insists on bringing enough cholesterol and nitrate laden meats to induce a heart attack. Jeff used to love this stuff, but there is no way that Sarah is going to eat any of it. She puts the packages in the refrigerator, and then starts the coffee pot.

"So I talked to Sal," Louise begins, "and he said you never stopped over. You know, honey, you could have at least asked him for dinner. He would have liked that. He and Jeff could have watched the Penguins game together."

Sarah looks at her mother. *She'll be so disappointed when she finds out.* Her mother has loved Jeff since Sarah first brought him home during spring break of her junior year, and Jeff and Sal really do get along well. Sarah puts out two mugs and the sugar bowl, and pours coffee. "Want to go out on the sun porch?" Click is spinning in circles in front of the door, letting Sarah know that he needs to go out. She opens the inside door and pushes back the slider. Click darts outside. Sarah sits down in the rocker, and her mother takes a seat on the wicker sofa.

"So, you're never going to believe what happened in Atlantic City. Guess." Louise acts like a kid with a secret. She pulls herself up to the edge of the sofa, and stares at Sarah expectantly. "Go ahead, guess!"

"I don't know, Ma. You won money."

"I did win money. Guess how much." She grins like the Cheshire cat.

"Why don't you just tell me how much?" Sarah feels bad, but she's just not in the mood to play games.

"Oh, you're no fun! Fine, I'll tell you, but you're never going to believe it."

"Try me."

Louise grips her hands in front of her heart. "Three-thousand, seven-hundred, and twenty-four dollars, can you believe it? I still can't believe it. You should've seen the look on Gladys's face as that machine just kept beeping and flashing, it was fantastic! I thought she was going to have a heart attack. She just kept screaming and carrying on. It made me wish that I had a camera.

I'm thinking that I'll take Sal on a vacation to someplace nice, like the Poconos."

Sarah chokes on her coffee. "The Poconos, that's the best you can do?"

"What's wrong with the Poconos? They have those champagne glass hot-tubs and heart-shaped swimming pools right in the rooms! I always wanted to go there. What, you don't think Sal will like it?"

Louise appears so disappointed so Sarah changes course. "No, Ma. I think he'll love it." Every passing moment makes her feel more and more awkward about discussing Jeff. There just doesn't seem to be a good time. Right then, Sarah realizes that her mother is asking a question. "I'm sorry, what?"

"I said that you're so distracted this morning. Are you sure I didn't wake you? Oh God, I didn't interrupt you guys, did I? Do you want me to leave, or did I already ruin the moment?"

"Ugh, Mom, no…don't go yet. Listen, I need to tell you something."

"Is it about Bethany? How is she? Did you talk to her at school?"

"I did, and she's fine. But it's not about Bethany, it's about Jeff."

"Jeff?" Louise asks. "Is he okay? He's not having that problem with his knee again, is he? I really think he should go to Dr. Moriarty. He really fixed Sal up good."

"Mom, Dr. Moriarty is a heart doctor. Besides, this is not about Jeff's knee." Sarah pauses to figure out what to say, but her brain is mush so she says the only words that will come, "Jeff left me."

"He left you? Why would he leave you? What did you do?" Louise looks confused.

Sarah's eyes pop and her mouth hangs open as she stares at her mother. When she can finally speak, she says, "I'm going to pretend that you didn't just ask me that. I don't know why he left, exactly. It was something about us deserving better, and being good examples for Bethany. If you don't think that makes any sense, that's okay, because I don't understand it, either."

Louise clicks her manicured fingernail on the wicker arm of the sofa as she comes up with a plan. Sarah can practically see the wheels turning inside her finely coiffed, blonde head. "Fine, I want you to go upstairs, and pack some things. You're going to come and stay with me and Sal for a few days."

"Mom, I appreciate that, really, but it's not necessary. Click is here, and..."

Louise looks offended. "When have I ever excluded your dog? Click can come, too. Sal loves dogs, and besides, maybe he'll take him on some walks. He could use some exercise."

"I walk him, Ma, he's fine."

"I don't mean Click, honey, I mean Sal! For goodness sake, I'm not leaving you here, so go get your stuff and don't make this more difficult than it already is, okay?"

Sarah knows her mom is not going to take no for an answer. It doesn't help that it is now eleven o' clock, and she is still in her robe. Louise knew something was off as soon as Sarah answered the door dressed this way. On a normal day, Sarah can't sleep past seven-thirty. Right now, she would go back to bed and stick her head under the covers, if she had the option. She imagines there can't be any harm in staying at her mother's. They live in one of those fancy retirement villages, with a pool that looks like it belongs at a resort in Florida. The guestroom is beautiful, and it might be good to hunker down in a place that has no memories of Jeff. After the car is packed, Sarah waters the plants in the sunroom, and grabs the head- cheese and liverwurst from the fridge. There is no way she is coming home to the smell of a Polish deli!

The ride toward Hershey is relaxing. Sarah feels some weight lift off her shoulders. She's glad for her mother's persistence. She texts Jeff and tells him that she won't be home for a few days, in case there's anything else that he wants to pick up from the house. Sarah considers suggesting that he stay there while she's gone, so that Donny and Amy can have some privacy, but then she changes her mind. She's still pissed at him, after all. Besides, Amy hasn't called her to see if she is okay, and she's sure she would have called Amy, if the situation were reversed. Let Jeff have their lumpy sofa, because she's going to be living it up at Hotel Mom.

The smell when they walk in the door is delicious. Sal is an excellent cook. His granny owned a restaurant in the Greenpoint section of Brooklyn when Sal was a kid, and he has some gourmet specialties to die for, like osso bucco and chicken cacciatore. He took over the cooking when he came into the family, which is a fabulous thing, since Louise's favorite gourmet meal is hot dog soup with boxed macaroni-and-cheese. Sal made it very clear after her first attempt at cooking for him, that there would be no more drinking of the hot dog water while he is living in the house. Sarah does love this about him.

Click runs into the kitchen and greets Sal before Sarah and Louise make it down the hall. Sarah hears his booming voice say to the dog, "Hey, Click! What brings you to my kitchen? Did you smell this stew all the way from Allentown?"

"It smells delicious!" Sarah drops her bags, and gives him a big hug and a kiss.

"Well, thanks kiddo! Are you staying for dinner? You'll get to have some." Sal glances at her suitcase in the doorway. "To what do we owe this surprise?"

Sarah looks at her mother. Louise looks at Sal. Sal looks back and forth, from one to the other. "Anyone have anything they want to say?" he finally asks.

Louise checks back with Sarah, to give her the opportunity to speak. When Sarah shakes her head slightly and looks down, Louise speaks up, "Jeff left her, honey. I couldn't just leave her in that empty house, so I brought her back here with us."

Sal looks at Sarah as if to confirm Louise's story. Her mother does tend to exaggerate, so Sarah understands his hesitation. "It's true." She shrugs her shoulders, at a loss for words. Before she knows what is happening Sal has his big arms around her, wrapping her in the most comforting and loving hug. Sarah begins to cry, and Sal just holds on tighter.

"Shhh," he whispers into her hair, "we got you."

Sarah didn't really know her father. He left Louise, or she kicked him out, when Sarah was four. Nobody knows what really happened except for Louise, and she's not talking. The only thing she will say, is that it was for the best, and she didn't need that good-for-nothing-turnip-picker to help her raise her little girl. Sal met Louise the year before Sarah found out that she was pregnant. He has no kids of his own, so he has a soft spot for Sarah and Bethany. Jeff is like the son he never had, and just thinking about it makes Sarah sob even harder in Sal's arms. She's so thankful for her family and friends. She knows that none of them want this for her, and that somehow, they'll help her get through this.

Lying in the guest room that evening, Sarah is trying to think about clouds when she hears the door click open. The room is dark, but she can see Sal peek in through the lighted crack. Click lifts his head from his spot on the bed, and his tail starts thumping.

"Hello?" Sarah lets him know she is still awake.

"Hey kiddo, you still up? Can I come in for a sec?" he asks.

"Sure. Come in." Sal walks over to the bed and sits on the edge.

"Listen, I don't know if it will help, but I wanted to share my story with you, if that's alright." Sarah nods and he continues, "I was married before your mother. I think you might have known that already. My first wife, Gloria, she was beautiful. Our families had known each other for a long time, and I always knew that I would marry her one day. After we got hitched, I was in the army for a while and we lived in eight different places in ten years. You would think it was hard, but we loved it. We had so many adventures, and the wives on base were close, so she always had friends.

We tried to have kids, but it just wasn't in the cards for us. Gloria had a couple of miscarriages, and after the second one, both of us knew it wasn't going to happen. I was pretty mad at God. My whole life, I tried to be a good person. When I was a kid, the threat of going to hell was reason enough, but as I got older, I realized that doing things for other people was what gave me happiness and made me feel good. I did everything for Gloria. She was the most important thing to me, you know? She was the most precious thing that I had, and I knew that she wanted a baby more than anything.

I started to drink a lot. At the time, I thought it made it better, because I couldn't see the pain in her eyes anymore. I started to do a lot of thinking, and the more I would think, the more trouble I would find. Eventually, Gloria left me for another guy, and I was asked to resign from my post. They were really bad times for me. I ended up living on my sister Maria's sofa, and I was miserable. One day, my mother called and told me that she heard from Gloria's mother, that Gloria had been in a terrible car accident, and she didn't make it. I felt like it was my fault," Sal paused and wiped his eyes with his shirt sleeve, "because I sometimes wished that she would die."

"It wasn't your fault, Sal." Sarah had no idea about any of this, and she hates seeing him upset.

"No, honey, I know that. The thing is, at that point, well, I was just so low. I didn't really think that things could get any worse for me, and I started to pray. At first, I was praying that God would forgive me for wishing Gloria to her death. Eventually, though, I just found it so comforting, that I started asking God to help me, you know, to help me heal. I didn't want to drink anymore, or think about my dead babies anymore. I asked him to help me find things to do that would make me happy, and eventually, years later when I felt whole again, I asked him to find me your mother, so I could share my happiness."

"God has a real sense of humor, huh?" Sarah smiles at Sal in the darkness, and she knows by the glow of his teeth that he is smiling back.

"You can joke all you want, but your mother is perfect for me. She's independent, she loves my cooking, and she loves to travel. But most of all, your mother needs love. I have lots of it, and because I give her what she needs, she loves me. And let's face it Sarah, love is all we need, right?"

"Like the Beatles."

Sal smiles again, "Just like the Beatles. So, know that you are loved. And give prayer a try, it just might surprise you." He winks at her in the dim light, and gives her hand a squeeze. "I'll let you get some rest now. Good night."

Sal ruffles Click's head and walks to the door. He pauses at the sound of Sarah's voice, "Thank you, Sal, for everything. And just so you know, I love you, too."

"I know kiddo. I'll see you in the morning." And with that, the door clicks shut.

Sarah stares at the ceiling and thinks about how lucky she is. Her heart still feels like a giant lump of lead in her chest, but Sal gives her hope. She closes her eyes, and asks God to help her heal. She hasn't ever really prayed before, beyond asking to pass a test, or receive what she wanted for Christmas, but she figures there must be a better way to pray than that. She asks God to help her learn to pray in a way that will make him happy, so that he can make her happy. It seems like a pretty good deal to her, and she closes her eyes and drifts off to sleep.

After a leisurely breakfast of licorice tea, quiche Lorraine and fresh cut oranges, Sarah takes Click for a walk. As she strolls past the man-made lake with the pair of swans that must be freezing, she comes across a bench and decides to have a seat. Her cell phone rings, and she's grateful to see Des' picture on the screen.

"Hey, you," she says.

"Why aren't you answering the door? I'm ringing your doorbell out here, like some crazy Avon lady who is hell bent on pushing lipstick! You're not still in bed, are you?"

"No, I'm not in bed, but I am at my mother's. I'm not going to answer, no matter how much you want to sell your lipstick." Des is so funny, and yet half the time, she isn't even trying. "You should come over here."

"Why don't you just call me when you get back? I don't want to interrupt your visit."

"I'm not sure when I'm going home, yet. Mom and Sal said I could stay as long as I want, and it really is nice here. The food's not half bad, either. You should come. It only takes an hour, and the leaves are beautiful right now."

"Are you trying to bribe me with fall foliage?" Des will come, even without the bribe.

"Yes, that and pasta e fagioli. Sal's got big plans for dinner."

"In that case, I'm in. I'll see you in an hour."

"Great. See you then." Sarah slips the phone into her pocket. She can use some time with Des, so this is a good thing. "Come on Click, let's get some exercise." As she walks through the tree-lined streets of the gated community, Sarah tries to focus on the beauty. Her mind keeps wandering back to Jeff, and the sick feeling in her stomach...then she'll have a moment when the leaves will rustle in the trees, or two squirrels will go chasing past, and she will feel like maybe it's going to be okay. Those moments are fleeting though, and Sarah knows this isn't going to be easy at all. As much as she wants to suck it up, and be the strong person that she always is for everyone else, she just doesn't know how she's going to get through this mess in one piece. How will she ever be the confident woman that she was in the past?

When Des pulls into the driveway in her fancy, white BMW wagon, Sarah is sitting in the rocker on Louise's front porch. Des steps out of the car looking as glamorous as ever, with her Louis Vuitton bag and Gucci sunglasses. How she ever manages to walk in those six-inch heels is a mystery to Sarah, and yet she does it with attitude and style. Des is one of those full-figured girls, and even though she is only five foot two, no one except her closest friends and family have any idea that she is so short due to her penchant for high-heeled shoes. Des walks up the path and leans over to give Sarah a quick hug and kiss.

"So, how are you?" Des inquires, slipping her sunglasses on top of her head. Sitting down in the empty chair, she sees that Sarah looks a little worn out, but she's smiling, and Des takes that as a good sign.

"I don't know, I'm okay, I guess. It's weird, because I feel like someone died, but no one did. I mean, I wish Jeff was dead, but not really. It wouldn't be better for Bethany if he were dead, but, for me, how can I see him and not be his wife? How do I just ignore that I love him, and I want to hold him, and have my marriage back? How do I do that when he is right there and I have to see him and just pretend..." She starts to cry again and Des pulls a wad of tissues out of her purse. After blowing her nose, Sarah continues, "He was my reason for everything, and now he's just gone! It's not fair. I deserve better than this from him and yet he acts like I want this. I don't understand how he can do this to me."

"I don't know, honey. I just can't begin to guess what he is thinking. Maybe it's a mid-life crisis."

"I asked him that. He said he guesses it's a crisis because something needs to change. Now everything has changed and I feel so lost."

"Honey, you just need to look at this as an opportunity to find yourself. I've known you a long time and I remember who you were before Jeff and Bethany, even if you don't. Somewhere inside of you is the same Sarah that tried to get me to jump out of a plane with her. Do you remember her? Or, how about the Sarah who called me at six o' clock in the morning the day her first article was printed in the Morning Call? Oh, and how about the Sarah who was only two belts away from her black belt when she found out that she was pregnant, and she cried because she would have to quit. Do you remember that Sarah? Honey, you're still that girl and you're so much more! Now is your time! You can have everything you've ever wanted, and you have nobody to answer to but yourself. In fact, it sounds so appealing that maybe I should leave Bob." Sarah shoots her a dirty look. "I'm kidding! I'll never find somebody who snores like Bob...he shakes the bed so much that it's like I'm getting a full body massage every night!"

"Jeff didn't snore."

"Well then, you don't know what you were missing. Good riddance, that's what I say. Seriously, though, what are you going to do?"

"What do you mean? I guess I'm going to get divorced."

"Well, I know that, silly! I mean what's next? You have to make a plan."

"I don't know yet. I need time."

"That's fair, but I wouldn't wait too long."

"Why?"

Des hesitates before she answers. Sarah is sensitive, and Des isn't here to upset her or push her further than she is ready to go. At the same time, the last thing she wants is to see Sarah fall into a depression so deep she can't shake herself free. "Honey, I just worry, that's all. I want to see you happy, and I don't know that sitting around in yoga pants or hiding at your mom's is the best way to go."

"You know, Des, you don't know. You don't know, because Bob is at work right now, and tonight he'll come home to your house and sleep in your bed because he still loves you. So, you don't know. I am doing the best that I can, and if that means I need to sleep at my mom's for a weekend, or a month even, then I'm doing it. I'm sorry you don't like seeing me sad, but I'm sad. Next year would have been my twenty-fifth anniversary, and I'm in mourning. I have to tell my daughter that her parents are getting divorced, and I even need to figure out what I'll be doing on Tuesday nights, because I certainly won't be hanging out at that damn bowling alley any more. Believe it or not, even that makes me sad, because I know those women well, and even if half of them do drive me crazy or bore me to tears, it was my life. I'm hurting, Des, I need you to get that."

"Honey, I do, I get it. I'm sorry, but I just want you to be happy. Yeah, I said it again. Please, I just want to help you."

"I know that, I do. I need to figure this out on my own. I'm going to pray about it, and I know that God will tell me what to do."

Des stares at Sarah, and wonders if she is losing her mind. Sarah was never a religious person. She was raised as a Catholic, but she hasn't been to church since she made her confirmation in sixth grade. "You think God is going to tell you what to do? What if he tells you to do something stupid, like move to Alaska? Will you do that?"

"What is wrong with you? He's God, Des, he's not going to tell me to do something ludicrous."

"Since when do you listen to God?"

"I don't know, since today, okay? It's not like I'm joining the convent. Maybe my life is so screwed up because I haven't been listening. Maybe this is my punishment, or a way for God to get my attention. So, I'm becoming more aware. I'm going to listen. Is that okay with you?"

"You know what? I think that sounds like a brilliant plan. If you think that's going to work for you, then go for it. In fact, I dare you."

"You dare me? You dare me to do what, exactly?"

"I dare you to do whatever God tells you to do. I want to see how this plays out. This should be entertaining."

Sarah looks at Des, trying to gage her level of sarcasm. "You're a jerk, you know that? Fine, I'll take your dare."

Des laughs out loud. "Fine, I'm a jerk. I kind of knew that, anyway." She sticks out her chest and shakes her shoulders back and forth, Vegas showgirl style. She winks at Sarah and says, "That's part of my charm."

Sarah can't help but laugh at her friend. "You're insane."

"Yeah, there could well be a little of that, too. You've met my mother!" The women laugh with each other. Des' mother makes Louise seem like a bore. She won the Powerball twelve years ago and has been living the wild life ever since. Right now she's in the Costa Rican jungle photographing howler monkeys and sloths, and from there she's headed straight to Guatamala.

After dinner, Des praises Sal for the wonderful food. They all feel ten pounds heavier, and Des is thankful to take home a bowl of his ricotta-mascarpone mousse with balsamic strawberries for Bob. After Des leaves,

Sarah helps her mother clean up the kitchen and heads for her room. It's an expansive second bedroom which Louise and Sal also use to store the bookshelves and massive desk that Sal needed before he retired from his sales job at Air Products. Sarah peruses the books, wondering at the eclectic collection, and trying to figure out which books are Sal's and which belong to her mother. A small blue book titled *Life's Little Energy Book* catches her eye, and she pulls it from the shelf.

Opening the cover, she turns to the first page and reads the opening line. "There is nothing over which you have control, and yet everything reacts to your energy. This knowledge gives you the power to make things happen. Even your thoughts are energy, and all energy vibrates at a certain frequency. Thoughts of love, joy, hope, and expectation vibrate at very high frequencies, whereas negative thoughts stemming from fear or hatred vibrate at very low frequencies. Like frequencies are drawn to each other, and understanding this provides you with the opportunity to put out only those thoughts which vibrate at a higher frequency, in order to attract those events and experiences which will create more high frequency thoughts."

Sarah closes the book and examines the cover. Of all the books she could have chosen, this one seems so appropriate. *Is this her problem?* Ever since Bethany began preparing to leave for college, Sarah has been miserable. Constantly worrying about money and whether or not Bethany will enjoy college is taking its toll. She's concerned about what she'll do with herself, and negativity has become the norm. Her bowling friends and daily routine leave her feeling trapped. Sarah thinks about her conversation with Sal, and wonders if this is her lowest moment. From here on out, maybe things can only get better if she just has a little hope. *What are those words?* She flips the book back to the first page and scans for them: love, hope, joy, and expectation. *I can do this!* She loves her friends and family, so that is easy. She certainly hopes things will get better. Then there is joy. How can she possibly be joyful right now? It's so hard to imagine. That one will take some work. The last word is expectation. What does that mean? The rest of the chapter breaks down the four words even further. It turns out that the love which the author is talking about doesn't have to do with just family and friends, but a bigger love that encompasses all things, and replaces all feelings of fear. It stresses the idea that we are all one, and so we must love ourselves and others unconditionally.

Sarah thinks about Jeff and how this gives her an excuse to still love him. The section about hope speaks about wanting positive things for everyone, including yourself and the environment. Sarah desires positivity in her life. The author encourages the reader to find joy in daily life, in routine tasks such as driving and cleaning, as well as the obvious activities that make us happy. Sarah isn't sure that she'll ever find joy in cleaning, so she moves on to expectation. According to the author, expectation is the sincere belief that the positive will occur. Nothing seems to be going right lately, though. This sounds like fantasyland to Sarah, but at the same time, fantasyland is oddly appealing in the moment. Sarah knows people who walk around acting optimistic all the time. *That is because nothing tragic ever happens to them, though.* Sarah pauses. In that moment, with that thought, she has a revelation. "Oh my God," she speaks out loud. "That's it!" *Nothing tragic ever happens to optimistic people, because they don't attract the negative!* She wonders how she can start incorporating this immediately.

Sarah walks down the hall toward the family room calling for Louise. "Ma?"

"Yeah, honey? I'm in the kitchen." Louise is pulling supplement bottles out of the cabinet, setting up her nightly regimen. "Magnesium?"

"What? No, thanks, do you have any paper?"

"Newspaper is in the bin outside the door."

"No, writing paper."

"Oh, there's a notebook in that drawer. Will that do? You should really take some magnesium. It will help you sleep, and almost everyone is deficient."

"I'm okay, really." Sarah shuffles through the drawer and finds a single-subject red spiral notebook. "Perfect. Thank you!" She hurries back down the hall, anxious to get started.

Sarah throws on pajama pants and a t-shirt, and climbs onto the bed. She pulls a pen out of her purse, and turns to the first clean page. On the top, she writes the words love, hope, joy, and expectation. Under that, she writes, "Today, I love my parents. I love my best friend Des and I definitely love ricotta-mascarpone mousse with balsamic strawberries. Who knew? Today, I hope that my life gets better. I hope that God gives me a sign as to what I should do next, and I hope that I recognize it." *Yeah, that will suck if I don't get the sign.* If only she had some idea what she was looking for, whether it was auditory, or physical. Perhaps the search can be part of the fun. She will pretend to be Nancy Drew, solving a mystery. Next is joy. *Yikes. Is it cheating to use ricotta-mascarpone mousse twice? After all, it does bring me joy.* Sarah puts her pen to the paper, "Sal's ricotta-mascarpone mousse with balsamic strawberries brought me joy today." *There has to be something else.* She looks around the room. *The book!* "Finding *Life's Little*

Energy Book brought me joy." *Or, was it hope? Whatever, it could be a joy.* She still needs one more. Click jumps up on the bed, and commences to lick her face. "What's the matter, baby, you want to play?" Click pushes at her with his paw, and she quickly flips him over and rubs his belly. He uses his mouth to gently bite at her hands, urging her to play along. Sarah smiles at him and says, "You're so silly. In fact, you're my third joy. Thank you for that." She ruffles Click's head and enters her last joy in the notebook. Now, what does she sincerely believe will occur? "I expect that the sun will rise tomorrow." That feels like cheating, but she is tired. "I expect to feel better one day." And finally, "I expect that God will help me."

Sarah closes the notebook and places it on the bedside table. After climbing under the covers, she switches off the light and lies back on the pillow. It's weird, but she feels lucky somehow. There's still a lump in her chest reminding her that something is wrong, but for the last ten minutes or so, she's almost forgotten what it is. She intentionally visualizes the clouds and tries hard to focus on them. She doesn't remember falling asleep, and when she opens her eyes again, the sun is beaming through the sheers.

"Oh, no, not again." Louise is flipping through the mail.

"What is it?" Sarah asks.

"Oh, it's the convent. They have this fall festival every year to raise money. Sal and I usually try to get up there, but for the last two years it's happened on the same day that we had other plans. Now, it looks like we won't be able to make it again because we'll be on that cruise with Maria and Tony." Louise's sister Theresa is a nun in Connecticut, so they don't see her all that often. When she was younger, the order was cloistered, and even the family couldn't visit, but they have changed a lot over the years, and are rather progressive now. Sister Theresa always spends the Christmas holidays at Louise's house, so Sarah has become very close to her. Sarah takes the postcard, and glances at the information. *October 27th, that's our anniversary.* Sarah just stares at the card. *Is this a sign?* After all, the last place she wants to be for her anniversary is here, near Jeff, so why not Connecticut? Being walled up with a bunch of women, who are smart enough not to get involved with a man, sounds like a brilliant idea.

"I'll go." Sarah blurts out.

"You will? Oh Sarah, she would love that! Oh, honey," Louise runs around the island, and throws her arms around her daughter, "this is perfect! I feel so bad when she doesn't have any family there. They make such a big deal of introducing everybody, and now she'll have you. Thank you! Now I'll be able to enjoy the cruise without feeling guilty."

"I'm looking forward to it."

"Well good, honey, that's the spirit. You can stay there, you know. Sal and I always sleep at the convent, and they put you up real nice. They have wonderful food there, too. That Sister Betty can really cook! Even Sal likes it, so you know it must be good!"

"What do I like?" Sal appears at the sound of his name.

"You like the cooking up at the convent. You said it was good."

Sal considers this. "Yeah, it's alright. I wouldn't write home to mother about it, but it won't kill you."

"Oh, come on, admit it. Remember that chicken with the oregano? You liked it!"

"Okay, it was good, alright? Why do I feel like we are arguing about this?" Sal shrugs at Sarah, looking confused.

"Aunt Theresa's festival is happening during your cruise. I said I would go, so Mom is trying to make it sound like I'm headed off to a weekend in the Poconos." She looks at Louise and grins, and her mother scrunches up her face and puts her finger to her lips. Sarah laughs,

"Anyway, I'm not expecting luxury. I was just thinking that it would be good to get away."

"Well, that sounds nice. I'm sure Theresa will be happy. Oh, and Sarah, just for the record, the food's not that bad, either." Sal grabs his coffee mug, winks at her, and leaves the room.

"Oh, shut up!" Louise chases after him, and smacks him on the butt. Sarah can't help but smile at their antics. She is so grateful that her mother has found Sal.

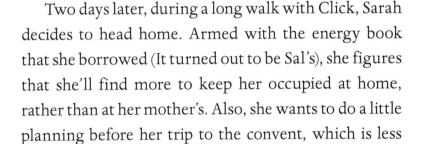

Two days later, during a long walk with Click, Sarah decides to head home. Armed with the energy book that she borrowed (It turned out to be Sal's), she figures that she'll find more to keep her occupied at home, rather than at her mother's. Also, she wants to do a little planning before her trip to the convent, which is less than two weeks away. There may be some cool places to check out on the way up to Wilton.

The house smells slightly stale when she enters. It's odd that you can't smell the scent of your own home until you leave it for a while. Sarah makes a mental note to swing by the craft store for some eucalyptus. She used to keep it in all of the bathrooms, but she threw it all away a few weeks back, when she noticed it was covered with dust. She loves the way it makes the house smell as if it's still the colonial era.

Click follows Sarah into her room, where she dumps her suitcase on the bed. She doesn't like unpacking, but hates living out of a suitcase in her own home. She places the energy book on her nightstand, and makes her way into the bathroom with the toiletries. Catching sight of her reflection, Sarah pauses. Does she look older, or is it just the lighting? Sarah feels well rested, but wiser, too. Life has a way of passing quickly, but she is determined to start paying attention. She must get back in the driver's seat, instead of allowing life to take her wherever it desires. Sarah nods at herself confidently. *I can do this. Life will go on regardless, so I may as well have a say in the whole process.*

———◦◦◦❧❦◦◦◦———

The next week is a pleasure. Sarah writes a letter to Bethany, which turns out to be a perfect way to communicate without fielding questions. She tells her about the book and reveals her plan to visit Aunt Theresa. She spends more time than usual with Des, who surprises her with tickets to see a show titled *Naked Boys Singing*. The two women giggle as they walk into the theatre and take their seats, but when the theater goes dark, the silence is deafening. All at once the lights are on, music is blaring, and a dozen naked men are dancing, singing, and swinging their stuff on stage. The audience is wild with screams and cheers, while Sarah and Des laugh so hard, that tears stream down their faces. Sarah forgets everything and has a fabulous time. Des is gratified to see her friend coming around a bit. There are still moments when she can tell that Sarah is ruminating about Jeff, but healing will take a while. In the meantime, Des wants to make her laugh as much as possible.

Sarah continues writing in the red notebook each night, and slowly it becomes easier to think of the joys. She appreciates that in the effort to come up with things, it forces her to focus on that which enriches her life. Last night she decided that she loves toilet paper, because truly, living without it would not be nearly as convenient as any alternative that she can devise.

Des gives her the information for the divorce lawyer. Lauren Zator is an old friend of Des' from grade school. Men fear her expertise in divorce negotiation, and Des trusts she will do right by Sarah. Sarah inserts the card in the zipper section of her purse, so that she doesn't have to look at it. She's certain that there will come a time when she'll need to call that number, but she just doesn't feel ready yet. Sarah doesn't want a divorce, and if Jeff does, he's just going to have to initiate the proceedings. As long as the bills are being paid, Sarah can live with the current situation, frugal as it is, simply paying for dog food, and her own meager lifestyle. At some point, money will become an issue, but she'll cross that bridge when she must. For now, the debit card on their joint account still works, and Sarah is considering different ways to earn a living. Writing is an option, but she hasn't done it for years; she has no idea where to begin. Thanks to Facebook, there are some connections from her past on her friend list that she could easily contact, and in a week or two, she'll reach out to them. She could always get a job somewhere, but first Sarah would like to figure out where it is that she wants to commit her time. At this point in her life, she refuses to work someplace that does not feed her soul. Even the thought of working in a restaurant or an office makes her want to crawl under a bed and hide. From now on, she wants her life to be interesting and inspiring, so she makes a pledge to herself to only make those types of choices. It isn't a full-fledged plan yet, but to Sarah it's a beginning. In these small moments of clarity, she's able to make huge decisions about her life, and it feels empowering.

—◦◦◦◦❦◦◦◦◦—

On the morning of her trip, she drops Click off at Des' house.

"Are you sure you don't want me to come with you? Bob would be happy to watch Click, you know that." Des doesn't like the idea of Sarah up at that convent all by herself. She can't imagine how being alone with a bunch of nuns is going to make her feel any better. "Tell me again why you're doing this?"

"Hey, this is your fault. You're the one who dared me to do whatever God told me to do, so I'm doing it." Des rolls her eyes. The fact that this little festival falls on the same day as Sarah's wedding anniversary is a coincidence, not some grand phone call from God. She told Sarah as much last week, when she asked if Des would watch Click while she was away. But Sarah gave her some song and dance about how God doesn't have a phone, and he's not just going to call her up and tell her what to do. Des thinks about how easily this dare could spiral out of control. What if Sarah starts believing that everything she decides to do is guided by God? Well, she imagines there could be worse things, but she just doesn't want Sarah living in a fantasy world. "Besides," Sarah says, "she's my aunt, and it must be terrible if your family doesn't show up to visit on the one day the convent has an event."

"I suppose you're right. And who knows, maybe they'll have movie night while you are up there." Des grins at Sarah.

"You are terrible." Sarah smiles at her friend. "Thank you for watching Click. I owe you. Come here, baby," she squats down and lets Click lick her face. "You be a good boy while I'm gone! I love you!" She looks at Des and says, "I need to go. Thanks, again." Sarah gives her friend a quick kiss on the cheek, and is out the door.

Sarah waves, hops in her Prius, and heads for the interstate. The drive up is uneventful, but Sarah's mind is racing non-stop. It is strange how much she thinks about God lately, considering that she hasn't given him much thought over the past thirty years. She hates to be one of those people who only talks to him in the bad times, but it's easy to forget about him when things are going well. The *Little Energy Book* has her thinking about using the power of intention to create the life that she wants. It speaks of God as the source of all energy, of which we are a part. As a result, we have access to the energy of God. Sarah marvels at the implications of this message. *Is she God?* She has heard that line from the Bible about how we are created in his likeness, but is this what it means? It makes sense to her. There's so much about religion that confused her as a child. As she grew older, she just couldn't bring herself to believe in the stories, and as a parent, she couldn't bring herself to teach those stories to her daughter as truth. Being raised Catholic, Sarah has plenty of guilt about this. She's always been spiritual, and believes there's something bigger than herself at work in the universe. She thinks Jesus is an amazing teacher, and love is the greatest of all things. Sarah passed those beliefs on to her daughter, and is proud of the thoughtful and spiritual young woman Bethany has become.

At exit fifteen, Sarah merges onto US-7 toward Norfolk. The GPS indicates there are only four more miles to her destination, and Sarah looks around carefully at the area where her Aunt has spent the majority of her life. Connecticut is beautiful this time of year. Most of the leaves have fallen from the trees, but a few persistent ones remain, hinting at the rich reds, golds, and browns that once sheltered their branches from view. Spotting the vast lawn of the convent on the right, Sarah turns into the driveway between the two modest white pillars. The lane is flanked on both sides by older pine trees, which seem to announce that something grand and important lay ahead. She pulls into the parking lot on the right, and shuts the engine. There are at least a dozen other cars, and Sarah wonders if they belong to the sisters, or to their guests. She leaves her suitcase in the car, grabs her purse, and heads for the entrance.

The Convent

WHEN SHE WALKS INTO THE lobby, Sarah is immediately greeted by an older woman with glasses and a short habit, who introduces herself as Sister Barbara. Sarah offers her name, and explains that she is here to visit her Aunt Theresa. Sister Barbara's face immediately brightens. "You must be her niece, Sarah. I haven't seen you since you were a little girl! How are you, dear?" Without waiting for a response, she says, "Please, come with me, and I'll take you to Theresa. She's anxiously awaiting your arrival." They pass a few nuns who are headed in the opposite direction, and the three women smile and nod when Sarah says, "Hello." She wonders about the rules. Is she supposed to talk to the sisters? Are they allowed to speak to her? Sister Barbara is friendly enough, but perhaps it's her job to greet visitors at the door. Sarah has no idea. She only knows that the nuns who drop Theresa off at her mother's for the holidays are always friendly and jovial. Sister Ruthie, one of Sarah's favorites, even tells jokes now and then. She always seems to be laughing and enjoying herself, so happiness can't be against the rules.

After a bit of walking, they enter a room that appears to be a combination cafeteria and living room. There are ten round tables set up, and a few seating areas with sofas, chairs, and coffee tables. Sarah even spies a television in the corner, and though she knows that her aunt always watches soap-operas when she comes home (she calls them her stories), it had never occurred to Sarah that Theresa was watching them here in the convent. It makes perfect sense, as how else could she know the storylines? Sarah easily spots her aunt among the sisters in the room.

Theresa entered the convent in 1944, at the age of sixteen. Back then, the School Sisters of Notre Dame wore habits that extended down to the backs of their knees. Their long gowns hung to the floor, and their hands were visible only when they were using them. While a majority of the nuns here are teachers, and participate with the outside world in some capacity, Theresa has always worked as the convent's laundress, and as a result, she leads a very sheltered life. She still wears the traditional habit and gown, even though most of her sisters have progressed to skirts and shoulder length habits, or no habit at all.

"Look who I have here!" Sister Barbara announces. A rotund Theresa rises from her chair. "Sarah!" They exchange hugs, and Theresa exclaims in her soft, sweet voice, "Everyone, this is my niece, Sarah." Around the room, she introduces her sisters, Assumpta, Betty, Eucharine, and Virginia. "And you know Sister Barbara."

"You can call me Ginnie, everyone else does." Virginia offers her hand. Sarah shakes it and returns Sister Ginnie's warm smile. She looks to be about Sarah's age, perhaps a few years younger, and Sarah wonders at what it is that drives someone to join the convent. The sisters who taught her catechism classes spoke of answering a call, but in her aunt's case, she knows that poverty was the deciding factor. Her grandfather had died in his forties, and her grandmother was forced to raise six children on her own. She cleaned apartment buildings to make money, but it was barely enough to feed them all. Theresa felt that it would ease her mother's burden if she were to dedicate her life to God. Back then, there was a lot of support for the church, and families were expected to encourage one of their children to enter a life of service. Louise had once told Sarah that it just seemed like the perfect opportunity for her sister, and that none of them ever considered that she was sacrificing anything by making this decision.

"It's so nice of you to come up and visit us." Sister Eucharine interrupts her thoughts. "Are you planning to stay for a while?"

"I would like that, if you'll have me. I..." Sarah thinks about Jeff and all that has brought her to this place. She isn't sure that now is the time to reveal her issues, so instead she continues, "I've been doing some soul searching lately, and I thought that this might be the perfect place for that kind of work." She smiles hopefully at Sister Eucharine.

The woman looks deep into Sarah's eyes, and with a knowing expression on her face, she speaks at last, "Oh, Sarah, this is indeed the perfect place for such work. God is everywhere, but we aren't always able to hear his wisdom wherever we are. Villa Notre Dame is an excellent place to listen to what God is trying to tell you. All of our earthly cares can fall away here, and our job is to focus on what God wants for us. I will pray that you receive your answers." Sarah likes Sister Eucharine immediately, even though her sense of all-knowing gives Sarah the jitters. Sarah has a feeling that there's no hiding the truth from Sister Eucharine.

"Thank you Sister, I do appreciate that."

"Would you like some coffee or tea, Sarah?" Sister Assumpta inquires. "Everything is set up on that table over by the wall, and Betty made a wonderful coffee cake that is there as well. Did you try that coffee-cake Theresa? I know you love your sweets. Shall I get you a piece?"

"No thank you, Assumpta. I already had two pieces this morning. I do love your coffee-cake, Betty. You should try some, Sarah. Nobody bakes like Betty," Theresa offers.

Sister Assumpta leads Sarah by the arm to the coffee table. "You can't be shy here, dear. God helps those who help themselves, you know." Sister Assumpta winks at Sarah. "Do you like coffee? I'm not a big fan myself, but I do love this Bengal Spice tea. Have you tried it? It has lots of cinnamon and will go great with Betty's cake. Here, let me cut a piece for you."

"Thank you." Sarah pours herself a cup of tea. "May I ask you something, Sister?"

Sister Assumpta seems surprised and honored, "Certainly! Ask me anything."

The nun looks at her so expectantly, that Sarah almost wishes she had a deep philosophical question to propose. Instead, she begins, "My mother told me that I would have to speak with Mother Superior if I want to stay longer than one night. How does that happen, exactly? Do I have to make an appointment?"

"Oh heavens, no, that's just a formality. Would you like me to take you to see her after you finish your cake? I would be happy to go with you."

"Would you? I would like to get it over with so that I don't have to think about it." She smiles sheepishly at Sister Assumpta, who squeezes her arm in response.

"You have absolutely nothing to worry about. It's not a test. Mother Superior just likes to know who is in the convent, and what their needs are, that's all. You will be fine." She leads Sarah back over to the others, and Sister Ginnie slides over on the pale blue, vinyl sofa to make room for Sarah.

"So," Sister Ginnie begins, "Theresa tells us your daughter is in her first year at Boston University. How does she like it, so far?"

Sarah swallows her crumb-cake and turns toward Sister Ginnie. "I believe she's enjoying it. She and her roommate get along, and she likes most of her classes, except for economics." She proceeds to tell the sisters about Sarah's roommate, Lexi, and her blue hair and pierced body parts. Interestingly enough, they aren't surprised at all, and Sister Ginnie even offers Sarah a new perspective.

"It makes me sad when I see young people hiding themselves behind a shocking appearance. We can only pray that one day soon they will realize their own magnificence, and shine forth in the glory that God gave them."

"That's beautiful, Sister. I like that way of thinking about it. Instead of considering them to be insecure, I always imagined them to be confident enough to do something crazy like that, and then walk around in public." Sarah can clearly remember walking into the dorm room, and worrying that Bethany was going to be in for a wild ride, with Lexi as a roommate. Now she realizes that Lexi just wants to be loved like everyone else, and she feels confident that Bethany is the perfect choice as a roommate for her.

"Yes, that's what they want you to think," Sister Ginnie agrees, "but the truth is, they're afraid they aren't good enough the way they are. Some even feel truly unlovable. It's important that we see the perfect soul underneath the shocking exterior, and praise them for their inner beauty. Only then will they begin to have confidence in the beautiful soul that they really are, on the inside."

"Are you ready to go see Mother Superior now?" asks Sister Assumpta, as she rises from her chair.

"Oh," Sarah looks at Sister Ginnie apologetically, "I hope we can talk more when I return."

"I'd like that. I'll be busy this afternoon, but you're welcome to join me in the chapel for vespers, and we can go to dinner from there."

"Thank you, Sister. I'll see you then." She looks over at her Aunt Theresa, who smiles broadly at her.

"Go on," she assures. "Sister Assumpta will take you down to see Mother. We can meet in the chapel later."

She walks down the long gray hall with Sister Assumpta, and eventually recognizes the lobby area. Sister Assumpta knocks on the door of a glass office, lined with long, gold draperies. Upon hearing Mother Superior's response, she pushes open the door, and Sarah follows her inside. The woman behind the desk is wearing a black skirt and jacket, with a white blouse that covers half of her neck. A long, gold crucifix hangs from a chain, and her dated, gold-rimmed glasses are the perfect accessory for her grandmotherly face. She's younger than Sarah had expected, probably in her late fifties. "Mother, this is Sister Theresa's niece, Sarah. Is this a good time?"

"Of course, Sarah, please sit down." Mother Superior indicates a chair across from her desk. "How was your trip? You are coming from Pennsylvania, if I remember?" Sister Assumpta silently slips from the room, and closes the door behind her.

"Yes, I'm from Allentown."

"Ah, yes, from the Billy Joel song. I have a cousin who lives in Bethlehem, have you heard of it?"

"I've been there, yes. The center of Bethlehem is only fifteen minutes from where I live."

"Really? What a coincidence. It's a small world, I always say. So, you're up for the family mass then. I know Theresa was very excited that you would be coming in place of Louise this year. How is your mother?"

"Oh, she's just fine, thank you for asking. She and her husband will be away on a cruise to the Virgin Islands, and she was very disappointed when she received the invitation for the festival."

"I'm sure. After all, who would want to go to the Virgin Islands when they can come here to lovely Villa Notre Dame in Connecticut?" She laughs aloud at her own joke, and then looks at Sarah with a slightly more serious expression. "Your Aunt told me about your husband. How are you doing?"

"Oh, I am okay, I guess." It seems as though Mother Superior is waiting for her to say more, but Sarah can't think of anything to add.

After a few moments of silence, Mother Superior nods, "I see." She pinches her lips together and says, "You know, Sarah, it is tempting to run from our problems, but the convent isn't meant to be a shelter from the storm." The scene from "The Sound of Music" flashes through Sarah's mind.

"Oh no," Sarah assures her, "I'm not running. Well, I am running, but if anything, I'm running toward God, and not away from my husband." Mother Superior offers an inquisitive look and Sarah continues, "I don't know, lately I've had these thoughts, about God, and it's just that I haven't spent much time over the years... okay, to be honest I haven't spent any time just thinking about God. So, it just seemed like it couldn't hurt to take some time, and..." Sarah looks up into Mother Superior's eyes. She shrugs her shoulders, hoping that she's built an appropriate case for herself.

"Well," Mother Superior says, "You're certainly welcome to stay. I hope that you can sort through your thoughts, and please, if you need me for any reason, my door is always open. Assumpta?" Sister Assumpta enters as quietly as she had left.

"Yes, Mother?" she asks.

"Please see Sarah to one of our guest rooms, and inform her of the schedule, will you?" She looks back to Sarah. "You are welcome at all of our activities, Sarah. I'm appointing Sister Eucharine as your spiritual advisor while you are here, so if you have any questions, she'll be able to help. I'm sure I'll see you around, and I hope you enjoy your stay here with us."

"Thank you, Mother Superior, I'm sure I will." Sarah rises from her chair and follows Sister Assumpta into the hall.

"How was it?" questions Sister Assumpta. "Not so bad, right?"

Sarah is honest. "I was a little nervous, but she was nice."

"Well, it's over now. I'll take you to your room. Did you bring a bag?"

"I did, but I left it in the car. May I go get it?" Sarah asks.

"Sure. I need to fetch my prayer book, and then I'll meet you back here."

"Okay, great." Sarah heads out the double doors into the fresh, fall air, and wonders about Sister Assumpta. She is definitely from another country, although Sarah can't be sure based on her accent alone. Are they going to pray when they get back to her room? This whole experience seems a little surreal. She really hasn't talked to her aunt yet, and the sisters she's met so far all behave as if she's come to visit everyone. They definitely act like a family, which is nice for Aunt Theresa.

Sister Assumpta is waiting inside the double doors and she leads Sara through a fire door, and up a flight of stairs. Before entering a long hallway, she places her fingers on her lips, and directs Sarah to the third door on the left. Once inside, she quietly closes the door behind herself and whispers, "I'm sorry, but upstairs we have silent prayer until vespers, so we have to be quiet. This is your room while you're here. Feel free to unpack your things in the dresser, or use the closet."

The room contains a small desk and chair, a tall dresser with five drawers, and a twin bed covered by an olive green bedspread. On the desk next to the bed is a small hurricane-lamp. Sister Assumpta pulls a printed piece of paper from the desk drawer, and places it on the desk in front of them. Pointing, she explains, "Morning prayer is from two to three in the chapel. Then, we return to our rooms and go back to sleep. At five, we awaken for private prayer, and at seven, we go back to the chapel for service. At eight, we eat breakfast, and at nine o'clock we celebrate mass. Our next service is at noon, and we eat immediately afterwards. From two to three is recreation hour for those sisters who work here in the convent. Many of the sisters gather in the chapel at three o'clock for thirty minutes of prayer before returning to work. We should head there now, if we don't want to be late. At five o'clock, we have vespers, and then supper follows. Our last service is at seven o'clock, and then it's back to our rooms for nightly prayer and bed. Feel free to join us at any time."

She smiles at Sarah, opens the door, and lowers her voice to a whisper. "Shall we go?"

The door to the chapel is propped open, and the two women enter, bless themselves, and sit down. This is the first time that Sarah is able to see the nuns gathered, and she is impressed by their numbers. There are at least seven wheelchairs in the aisles, and a few of the older sisters look as though they might be sleeping, instead of praying. Sarah folds her hands in her lap, and bows her head. For the first fifteen minutes, prayers are recited out loud. After that, the room is silent, and when ten minutes pass, Sarah begins to look around. *What are they all thinking?* Sarah notices Sister Barbara to the left of her, and while her eyes are closed, her lips are moving furiously. *What or who is she praying for so fervently? Especially since this is the fifth, or sixth, time set aside for prayer today?* Sarah doesn't think she could ever be a nun, and she wonders if she should have waited before she asked Mother Superior's permission to stay. When the bell finally rings, Sarah rises along with the other sisters, to head out of the chapel. She sees her Aunt Theresa walking with a few other nuns, and makes her way over through the sea of black and navy blue. Theresa introduces her to the surrounding sisters, and they proceed into the gathering room.

"I have some things to finish in the laundry room, Sarah. You're welcome to join me there if you'd like, or, perhaps you would rather go to your room? Are you tired after the drive?" Aunt Theresa asks.

Sarah contemplates her options. While she would love to spend some time with her aunt, this is all such a whirlwind, and the thought of lying down does sound appealing. "I think I am going to rest for a bit. Where am I supposed to be next?"

Aunt Theresa laughs. "Vespers is not until five o'clock in the chapel. I'll see you then?"

"That sounds perfect. Thank you for this." She gives her aunt a quick hug, and turns back to look for her room. The convent's layout is simple, and she easily finds her way. The silence here is lovely. Aside from the slight buzzing of an exit sign in the hallway, she can't hear a sound, and she finds it refreshing. Jeff always had the radio or the television blaring, and she realizes just now how hard it is to think with all of that distraction. Sarah sets her phone alarm for 4:45, and lying back on the pillow, she contemplates the life of a nun. *Do they really wake up at five o'clock every morning? Today is Saturday, so the thought that they do this, even on the weekends, seems insane. Tomorrow is Sunday, though, so maybe they are not as strict. After all, you aren't supposed to work on the Sabbath, right? Don't all religions practice that?* Sarah closes her eyes and contemplates afternoon prayer, and how difficult it was to sit there. Thoughts were racing in her head, and it reminds her about the monkey mind. She will need to get those monkeys under control if she is going to survive even a few more days of these prayer sessions.

When her alarm sounds, Sarah isn't sure where she is. She'd been dreaming her shoes were missing, and she was digging a hole to find them, when suddenly her shovel hit a book. Sarah used her hands to expose the cover, and realized that it was a holy book. She was trying to text Sal to see if he could bring a decoder, when she was awakened by the sound of the alarm. *Weird, I would like to talk to a dream analyst about that one!* Sarah sits up and slips her feet into her shoes. She runs a brush through the back of her hair, and shoves a tube of lip balm in her pocket.

—◦◦◦)◦◦◦—

Sarah makes her way down toward the chapel, and nearly bumps into Sister Assumpta as she rounds the corner past the stairs. "I'm sorry, Sister, I wasn't paying attention."

Sister Assumpta smiles at her. "Hello, Sarah, how are you?"

"I'm fine, thank you for asking." Sarah marvels at the kindness in Sister Assumpta's eyes.

"Are you heading to vespers? They're my favorite."

"I am indeed. What makes them your favorite?" inquires Sarah.

"Oh, you'll see. I love the singing."

Together they make their way into the chapel. Sister Assumpta walks all the way to the front, sits in the second pew on the right, and Sarah follows. Mother Superior stands on the altar, smiling as she makes eye contact with Sarah. Sarah bows her head, and asks God to help her feel comfortable in prayer today. She pleads with him to quiet her monkey mind, and to help her to focus on the work that needs to be done. It feels awkward. What work is she talking about? She isn't exactly sure, but she knows it has to do with herself. She wants to be on the right path, and certainly God must know what that path looks like for her? *If only he would speak to me and spell it out.* The sisters begin singing in Latin, in an offertory and response pattern. Sarah has no idea what they're saying, but it sounds comforting, and she can understand why Sister Assumpta finds it enjoyable. She wishes she could sing along, but finds that by focusing on the singing she's able to quiet her mind and pass the time. Before she knows it, the bells ring and the sisters all bless themselves and start toward the exit. Sarah follows along to the dining room, and looks for a familiar face. She finds her aunt, and pulling out a chair, Sarah asks if she will be sitting in someone else's spot. "Don't be silly," says Aunt Theresa. "This is the seat the Lord hath made, sit in it and be glad." The sisters who hear her laugh out loud at her twist on Psalm 118:24.

"That is a good one, Theresa!" Barbara comments.

"Ha," says Theresa, "I know! I'm on roll today."

"You should have been a comedian." says Assumpta.

"I know. I could have been on Johnny Carson. I really liked his show."

"Who's Johnny Carson?" asks Sister Kelly. Kelly is the youngest nun in the convent. At only 24, she is a postulant, which means that she participates in all forms of the community, but she hasn't yet taken vows.

"Stop making us feel old, Kelly!" Barbara laughs. "Johnny Carson was a talk show host, like Conan O'Brian."

"Oh," replies Sister Kelly, "I've never heard of him."

The older sisters at the table exchange glances, and burst out laughing. When they finish, Theresa says, "Who's Conan O'Brian?" and they all giggle again.

Sarah has a great time at dinner. The nuns are funny, and the rosemary chicken is very good. Sal would have approved. Sarah talks with Aunt Theresa about the latest news in the family, and gets some updates on a few of her cousins that she hasn't heard from in years. One thing about Aunt Theresa is that she never forgets a birthday. Faithfully every year, a notecard will arrive in the mail, and she'll fill every blank space with her sincere wishes, and her latest interactions with family members. Sarah will usually write back, and she realizes now that she's not the only family member who enjoys Aunt Theresa's annual missives.

After they finish eating, Sister Ginnie shows her where to place her dishes, and asks if she'd like to join her for a walk. Sarah is pleased to be outside, and they walk along the path that wanders around the building and through the gardens. After talking about the beautiful weather, and the unusually warm fall temperatures, Sarah decides to ask Sister Ginnie about prayer. She seems enthusiastic about the topic, and Sarah can tell immediately that it's something she's passionate about.

"Prayer is what keeps me close to God," says Sister Ginnie. "It is how I know what he expects from me."

"See," says Sarah, "that's where I'm lost. I don't know what God expects from me. I feel as if I'm not doing it right. I mean, what are you all praying about when you are in prayer for so much of the day? I just don't see how there can be that much to pray about."

Sister Ginnie looks pensive. She wants to give Sarah advice that will help her, but she isn't sure of the best place to begin. "First of all, I don't think you should worry about whether or not you are doing it right. There is no wrong way to pray. One thing that Matthew 6:7 states is that, "When you pray, don't babble on as people of other religions do. They think their prayers are answered only by repeating their words again and again." So, what that means to me, is that it's not necessary to know a specific set of words to say. Speak from your heart, and ask God to guide your hand. The more time you spend in prayer and reflection, the more you will become aware of those things which are holding you back from being the person that God wants you to be. So, then, you just ask God to help you change those things. Once you are comfortable with yourself, you will know that God is happy, too. If he isn't, you won't feel happy deep inside, either. Then you can start asking God to put you in those situations where you can be of service to others. For me, once I started serving others, that was a turning point. Have you been in your room yet?"

"Yes, I was there after mid-afternoon prayer," replies Sarah.

"Did you notice that there's not a mirror? Sister Ginnie asks.

"Yes, you are right, there isn't one." Sarah realized there wasn't a mirror in her room when she was getting ready for vespers. At the time she thought it was unusual.

Sister Ginnie sits down on a bench in the garden, and motions for Sarah to join her. "We are taught to turn our attention to others. But it's not only that. In order to teach us that it's what's on the inside that matters, we have to go into the world confident that we are beautiful on the inside, too, because God made us this way. If our inner beauty shines brightly enough, our outer appearance will be irrelevant. We see this in figures like Mother Theresa, Padre Pio and Ghandi. Their inner lights are so bright that it would not have mattered if they were hideous. Prayer is the time when we can talk to God and discover how to grow our inner light. As Matthew 6:6 states, 'But when you pray, go into your room, close the door, and pray to your Father who is unseen. Then your Father, who sees what is done in secret, will reward you.' God wants us to pray together, but he wants us to pray alone, too. When we pray alone, it is the most honest and sincere prayer. It doesn't matter what you say, or how you say it. It only matters that you do it frequently."

"I will do that then, thank you. I guess there's really not a big secret to it. Just ask for my own healing, and then ask for that for others."

"Exactly! I usually pray for myself, and for God's guidance in all I do. After that, I pray for all of my family and friends. Then, I pray for my sisters and our ministries, and then the religious all over the world and their ministries, as well. After that, I pray for all of the people who have no one to pray for them. I think it's most important to remember those that are forgotten. Jesus always helped the outcasts of society, and we should, too."

Sarah thinks about that. She always wanted to do meaningful volunteer work. Volunteering for the PTO was beneficial for her daughter and the other kids in the school, but she never found the work very rewarding. The other mothers there loved to gossip about each other, and Sarah avoided them as much as possible. When she returns home she will try to find someplace where she can make a difference.

"Sister Ginnie? How did you know you should join the convent? I mean, if it's not too personal."

Sister Ginnie's face glows. "It's very personal, but I am happy to share it with you." Sarah exhales with relief and Sister Ginnie continues. "I wish I could tell you that it was one event that caused me to decide, but it wasn't like that. I wasn't raised in a very religious family. I was baptized and confirmed as a Catholic, but my parents never went to church. They were hard workers, though, and they taught me the same work ethic. I went to college to be a nurse, but I somehow ended up with a degree in psychology. I guess I always had a desire to help people. One day, I went to a psychic with a friend, and it was amazing. She was spot on about everything, and when I went home afterward I was looking at a brochure that she gave me about past life regression. I decided to make an appointment, and during those regressions, she brought me up to the light between lives. While I was there, it was the most incredible feeling of peace and love that I have ever experienced. My physical body was gone, and I was a ball of energy. I saw my grandmother there, who was also a ball of energy. We didn't speak with words, but we absolutely communicated our happiness to see one another. The psychic asked me if I could see God. While I didn't see anyone who looked like my expectation of God, you know, the old man with the long beard, I did sense this large ball of energy in the distance. It was so immense that it appeared to be a giant wall, but I knew that it was God. She asked me to go and sit on God's lap. I couldn't really do that, because there was no lap, but I moved closer, and merged myself into the larger energy. It was so wonderful, like nothing I have ever experienced before, and I never wanted it to end. The psychic asked if there was anything that I wanted to say to God, and I physically cried, as I told him without words that I always knew he existed. She asked, 'And what did God say to you?' I was sobbing because God said that he always knew that I knew. He wasn't angry that I went through stages of doubt. Instead, I was made aware of his unconditional love for me, and for all existence."

"Wow," says Sarah, making a mental note to have a past life reading, "that's incredible!"

"I know! And the thing is, after I had that experience, I couldn't go back to not believing. I couldn't even say that I was agnostic, because after that point, I just felt sure. I know there's a God, and I know that he loves me unconditionally. I even know that I'm created in his likeness, and that my goal is to one day join again with him. In the meantime, though, I had this life on Earth to contend with. I loved my work, but I just felt that I wanted something that would support me in growing my relationship with God. I started to do a little research, and the School Sisters of Notre Dame seemed like the best choice. It's almost fifteen years later, and here I am with no regrets."

"That's a wonderful story. So you never actually wished that you had a husband, or children?"

Sister Ginnie laughs, "Absolutely not! I mean, sure, I thought about the what-ifs a lot before I took my vows. I had some boyfriends, so I knew what it was like to be in love, and I was a little unsure if giving that up was the best idea. I worried that I might meet the man of my dreams after I took my vows, but what I knew for sure, was that divine love is so much more powerful than carnal love. Once you experience it, you realize that it really is all you need. To see the good in everyone, and know that everyone is worthy of love, it's like a miracle. If everyone could experience it, there would be no more crime, or poverty, or war. To harm another individual becomes a pain that you inflict upon yourself, which makes it impossible. Oh Sarah, no, I have no regrets."

"You're so lucky, to know what you're doing. I feel so lost. I always knew my place in the world, and now I just don't. My husband left me. Bethany is at college, and now I'm all alone, and it's so weird."

"I'm sorry about your husband, I didn't know." Sister Ginnie looks sincerely pained.

"Thanks. I just don't know what to do."

"Sarah?" Sister Ginnie reaches for Sarah's hand and squeezes it. "God knows exactly what you should do, and all you need to do is ask him."

"It's funny you should say that, because that's exactly how I ended up at this convent."

"Well then, you are right where you need to be. Talk to God, and listen with your heart and I promise he won't fail you. I think you are much closer to receiving your answers than you think."

"Sister, may that go from your lips to God's ears!" The two women laugh, and Sister Ginnie stands up and pulls Sarah off the bench.

"Directly! Now, we should get back inside." Sarah is content as she walks along with Sister Ginnie, marveling at the fact that she's strolling along a convent path with a nun, on her way to evening prayers. Life can be so unexpected, and she's actually beginning to enjoy it!

———◦◦○ ✹ ◦◦———

The next morning when Sarah's alarm sounds at four forty-five, she sits up immediately and runs her fingers through her hair. Last night after returning to her room, she prayed for a bit, had a short text conversation with Des, and then spent the remainder of the evening staring at the ceiling while trying to fall asleep. A night owl by nature, these early bird hours are a shock to her system. She finally drifted off around ten o'clock, though, so she is hardly lacking for rest. Sarah dresses, brushes her hair, and wanders out to the hall bathroom with her toothbrush. A number of sisters are moving about, and Sarah spots a familiar face in the bathroom.

"Sister Ruthie? Hi!"

The nun turns to face Sarah. "Sarah, is that you? What on Earth? Fancy meeting you here in the bathroom at five in the morning! How are you? Give me a hug!" The two women embrace like old friends, and Sarah begins to brush her teeth. "So are you here for the mass, then? I just got back from a business trip to our sister convent in Illinois. How fortunate it is that I didn't miss you!"

"I know!" Sarah is sincerely happy to see Sister Ruthie. "I was just lying in bed last night wondering where you were and reminding myself to ask Aunt Theresa about you today. How have you been?"

"Acht," Sister Ruthie waves her hand, "I'm fine. You know, still teaching after forty-six years. There ought to be some sort of rule about that, but I would probably just break it anyway, who am I kidding? If I couldn't teach, what would I do all day, pray?" Sarah looks around, hoping none of the other sisters hear her. "What's the matter, you afraid someone is going to hear me? Don't worry, Sarah, the only one I have to answer to is God, and he knows full well how I feel about praying all day.

We check in with each other plenty, there's no need to sit around with idle hands when there is so much work to be done. I have an inkling that God is on my side about this, so I don't worry myself much about it. One day when I am forced to retire, that's when I'll worry. Until then, I just ask God to keep my body capable, and my mind fit. You know what I mean?"

Sister Ruthie is just as she remembers and Sarah grins at her and nods her head. "I think I do."

"Atta girl. Let's get out of here." Sarah pops into her room to return her toothbrush, and once again she is off to the chapel.

The sun isn't up all the way yet, but Sarah can see through the front doors that it's going to be a beautiful, sunny day. She's looking forward to the activities, as this is her first fall festival. She notices a few other lay people in the chapel this morning. Sarah wonders if she might be able to snag a quick shower after this, when the rest of the sisters will be in their rooms in private prayer. Rinsing off quickly in some hot water would feel marvelous. She's trying to decide what to do as she walks back to her room, when Sister Eucharine stops her in the hall. "Good morning, Sarah."

"Good morning, Sister Eucharine."

"I was wondering if I might talk with you for a bit after breakfast."

"Certainly, where shall I meet you?" Sarah asks.

"I will be in the chapel."

"Okay, I'll see you there."

Sister Eucharine nods her head, and floats away. Sarah assumes this meeting has something to do with her role as Sarah's spiritual advisor, and contemplates what they might discuss. She decides to skip the shower for now, and make an attempt after breakfast, while the sisters are working. Sarah wants to call Bethany, but it's only six-thirty in the morning, and no college student would be up at this hour. She chooses to use the time as it is intended, and enters into a conversation with God.

"So, here I am, at the convent where you sent me. If there is something that you want me to learn here, I hope that you'll bring it to my attention. I don't want to waste my time anymore, God." She thinks about her schedule at home compared to the one here. At home, she sleeps until eight or eight-thirty, has a cup of coffee, watches the morning show, reads the paper for a while, takes a shower, and is possibly dressed and ready to head out the door by noon; if she's lucky. She tries to get her errands done by three so that she can be home with Bethany, and then she starts dinner, finishes any laundry that she might have started, straightens the kitchen and then watches some television before bed. These nuns, they pray eight times a day and they still manage to socialize, exercise, work, and create. It is disappointing to realize how much time she wastes on eating, and contemplating her extra weight. "I want it to be different, God. I want to have purpose," she remembers Sister Ginnie's words, "please guide my hands."

———◦◦◦✢◉✢◦◦◦———

At six fifty-five, Sarah closes her bedroom door, heads down to chapel, and sits in the last row next to an older sister whose name escapes her. Father Murphy is there to say the mass and distribute communion to the sisters. He is clearly Irish, in appearance as well as name, and his homily doesn't put Sarah to sleep, which she appreciates. She doesn't go up for communion, since she hasn't been to church, or confession, for years. Her grandmother always taught her that she didn't need a middleman between herself and God, and confession always seemed unnecessary to her, for that reason. At the same time, her catechism teachers told her that if she didn't go to confession, and she died, she would go directly to Hell. It was difficult as a child, not knowing whether to believe her family, or the church. Sarah was determined not to raise Bethany with such moral dilemmas. Her solution was to avoid organized religion all together, and to teach her daughter about a kind and loving God; the type of God that Sarah would like to believe exists. She may not be absolutely sure about what she does believe, but she is clear on what she doesn't. Hell falls into the latter category, and Bethany never worried about the devil stealing her away to a fiery afterlife.

The mass is long, just as Sarah remembers, and she's grateful when it ends. She walks out with Sister Assumpta, who is genuinely happy to see her again. Sarah can see why her aunt is close with Sister Assumpta. As they walk to breakfast, Sarah remembers her appointment with Sister Eucharine, and she decides to see if she can weasel any information out of Sister Assumpta. "So, Sister, I have another question for you."

"Okay, great! What is it?"

"Yesterday at my meeting, Mother Superior had told me that she appointed Sister Eucharine as my spiritual advisor. What does that mean, exactly?"

"Well, Mother Superior usually appoints a spiritual advisor when someone is staying here to work out a problem. Sometimes it's because somebody close to them has died, or maybe they lost their job, or their home, and they need to reconnect with God. I'm not sure why she would appoint an advisor if you are only visiting." She looks at Sarah as if Sarah herself might have some idea that she might like to share.

Sister Assumpta has been kind to her, so she indulges the nun with the information she's looking for, "My husband has left me. Today would have been our twenty-fifth wedding anniversary."

The nun's smile instantly turns to a frown. "I'm so sorry, Sarah. I'll pray for you." She hesitates, and then adds, "Sister Eucharine is a wonderful advisor. I'm sure she'll be able to help you, if you decide to confide in her."

"I am meeting with her after breakfast. She makes me a little nervous, though."

"Sister Eucharine? That's because she's German. She's a tough cookie on the outside, but her heart is warm and loving. You'll see, she'll be like the grandmother you wish you had, before she's done with you. Mark my words."

Sister Eucharine, a warm-hearted Grandmother? Sarah can't quite conceive it, but it puts her mind at ease. "Thank you, Sister Assumpta. You always know just what to say."

"You're welcome. Now let's go find a seat with Theresa." They make their way over to her Aunt's table, and a breakfast of pumpkin pancakes, fruit, and sausages.

"Why don't you say grace, Theresa," suggests Barbara.

They all bow their heads and bless themselves as Theresa begins, "In the name of the Father, the Son, and the Holy Spirit. Rub a dub dub, thanks for the grub." And then all the sisters throw their wiggling hands up into the air and shout, "Yay Lord!" Sarah is in shock, and she almost laughs out loud, but the nuns just start eating as if nothing out of the ordinary has just occurred. Sarah realizes that the relationship that the sisters have with God is real. There's no reason to impress God with formalities and pomp. God knows what's in your heart, and these sisters are thankful, and they have a great sense of humor. Sarah feels overwhelmed with love for all of them.

After, breakfast, Sarah puts up her dishes, and makes her way to the chapel. Sister Eucharine isn't there yet, so she takes a seat about half-way down the aisle. She starts to think about Jeff, and what she might tell Sister Eucharine, when she hears the chapel door open. The nun makes her way down the aisle, and sits beside her. After greeting each other, Sister Eucharine begins, "You may be wondering why I have asked you here.

Did Mother Superior mention anything to you about a spiritual advisor?"

"Yes, she did tell me that she had appointed you."

"That's right. As your spiritual advisor, it's my job to listen to your story, and then offer you scripture-based guidance as I am able. Would you like to share your story with me?"

"You want me to tell you the story about my husband leaving me?"

"Yes, and anything else that you feel inclined to share. Tell me how it all began."

"Well, see, that's the thing, I feel like I don't know how it happened. My daughter went off to college this year, which was a big deal for me. She is my only child, and we are very close, so I have been feeling a little down. As for my husband, I'm at a loss. Today is our 25th wedding anniversary," Sarah's eyes fill up with tears, "and I'm sitting here in this convent telling you about how he doesn't think we belong together anymore." Her chest tightens, but she continues, "The weird thing about it is that he talks as if I wanted this too, but I didn't! I had no idea that he was even thinking anything like this, and yet he is. He seems to think that I believe this is the best thing for us, and I don't agree with that at all!" Sarah's tears flow freely down her cheeks, and Sister Eucharine listens patiently. "I thought maybe he just wanted a separation, but when I tried to talk about it, he made it clear that there is nothing to fix. He's finished."

"That must have been very difficult for you to hear."

"It was. I thought that he loved me, and that we were going to be together forever. We got married in a church." She waves her hand around the chapel to make her point. "What God has put together and all that... and he just threw it away."

"You're right. I don't believe that God intended for us to marry and part before death, yet this is something that happens all the time. When something tragic like this occurs, the best thing that you can do is forgive, and move on. Staying in this place of questioning, of asking 'what if', and resenting your husband, will make you bitter. It will burn up your insides, and make you sick. Forgiving him, well, it's not about him. You don't do it to make him feel better. You do it for yourself, for you will know that you are right in the eyes of God. According to Mark 11:25, '...whenever you stand praying, forgive, if you have anything against anyone, so that your Father also who is in heaven may forgive you your trespasses.' If we're going to ask God to forgive us, we must first be forgiving."

"It's just so difficult, Sister, I don't know if I am ready to forgive him."

"I understand that you feel that way, but know this, the anger that you carry in your heart, it's hurting you, and not him. Nelson Mandela once said, 'Resentment is like drinking poison, and then hoping it will kill your enemies.' You must let it go, Sarah, and the only way to do that is through forgiveness."

"I hear your words, and they make sense to me, but I know that if I were to say that I forgive him, it would be a lie."

"That's because you are forgetting that you have God on your side, and the strength of the Holy Spirit that you can call upon. In Psalm 55:22, it clearly states, 'cast your burden upon the Lord, and he shall sustain you.' You can do this Sarah. Tell God that you don't have the strength to forgive your husband while this pain burdens your heart. Ask him to take the pain for you, because you can no longer carry it by yourself. Think of that beautiful footprints poem, when the author wonders aloud to Jesus about the most trying times in her life, when there were only one set of footprints in the sand, and she wants to know why Jesus would abandon her, in her most difficult moments. Jesus tells her that there is only one set of footprints, because those were the times when he carried her. You can let Jesus carry you right now. God always wants to help you ease your burdens, all you need to do is to recognize the gift of his love, and return that love to others."

Sarah thinks on this for a moment. All she needs to do is recognize the gift of God's love, and return that love, not to God, but to others. It seems to ring of the message of interconnectedness in *Life's Little Energy Book*. We are all parts of God, and by loving one another, we love God.

"I want to try. Can you help me? Will you pray the words for me?" Sarah looks at Sister Eucharine with hope. She has to believe that this pain in her heart can be carried by God.

Sister Eucharine blesses herself, and Sarah follows, "In the name of the Father, the Son, and the Holy Spirit." She grasps Sarah's hands, and continues, "Heavenly Father, it is with a heavy heart that Sarah comes to you, asking for your help. Please carry her burden for her, so that she may be relieved of the pain of separation from her husband. Help her to find the strength to forgive him, so that she may be acceptable in your eyes. Allow her to find peace, so that she may move forward, free of the pain and the grief that this event has caused in her life. Help her to know your purpose for her, Lord, and guide her in her search for meaning and fulfillment. We ask this in the name of the Father, the Son, and the Holy Spirit, Amen."

"Amen." Sarah looks up at Sister Eucharine. In that moment, she feels such relief, as if her burden really has been lifted. She isn't positive that the heavy feeling in her chest won't return, but for now she feels lighter.

"May I hug you, Sister?" asks Sarah.

Sister Eucharine looks flustered, but she nods her head, and Sarah leans over and wraps her arms around the nun. "Thank you" she whispers into Sister Eucharine's ear.

"Thank you, my dear." Sister Eucharine whispers back.

Sarah returns to her room, and pulls the red notebook from her suitcase. Propping the pillow against the wall, she stretches out her legs in front of her, and begins to write, "Dear Jeff, I still can't believe that you've decided to end our marriage. When I met you at my cousin's St. Patrick's Day party, I thought you were the kindest man. The way that you listened to me that night while I was rambling on about politics and social justice, I couldn't help but picture us together. I was so happy when you called me to go to the carnival with you the next day, and that date marked the beginning of our life together. I love all of our memories: our wedding, the vacations, Bethany- all the triumphs and the struggles that brought us even closer. Thank you for all of those things. I will never understand why you decided to end our marriage, but whatever the reason, I forgive you. I love you and I want you to be happy, and I want to be happy, too." A tear lands on the page and Sarah realizes she truly does want Jeff to be happy. She loves him enough to let him go, knowing that he may never return.

When Sarah enters the chapel for midday prayer, she is surprised to see so many people. There are not only nuns. The pews are filled to capacity with lay people. Father Murphy is back, and Mother Superior stands at the podium, and begins to speak, "Let us begin, as we begin all things, in the name of the Father, and of the Son, and of the Holy Spirit. Amen. I would like to welcome everyone to the Mass of Thanksgiving for the friends and family members of the School Sisters of Notre Dame. Our mission, to proclaim the good news and direct our entire lives toward that oneness for which Jesus Christ was sent, could not be accomplished without the love and generous support of all of you. We are thankful for each and every one of you and we pray that the Lord God will bless you all. I would like to invite all of you to lunch in our gathering room after mass. Thank you." Sarah sits through her second mass of the day. This is certainly a record, and one that she hopes never to break. Two masses are one-and-a-half more than she feels necessary. She will admit, though, that Father Murphy is keeping it light and humorous.

At lunch she sits next to Sister Ruthie, who tells a story of her birth sister, who was digging in her garden when her shovel hit something hard like rock. It turned out to be an old Native American burial ground. They have since found many interesting items, and Sister Ruthie goes on to describe a few of them. Sarah is reminded of her dream, and speaks up. "That's interesting, Sister Ruthie. I actually had a dream recently where I was looking for my shoes, so I started digging in the yard, and I hit a book. As I uncovered it, it turned out to be a holy book of sorts, so I texted my stepfather so that he could get me some information."

"Oh, Sarah, that's a good one! I've read a number of books about interpreting your dreams, and when you dream about excavating something, it means that you are making new discoveries about yourself and uncovering your potential. A textbook in a dream implies that you still have a lot of knowledge to gain, and a text message represents your connection to others, or a message from your subconscious. They say that if you can remember the subject of the book, it can give you clues. So, that could mean that your subconscious is trying to tell you that you are discovering that you still have a lot to learn about the Bible. What do you think?"

"That's so cool! I imagine it could be true. It certainly makes sense." Sarah looks around at the other nuns. They all agree that it is interesting.

"I love to dream that I can fly. What does that mean, Ruthie?" asks Sister Kelly.

"That means that one day you might get your own T.V. show!" blurts Aunt Theresa. Everyone else laughs along with her.

"Really?" asks Sister Kelly, looking very excited.

"Oh for heaven's sake, Kelly, do you really not know about the Flying Nun?" asks Sister Barbara.

"The Flying Nun, who is that?" she asks. Everyone laughs some more, and Sister Kelly turns red with embarrassment.

"Never mind them, Kelly," says Sister Assumpta. "The Flying Nun was a T.V. show, from way before you were born. They're just jealous because you are young." The sisters laugh again. As usual, Sarah is impressed by the kindness of Sister Assumpta. She is always trying to make people feel comfortable.

After lunch, Sister Betty brings out a large, white sheet cake that reads, "Thank you friends and family of the S.S.N.D." The sisters who have family members visiting pose for pictures behind the cake, and Sarah and Aunt Theresa have their turn. Everyone chats, and drinks warm apple cider from crock pots. At three o'clock, the sisters that don't have visitors make their way to the chapel for prayer.

"Do you want to go pray?" she asks her aunt.

"Oh, no, I prayed twice as hard this morning to make up for it." Aunt Theresa grins at her, and Sarah can't help but be amused by her aunt's wit. How wonderful it must be to never have to wonder about how you will pay the bills, or if you have saved enough for retirement. It's incredible to Sarah, that in this day and age, when one is taxed for everything, there is still a way to live a life devoted to God without any earthly cares. Perhaps if there weren't so much church involved, Sarah could get used to this.

Sitting with her aunt, Sarah's mind wanders as she thinks about Bethany and Jeff. She wonders how Click is doing with Des, and if he is getting along with Des' Chihuahua, Taco. The two dogs have been fine in the past, but that's always been on Click's turf, and Taco usually spends that time in Des' lap, or in her Gucci dog purse. When Sarah realizes that she's lost her focus, she brings her mind back to God. She asks if she should go home yet, but she immediately knows that the answer is no. She wonders if this is God's answer for her, or if it is just a deep knowing inside her soul that it isn't the right time to leave. She reasons that it really doesn't matter either way, since no is the answer that feels true to her, and she decides to listen.

Three days later after lunch, Sarah says goodbye to her aunt and her new friends. She thanks Mother Superior for allowing her to stay, and Sister Eucharine for her guidance. Sister Ruthie gives her a book on dream interpretation, and Sister Ginnie offers to walk with her, to her car. On the way, Sister Ginnie asks her how she feels about her stay at the convent, and Sarah pauses for a moment to gather her thoughts.

"You know, Sister, before I came here, I had hoped that faith in God could help me get through this situation. What I think I have learned, though, is that it's my relationship with God that will get me through my life. It's easy to remember God in the bad times, and to beg him for help when it doesn't seem like there are alternatives. Watching all of you, though, and seeing how you not only share your sorrows and joys with God, but also things that seem trivial, like folding the laundry. The way you're all constantly asking him for guidance, I hope I can take that with me. I do want to."

"Well, then I'm sure you will. You know Sarah, as nuns we have formal prayer times so that we can constantly keep God in front of us. He is the first thing that we think of when we awaken, and the last thing on our mind before bed. This faith, it's not about worshipping Jesus, it's about becoming more like him. When he said 'follow me,' he meant that we should do what he did. If you can forgive your husband, you can be forgiving like Jesus. It will bring you peace."

"You're right," Sarah agreed. "Sister Eucharine said the same thing. I think I am almost there...you know, fake it until you make it, right?" She opens her arms for a hug. "I should go."

The two women embrace, and Sister Ginnie says, "Be well, Sarah. And, keep in touch, okay?"

"I will. Thank you for everything. I really appreciate it."

"It was my pleasure. You drive carefully!"

"Okay, bye!" Sarah slips into her Prius, and waves as she pulls away.

The drive home is strange. Sarah is glad to be on her way to see Des, but she also feels sorrow about leaving the routine, and the undeniable sense of peace and joy, that she experienced in the convent. She didn't have many expectations coming into this trip, and her experiences far surpassed what she could have hoped. The sisters are such a good example of how to be with yourself, God, and others. At the same time, Sarah wonders how easy it will be to carry their example into the real world. She feels badly wording it that way.

Certainly, the nuns live in a world that is real for them, but she can't help but think about how much easier life must be if you don't have to worry about money, or loneliness. Interestingly enough, the nuns spend so much time in prayer, that they really only get to socialize for eight hours per day including their meals, and work time. Some of them work at solitary jobs, so that leaves them with only three and a half hours. And yet, they don't seem lonely at all! They are all so centered and joyful, that there must be something very rewarding in having a relationship with God. Sarah needs to work on that. She isn't ready to jump back into the Catholic Church just yet, though. The repetitive praying of the Our Father and the Hail Mary mean nothing to her. There has to be more to building a relationship. Even that Bible verse that Sister Ginnie quoted spoke of praying without repetitive words, which makes sense to Sarah.

Sarah pulls into Des' driveway and grabs her purse. She rings the bell and inside, the dogs bark like mad. "Come in!" she hears Des yell from far away. Entering the house, Sarah is accosted by Click, who is leaping in the air with every bit of poodle genes that he can muster.

Being so large, he can still jump as high as a circus dog when he's excited. Sarah calms him down, while Taco stands barking in the doorway of the kitchen, nervous and fierce, at the same time.

"Hola, Taco. Como estas?" She asks the Chihuahua. Hearing his name, the dog wags his tail, and jumps up on Sarah's shin. She scoops him up with one hand, tucks him under her arm, and finds Des in the kitchen, with her hands elbow-deep in flour. "Hey, what are you making?"

"Onion bread, remember that recipe of my mother's from back in her domestic period? I loved that stuff, and you just can't buy it anywhere. So, here I am, like freaking Julia Child, covered in flour and wearing an apron."

"Yeah, I was going to say, that thing is hot." She winks at Des.

"Oh shut up, Sister Mary. I see the nuns didn't make you any kinder," she laughs out loud. "How was it?"

"It was good. We prayed, a lot. I didn't like that part so much, but some of the nuns are real characters, so I had a good time."

"So did you talk to God while you were there? Did he tell you what to do next?"

"Yes, he did." Sarah replies.

"Really, what did he say?" her eyes are wide, as she waits for Sarah's response.

"Well, he told me I should come here and pick up my dog, so here I am!" she smiles at Des. "Do you have any wine?"

"Did he tell you to drink my wine, too?"

"Ha ha, very funny, and yes, he did. In fact, he told me to tell you to stop buying this cheap crap, because I deserve better." She pours a glass for herself, and one for Des as well. Handing her the glass, Sarah clinks hers against it and says, "Cheers." It's good to be home.

After Sarah fills Des in on as much convent coverage as she thinks her friend can handle, she looks at Click and says, "Ready buddy?" The dog pants and runs to the front door at the sight of his leash. "I'll take that as a yes. Thanks so much for watching him, Des. I couldn't have done it without you."

"I was glad to do it. I think he had a good time. Taco is going to be lonely now, right baby?" The Chihuahua looks up from his doggie bed at the sound of his name, and quickly puts his head back down.

Sarah laughs, "Oh yeah, he looks distraught."

"I know, right? He might need anti-depressants, he looks so sad. Do you have any plans for tomorrow?"

"No, why, did you have something in mind?"

"Not really. I'll call you in the morning."

"Sounds good, thanks again!" Sarah waves good-bye and closes the door.

—∘∘◦}◎{◦∘∘—

When they arrive home, Click runs all over the house sniffing and making sure there aren't any changes. Sarah throws her purse on the hall table, hangs up her jacket, and heads to her room to unpack. After she throws on a pair of her favorite yoga pants and a sweatshirt, she curls up on the couch and hits the flashing button on the answering machine.

"You have two messages. First message, Saturday, two-fifteen pm: "Hey Sarah, this is Laurie. I am so sorry about you and Jeff. No one tells me anything! When you didn't show up last night at the tournament, I thought it was weird, but then the next thing I know, Jeff is playing with Kate's hair! I was like, 'What the heck is going on here?', so Amy had to fill me in on everything when Kate went to the bathroom. It's just so crazy. Call me! Bye." Beeeep. Next message, Sunday, nine forty-seven am: "Hello, this is Patricia from the Morning Call. We are running a special, and you can now receive Thursday-through-Sunday delivery for the same price as you are paying for the Sunday edition. If you would like to take advantage of this offer, please call us at 1-800-get-news. Thank you, and have a nice day." Beeeep. To listen to these messages again, press nine. To erase, press erase all."

Sarah stares at the answering machine, with her mouth ajar. *Oh my God! Kate? Why Kate?* It never even occurred to her that there might be someone else, but it would have never occurred to her that it could be Kate. *What about Mike? Does he know? This can't be happening! And, of course, I have to hear it from Laurie's big mouth. She probably couldn't wait to call and let the cat out of the bag. How long has Amy known this?* Sarah has to know. She picks up the phone and dials Amy's number. She panics slightly as the phone starts to ring. *What should I say if Donny answers?*

"Hello?" It is Amy.

She takes a deep breath, "Amy, this is Sarah."

"Sarah," her voice gets very quiet, "oh my goodness, hold on." There are fumbling sounds, and Sarah hears doors opening and closing. "Okay, I'm sorry. I didn't want to talk in front of the guys." Sarah isn't sure what to say, so there are a few awkward moments of silence. "Sarah? Are you there?"

"I'm here. Amy, Laurie left a message on my phone. Is it true about Kate?" There is more silence. "Hello?"

"Sarah, I'm so sorry." Amy feels so uncomfortable, and it's obvious.

"You're sorry that you haven't called me to see if I'm alright, even though my husband moved onto your sofa, or you're sorry that he's having an affair and you didn't tell me? Which one are you sorry about, exactly?"

"Please, don't be like this, Sarah. I couldn't tell you. I didn't know!"

"You didn't know he left me? You thought he was a hologram of himself on your couch for the past month? Give me a break, Amy."

"Sarah, Jeff hasn't been on my couch. I swear to you, I would have called you!"

"He hasn't been on your couch? Well then..." Understanding crashes over her like a tsunami and she is overwhelmed by nausea.

"I'm sorry, Sarah. I really had no idea. You know how Donny is, that man doesn't tell his left hand what his right hand is doing. He would never break Jeff's confidence. And, I'm sure he knew, because when I started asking questions, he got all awkward. He finally broke down and told Jeff last week that he needed to tell me something, so I guess Jeff gave him permission to tell me that you guys split. But I swear, I didn't know about Kate until Thursday, when Mike showed up here."

"Mike showed up at your house?"

"Yes! It was so strange, because we don't usually see him outside of bowling, but he came in, and Donny grabbed a couple of beers, and they sat down at the table. I was finishing up the dinner dishes, and Mike just went on like I knew everything. I couldn't believe what I was hearing."

"What did he say?" Sarah asks.

"He's pissed at Jeff. It sounded like he's mainly mad because he can't bowl on their team anymore, because he really didn't say too much about Kate."

"They kicked him off the team?"

"No, I think he just doesn't want to be around Jeff and Kate."

"I don't blame him. This is so messed up."

"I know." Amy thinks back to Friday night, and how uncomfortable it was to watch Jeff with Kate. He was smiling and flirting, and she was just giggling like a teenager. Sickly Kate, with her headaches and ulcers, is gone. This is a new woman, and she expects everyone to be happy for her! Amy can't tell Sarah any of this, as she is sure it will make her feel worse. "Oh, Sarah, are you okay?"

"I just can't believe it. Did you see this coming? Am I just stupid?"

"No. No, you're not stupid, Sarah, you're not. This whole situation, it's so awful."

"Is he living at her house? Oh my God, did she kick Mike out?" Sarah wants to know. She is thinking of calling Mike, but she isn't sure if that's appropriate. *Screw it.* "Do you have Mike's number?"

"I only have Kate's cell phone number in my phone. Are you going to call him? I can ask Donny for the number, hold on." Kate puts the phone down, and Sarah tears through her purse for a paper and pen. She finds an old receipt with a piece of chewed up gum stuck inside, but it will work. She can hear Donny in the background. He and Amy are going back and forth, but she can't quite make out what they are saying. He doesn't sound angry, though. It's odd to think that Donny is out of her life now. They can't be friends after this. Jeff would obviously win Donny in the divorce, which is a shame because she always liked him. "Okay, are you ready?"

"Yes."

Sarah writes down the number and thanks Amy. She is going to call Mike right now.

"Sarah? I hope this doesn't change anything between us."

"I know. We'll see. I'll talk to you soon, and thanks again." Sarah hangs up the phone. She wants to think they can remain friends, but she knows how it works. She has seen too many couples divorce over the years, and it's impossible. She doesn't want to be a third wheel, and she wouldn't want Jeff hanging out with Bob, at Des' house, so she isn't going to go into Jeff's territory.

Sarah enters Mike's number into the phone. It rings twice, and he picks up. "Hello?"

"Mike, hey, this is Sarah."

"Sarah, hi, I'm glad you called. I wanted to call you, but I didn't know…" there is a long pause as he searches for the right words.

"I know, it's weird. I would like to talk to you." She finishes his thought for him.

"Yeah, me too. Hey, do you want to get some coffee or something?"

"You know, Mike, I just drove home from Connecticut, and I am dressed like a slob, but you're welcome to come here. I make lousy coffee, apparently, but I have all the makings, and there's always tea." Or scotch, thinks Sarah. *Scotch would be good now.*

"Alright, I'll be over in a bit. I just have to let the dog out before I leave."

"Okay, whenever. I'll be here."

"Great. See you soon."

"Okay." Sarah puts the phone down on the end table. This is so odd. Mike is coming to her house! She contemplates changing, but then she remembers that she already told him that she's dressed like a slob. Besides, it's not as if she needs to impress him.

Click comes over, sits in front of her, and gives her the look. As soon as she makes eye contact with him he starts panting, and his tail begins pounding the floor. "What? What do you want? Do you want to go outside?" Nothing. "Okay, do you want to eat?" Click barks in response, and runs to the kitchen, looking back to make sure that Sarah is following. "I'm coming, you hairy beast. Let's get your food." Sarah opens the pantry door, pops open the ten gallon plastic container, and places a heaping scoop of nuggets in the dog's bowl. Click wastes no time chowing down. "There you go, buddy." After about twenty minutes, the doorbell rings. Sarah checks herself in the hall mirror and opens the door. "Hi. Come on in."

"Thanks." Mike hands her a bag from the donut shop. "I brought munchkins."

"Munchkins? Okay, thanks. I'll put them in a bowl." She was glad he didn't bring a whole box, because she would eat all of them after he leaves. Mike follows her into the kitchen.

"I only got chocolate, I hope that's okay."

"Is that the only kind they had left?"

"No, that's the only kind I like. I hope you don't mind."

"No, why would I mind? I mean, what girl doesn't like chocolate?"

"Kate." Sarah looks up from what she is doing. "Yeah, Kate doesn't like chocolate. It gives her a migraine. I guess I don't have to worry about that anymore, though, right?"

"I suppose not. So, can I ask you how you found out about all this?"

"Sure, I've been wondering the same thing about you. It's going to be over a month now. I came home one day and there was this note." Mike pulls his wallet from the front pocket of his jeans, takes out a slip of paper and slides it across the counter and then he nods at the note to indicate that she should read it. Sarah slowly unfolds it, and imagining Kate's nasal voice, she reads it out loud:

> Mike,
>
> I'm sorry to do this, but I am too ashamed to face you. You have been a good husband to me through all of my problems, and I am thankful for that. The thing is, I just don't want to be married to you anymore. I took the money from my mother out of the savings account, and I want a divorce. I'm getting an apartment, and you can stay in the house

until it sells. I think this is fair, don't you? I
got a lawyer, and he'll send you the stuff in
the mail for you to sign.

I'm SO sorry!

Kate

Sarah folds the note. There was no mention of Jeff,
so how their relationship came to be is still a mystery.
At least Jeff had the nerve to tell Sarah in person, even if
he did fall short of telling her the entire story. She hopes
he realizes the kind of person he is getting himself
involved with. She looks up at Mike, "I don't know
what to say."

"Really, because I was like, wow, what kind of
woman leaves a note like this on the counter, and
doesn't expect to have to say a word to her husband
of twenty-three years? What the hell? Did you get a
note, too?"

"No," Sarah almost feels guilty, "I did not."

"That's exactly my point. You don't do that to
somebody. So, what did Jeff tell you?"

Sarah pours the coffee, and gets the milk out of the
refrigerator. She drops a sugar cube in her cup, and tries
to recall how this whole mess began. Carrying her cup
over to the sofa, she indicates that Mike should sit. "I was
cooking. It was the day after we had dropped Bethany at

school, and he came home after work looking nervous. I thought he had big plans for us, but surprise! He said something about how he couldn't do this anymore, and it had nothing to do with me. Honestly, Mike, I didn't even know what the hell he was talking about. I even worked myself into this whole imaginary situation the next day, where I thought he just wanted a separation, so we could figure out what we needed from each other. But no, he made it very clear to me that he did not want me back, no matter what. He said something about things just not being right, and that something was missing."

Sarah leans back against the sofa and pulls her knees up to her chest. Remembering this is more painful than she thought it would be, and her head is starting to pound. She looks at Mike, and notices for the first time that he looks like crap. He is a handsome guy, and all the girls wondered how Kate had managed to land him, but tonight he is unshaven and appears drained. "Anyway, as much as he wished I could be the missing thing for him, I'm just not. When did you find out that they are seeing each other?"

"About a week after she left. Kate had locked her keys in the car, and she came by the house for her extra set. I was down in the basement, and heard her rummaging around in the kitchen drawer. I thought someone was robbing the house, so I grabbed a plunger, and crept upstairs." Sarah can't help but smile at the visual. "Kate wasn't happy that I caught her. She tried to look innocent, and told me about the keys. I said that we needed to talk, but she told me there is nothing to talk about, and walked out of the house. When I followed her, I saw her jump into what looked like Jeff's car, so I hopped in my own. I was curious about where she was living, you know? They went to the grocery store, and then they rented a movie before they finally headed back to those apartments off Tilghman Street. You know, over by the grocery store."

"They're living so close!"

"I know, I thought the same thing. I sat in the car after they went in, figuring that when Jeff came out I would talk to him, and find out what was going on, but then he never came out. I sat there like an idiot, all night long, until I literally had to leave so I wouldn't be late for work. It was probably three a.m. before it even occurred to me that something might be going on with them. Am I a moron? I just figured that you guys were fine, so I never even thought about an affair. I feel like an idiot."

Sarah understands all too well. "I know what you mean. I didn't find out until this morning. Laurie left a message on my machine. She might have thought I already knew about them, but knowing her, she just wanted to be the person to tell me. I called Amy to get your number. I just don't want to listen to any more lies. Jeff made it out like he was confused and searching for something, but I guess he knew all along what was missing, and he just couldn't have it while I was in the picture. Have you talked to Kate since then?"

"No, but my lawyer has. Did I tell you that she took the furniture?"

"And, you let her?"

"Hell no! This was the same day that she wrote the note. I wasn't even home!" Sarah's eyes go wide with disbelief. "I kid you not. She took everything in the living room, except the recliner and the television. The kitchen table and the dressers were gone. She left me the bed and the dining room set, probably because it wouldn't fit in her damn apartment."

Sarah feels terrible for him. They have an open concept floor plan in the house, so it must look ridiculous with just a recliner and a television. "You should have seen Bronx when I came home from work. He usually lays on the back of the sofa so he can watch out the window, but the poor guy was stretched out on the hearth rug by the fireplace, looking like he failed me. I have to get him a couch." Sarah thinks it is sweet that he is thinking of the bulldog. "You know what's so strange, Sarah? I don't miss her as much as I thought I would. It wasn't always easy living with Kate, but she was my wife, and I accepted that I would always have to take care of her. She was sick a lot, and sometimes she didn't get out of bed for a week. I would have to do everything: all the cooking, cleaning and laundry. It wasn't easy."

"No, I can't imagine it was." Sarah recalls the cooking, cleaning, and laundry that she has done over the years, but she never had to work full time simultaneously. Mike deserves sainthood. "Are you okay with it then? Her leaving, I mean."

"Am I okay with it? That's a good question. It's too new, and the wounds are still fresh. But I do think that in time, I might see it as beneficial. I never hoped that my life could be anything more. We weren't able to travel, because Kate never felt well. The kids only come home for holidays, since it's not much fun at our house. Now, all that can be different. At first, I was really angry, and I felt like she owed me. I sacrificed so much for her. I'm starting to think about the future though, and there's a chance that she did me a favor." Kate certainly didn't do Sarah a favor. If only Jeff could hear this, she is sure he wouldn't want Mike's life. "So, I called a lawyer, and I'm filing for divorce. It never occurred to me to end my marriage, but now that Kate has opened the door,

I'd be a fool not to walk through. How about you? Are you okay?"

"I don't want to be divorced from Jeff. I would take him back in a heartbeat if he would have me. No offense, but I don't think he's going to be happy with Kate, so part of me feels like I might be able to wait it out, until they split. This morning, before I knew about them, I think I was on a healing path. But now, I can't help but wonder if this will be a brief affair. It seems he just isn't thinking straight." Mike is silent. He looks down at his hands, and picks at some dead skin on the side of his thumb. "What?" Sarah asks. "What are you thinking?"

"I don't know..." Mike begins.

"You think I'm stupid."

"Not stupid. No. I just don't understand how you can want him back after he's done this. How can you ever trust him? I would've never believed that Kate would cheat on me, but now, how do I know she won't just cut and run if some guy looks at her the right way."

"I get that, I do, believe me." Sarah continues, "It's just that my marriage was good. Maybe Jeff didn't think so, but I know there was a time when he was happy. I think I can forgive him. I don't know." Her conversations with Sister Ginnie and Sister Eucharine are running through her mind in loops. "I made a commitment to him, for better or for worse. This is the worst, for sure, but he's still the man I love. It's interesting, but I always used to think that if Jeff ever had an affair, I wouldn't want to know. I don't mean a love affair, but if he just cheated on me one night, when he was drunk. That wouldn't be worth destroying our marriage."

"Yeah, but Sarah, open your eyes. They are living together!" Mike is frustrated and sorry for her.

"I know that! But I haven't talked to him yet. I need to hear it from him."

Mike wants to shake her. "Hear him say what? You already told me that he said it was over, and that he made it clear that he doesn't want you back, no matter what. Kate doesn't change that. You need to let him go, for your own sanity." Sarah feels the tears welling up. She doesn't want to cry in front of Mike. He's been on the bowling team for the last four years, but most of the time he was with the guys, while she was at a table with his wife. She really only knows what Kate said about him, and even that isn't much. She looks down at her knees, and feels the warmth of the tears as they stream down her cheeks, and drip from her chin to her hands. "Aw, Sarah, I'm sorry." He slides next to her on the couch, and strokes her hair.

"No, it's not your fault. The truth hurts, that's all." She wipes at her cheeks, and rubs her hands on her pants.

"I didn't want to make you cry." He is twirling her hair in his fingers now. "You have beautiful hair, you know that?"

Sarah thinks of how much Jeff loves her hair, and how she enjoyed when he would play with it. Her shoulders start to shake, as the tears flow again. Mike leans over, and kisses her cheek. "Don't cry," he whispers in her ear, and then he kisses her there. "Your eyes are too pretty to cry." He leans around, and kisses her on the lips.

The hairs on the back of Sarah's neck stand up, and her whole body becomes tense. She doesn't want to hurt Mike's feelings, but this is not what she wants. She uses her hands to push him away. "Mike, don't." Sarah stands up, and so does he. "You should go."

"Sarah, I'm sorry. I shouldn't have done that."

"No, you shouldn't have." It sounds harsher than she expects, so she softens her tone. "Please, Mike, let's just pretend this never happened. We've both been thrown into a situation that neither of us expected, and you're the only person who knows what I am going through. Thank you for coming here tonight."

Mike feels like an ass. What was he thinking? In the moment, he was only focused on how sad Sarah was, and how they could make each other feel better. Subconsciously, he probably wants to kiss Jeff's wife, the way that Jeff is kissing Kate. Still, that's not Sarah's fault. "Sarah, please accept my apology. I'm not usually a jerk. Please."

"Thank you, Mike, really, I'll be fine. I'm tired, my head hurts, and I just want to go lay down." She opens the front door, and smiles at him half-heartedly. "Thanks for coming, and for the munchkins."

"You're welcome. Get some rest. Goodnight."

"Goodnight" says Sarah, and she closes the door.

Sarah leans back against the door, takes a deep breath and exhales. Talk about sensory overload! Her head is pounding, and she's sure that she can hear the blood rushing through her ears. She can still smell the faint scent of Mike's cologne on her face. *What is wrong with men? Why would he want to kiss me with snot dripping out of my nose?* Sarah locks the door, flips off the lights, and trudges upstairs to shower.

Feeling clean and wearing her favorite sock monkey pajamas, Sarah reaches for her red notebook and climbs into bed. She's exhausted, but today of all days, she needs to spend some time focusing on the good things. Deciding to write just one thing for each of the four categories, she stares at the blank page for a few minutes, and then begins to write. "I love the smell of the tangerine soap in my bathroom. I hope Jeff will see Kate for the woman that she is. Warm water in the shower brings me joy. I expect that tomorrow will be a better day, because it can't get any worse than this one." She erases that last part. Sarah is starting to realize that whenever she says that it can't get any worse, God seems to feel the need to prove this untrue. Her parents could fall ill, or Bethany could drop out of school. There are definitely worse things that could occur, and Sarah isn't taking any chances. Before she closes the notebook, she raises her eyes and says, "God? Please help me to deal with this Kate situation, because I honestly don't think I can do this myself. Help me to know how to handle this. Just tell me what to do, please. Amen." Sarah can't stay awake for another moment, so she turns off the light, and goes to sleep.

Click wakes Sarah at one-thirty in the morning, and again around three and five-twenty. He must have enjoyed too many new treats over at Des' house, because he goes outside to eat grass for twenty minutes, and then comes back inside and vomits as soon as Sarah is snug in bed. The clock becomes her enemy, as she peeks at the red glowing numbers, and realizes that she is still awake. When Click begins whining at the side of her bed at seven-fifteen, she gives up on sleep, and decides to start her day. She throws on her pink robe, slides into her slippers, and heads downstairs to make some tea. The sun porch is just too cold this morning, so she sits at the desk in front of her laptop, and signs on to Facebook. Sarah isn't the type to post status updates often, but she's feeling alone this morning, and thinks it might help to be acknowledged. She ponders for a few moments and then types, "Everyone is just looking to feel loved." Within five minutes, thirty-three people have liked her status, and eighteen of her friends comment about their love for her. In fifteen minutes, the likes have climbed to fifty-seven. *Huh.* Sarah is amazed at the sheer power of social media. More than that, though, she is surprised by the response. In the six years she has been on Facebook, she has never had such a large response to a post. Obviously this one strikes a chord with people.

Sarah can't be the only one out there feeling unloved, or wanting to reach out and love other people. Not romantic love, but that divine universal love that is discussed in "Life's Little Energy Book." Feeling better, she trots upstairs to dress and fix her hair. When she returns, she checks Facebook one last time, before she takes Click for a walk. He's lying under the kitchen table looking less than lively, and she thinks that the fresh air will do him some good. She also wants to make sure he is tired tonight, because she is hoping for a full eight hours of sleep.

—∘∘∘❖∘∘∘—

Sarah sits down at the desk, moves her mouse, and brings the laptop to life. Sixty-three likes and a private message are waiting. *How exciting!* Sarah clicks on the message bubble at the top of the screen, and sees that it is from her cousin Carol.

Sarah and Carol were close as children, and Sarah still considers her a good friend. They don't get to see each other very often, because Carol lives outside of Pittsburgh, six hours away. Her father was disabled, during a fall on a job site when he was in his early thirties, so they never had a lot of money. Even so, there was plenty of love in their family, and Carol was well educated. She had a full ride to the University of Pittsburgh, and then continued on to become a doctor. Her volunteer work has taken her all over the world, including Africa and South America, and Sarah is impressed by her motivation and courage. More than that, Sarah always admired Carol's unwavering faith in God. She's a very spontaneous person, unlike Sarah the worrier. Carol is always confident everything will be fine. Even when she brought her family to Africa with her one summer, the whole extended family was terrified that they would contract a horrible disease, but Carol had faith.

Sarah reads the e-mail:

> Hey Sarah! I hope all is well out in Allentown. Just wanted to touch base, and see how everything is going with Bethany. I hope she's enjoying her freshman year as much as I enjoyed mine (Okay, maybe not that much!) Anyway, you have always been so interested in my mission trips, and I'm going to West Virginia on Saturday, for two weeks. We'll arrive home a few days before Thanksgiving, and I wondered if you'd like to join me? I apologize for the short notice, but I just found out that I would be going myself. My friend Shirley runs the mission, and they have four spaces open. We could fill two of them, if you are up for it. What do you think? Let me know! xoxo, Carol

What a crazy idea. Sarah wonders what she would do on a mission. Carol is a doctor, but Sarah doesn't have any special skills. Dismissing the idea, she grabs Click's leash and calls for the dog. Slowly, he drags himself out from under the table, puts his paws out in front of him, his butt in the air, and stretches for a good, long time. Finally, he makes his way over to where Sarah stands waiting at the front door. "My goodness, Click, you really aren't feeling well, are you boy?" Sarah pats his head, hooks his leash, and heads down the street. They walk past Mr. Grady's house, and his old, blind German shepherd wanders over to the curb to greet Click. Sarah lets them have their time together, and wonders about Jeff and Kate. *They can't really last, can they? Why on earth are they together? If Jeff and I can't last, there is no way Kate can be the one for him. When did this all start?* Sarah still doesn't know the answer, and the only way to find out is to ask Jeff. Will he tell her the truth? She's not sure, but she needs to try. There's no way she'll move past this without some answers, so once Jeff gets home from work, she will call him.

The sun feels good on Sarah's skin. Even though it's nice for a fall day, she's glad that she's wearing her heavier jacket. As they continue to walk and chat with neighbors, Click finally leads them home again. According to Sarah's calculations, they've been out for at least an hour-and-a-half, which should tire him out. When they return, Click crawls back under the table, and Sarah checks her phone. Des has called, and she needs to call her back, to tell her about Kate and Mike.

Sarah wishes she could be the bearer of good news, but instead, it's just more of the stuff that makes her head ache.

After the third ring, Des says, "Hello?"

"Hi" responds Sarah. "What's up?"

"Listen, I am in the car, but I am on the way to grab some lunch. Can I bring you something?"

"Sure, that sounds great."

"Okay, I am going to the deli. What do you want?"

"The deli? I don't know, a corned-beef sandwich?" Sarah sounds hesitant.

"Corned-beef? You should get pastrami. It's better. And I'll get you some coleslaw to put on top."

"Why do you always ask me what I want if you are just going to order for me anyway?" asks Sarah.

"Because I know you better than you know yourself, duh! Have I ever steered you wrong?"

"No, I guess not."

"Exactly my point." Des sounds proud.

"Except that time you got me the tongue sandwich. That was gross."

"That was Halloween, and it wasn't gross. You were just too chicken to eat it."

"You're damn right."

"Well, you don't know what you're missing, smarty pants. Tongue is a delicious meat, and it's very tender with no fat or grizzle."

"Enough! No more talking about tongue. Gross."

Des laughs out loud. "I'll be there in fifteen minutes."

When they hang up, Sarah starts thinking about Jeff. If she calls him after work, Kate might be there. She decides to text him so that he can call her back when he has some privacy. She picks up her phone, and types in, "Hey. Can you give me a call tonight when you get a chance? Thanks." A few seconds later the phone vibrates with his response.

"What's up?" he asks.

"I just need to ask you about something," she replies. It's vague, but she is trying to pique his interest without scaring him away.

"Sure. Later." The doorbell rings and Sarah shoves the phone into her purse. She is positive that Des won't approve of her plan to get Jeff back, so she decides to keep this information to herself.

"Oh my God, the deli was a disaster! Remind me never to go in there at lunchtime again. The crowd was so thick, and some guy pinched my ass."

"What? Are you kidding?" Sarah laughs.

"Why would I kid around about something like this? No! He really pinched me, but the worst part is that

when I turned around there was this young, hot guy
that looked like that construction worker from the Diet
Coke commercial. Do you remember him?"

"Why is that bad?" Sarah asks.

"Well, there was also this older guy with a pot belly,
a baseball cap that said 'World's Best Grandpa', and a
few missing teeth. I didn't know which guy it was, and
they weren't giving me any clues, so I had to act all
nonchalant in case it was the cute guy."

"Did you think he was going to ask you out or
something?" Sarah doesn't understand.

"I'm married!" Des pretends to be offended.

"I know that, which is why I don't understand why
you didn't say something about him pinching you."

"I didn't know which one did it!"

"Then you ask!" It seems obvious to Sarah.

"Well, I didn't want to offend Diet Coke Guy if it
wasn't him."

"Whatever. Where's my sandwich?" Sarah looks at
the numerous bags on the counter. "What is all this
stuff?"

"I was bored, so I did a little shopping. Your sandwich
is in the plain brown bag." Sarah pulls it out, tosses the
wrapping, and places her sandwich on a plate.

"Look what I bought!" Des pulls a dark orange
sweater from its bag.

"Is rust the new black?" asks Sarah.

"It's not rust, it's pumpkin. For Thanksgiving, get it?" Des holds the sweater against her. "It's nice, right?"

"Sure, it's great." *If you're going for that convict look.* Des has her own sense of style, so there's nothing Sarah can say to convince her that the sweater is anything but perfect. Knowing Des, she'll glam it up with accessories, and be the envy of all who attend.

"Are you missing convent life? I bet you slept past five today." Sarah thinks back to her night with Click, and a frown washes over her face. "What? Don't tell me you really miss it there! Oh my God, I knew this was going to happen. They brainwashed you, didn't they?"

Sarah laughs, "Would you shut up. They did not brainwash me, and I haven't really had any time to miss it yet. I just left yesterday! So much has happened since then, though, that it seems like a week ago."

"So much, like what?" Des inquires. "I just saw you last night."

"Well, after I got home from your house, I listened to the messages on the answering machine. Do you remember that woman Laurie, from bowling?"

Des scrunches up her face in thought, and shakes her head. "I don't think so."

"She's the whiny one, who knows everybody's business."

"Yes," Des remembers, "With the cranky husband!"

"Yes. So she leaves this message. You know what? I should just play it for you…here." Sarah pushes the button, and they both listen to Laurie's nasal voice. Sarah looks at Des, whose mouth is hanging open in shock.

"Is Kate the hypochondriac?" asks Des. Sarah nods, and Des continues, "I don't believe it! I have to tell you, Sarah, I never thought Jeff had any of this going on in his head. An affair! How long has this been happening?"

"I don't know. I called Amy after I listened to the message."

"What did she say?" Des knows that Sarah has been upset that Amy hasn't called.

"You know, it was better than I thought it would be. She told me that she had no idea about Jeff leaving, because apparently he never went to Donny's after all. It turns out that they are living in an apartment next to the grocery store."

"Are you serious? You're telling me that he's living with her. I can't believe this!"

"I know."

"So, what else did she say?" Des wants to know everything.

"She didn't tell me about the apartment, that was Mike."

"Who's Mike?"

"Mike is Kate's husband."

"You talked to her husband? Oh my God! Did he call you?"

"No, I called him. I got his number from Amy, and when I called, he asked if I wanted to go get some coffee. I looked like crap, though, so I invited him to come here."

"And he did?" she presumes.

"Oh, yes, he did. It was so weird, Des, I don't know how this stuff always happens to me."

"What do you mean? What happened?"

"Well, he let me read this note that Kate left on the counter when she split. Can you believe she wrote him a note? I would have killed Jeff if he did that to me. Anyway, he said that she stopped by one day to pick up her extra set of keys, and he saw her get into Jeff's car with him when she left. Long story short, he followed them, and discovered that they were living together when he sat outside the apartment building all night, and Jeff never came out."

"Un-freaking-believable!" Des is in shock. *Poor Sarah, this keeps getting worse for her.*

"It gets worse."

"It does? How? Oh my God, is she pregnant?"

"What? No, at least I don't think so. She has two grown kids already." Sarah didn't even consider pregnancy.

"So, what's worse?" asks Des, clinging to the edge of her seat.

"Mike kissed me."

"What? No way! Holy crap, did you kiss him back?"

"No! Why would I do that? No. It was so awkward. I was crying. At first, he was comforting me, and before I knew it he was kissing the side of my face, and then my lips, ugh! I don't even want to think about it." Sarah shivers at the thought.

"That's crazy. Did you kick him out?"

"I did. I wasn't mean about it, but I told him that he should go, and I made it clear I was uncomfortable. He did apologize for being a jerk, which made me feel a little better."

"Men," Des sighs, "what is wrong with them?"

"I know," Sarah agrees. "I thought the same thing."

While out raking the leaves, Sarah's phone rings around seven-fifteen. She throws down the rake, pulls the phone from her coat pocket, and heads for the house. "Hello?"

"Hi. What's up?" Jeff sounds rushed.

Sarah fumbles with the door handle. The last thing she wants is to have this conversation on the front lawn. "Hey. I want to talk to you. Do you have a minute?"

"Sure." He doesn't sound remotely enthused.

"Okay. Look, I don't know how to say this, so I am just going to come out with it. Are you really having an affair with Kate?" Sarah feels sick as she waits for his answer. Her whole body is shaking, as it does when she is nervous.

"I wouldn't call it an affair. We're separated, Sarah, but yes, I am living with Kate."

Sarah's head is buzzing. *He wouldn't call it an affair? Why not? Is he not sleeping with her?* "You are just living with her."

"We are living together, yes."

"Are you sleeping with her?"

Jeff is silent for a long time. "Don't do this, Sarah."

"Don't do what? You said you're not having an affair. I think it's a fair question."

"Look, I'm not going to discuss my sex life with you. I didn't cheat on you, if that's what you want to know."

"Did your lawyer tell you to say that?" Sarah has no idea where that came from, but she's mad. "Come on Jeff, am I supposed to believe that you and Kate just happened to leave us on the same night, and then decided to move in together, because you had no place to go? I'm not a moron. Somebody rented that apartment, and preplanned this. Are you in love with her?"

"Sarah, stop." *Ugh, why can't she just let this go and accept it? Why does she have to make it worse?* Jeff does not want to do this to her.

"So you think you are, then? Because here's the thing...I know Kate. While you spent your time bowling every week, I sat listening to her latest complaints. She's miserable, and she's never going to be happy. She's going to drag you right down with her, and then when you're down there, you're going to look up, and realize that you threw away the best thing that ever happened to you. We were good together, Jeff. I know you know it! What is it about her that could possibly attract you?"

"Sarah, stop. I'm not going to let you talk about her like this."

"Excuse me? I'm sorry, but you're her great defender now? Fine, but I need you to explain this to me. I need to understand why you would leave me for someone like her. Tell me anything, but tell me something, please."

Again, she is putting him in a no win situation. *Fine, if she wants to know, I'll tell her.* He hates the thought of hurting her further. At the same time, he knows she will never stop nagging unless he tells her the truth. "First of all, I didn't leave you for Kate. I decided when

I went skiing with Donny, two years ago, that I was going to leave after Bethany went to college." Sarah's face falls and he can hear her gasp lightly. He knew this would shock her, but he continues. "The thing with Kate, well, it just happened. You never wanted to come out with us on Thursdays, but Kate was always there. We talked about a lot of things, and I just got to know her. Can you understand?"

"No, I don't. Please tell me." Sarah can't believe what she is hearing.

"There were a few times when Mike couldn't make it, but Kate would show up anyway. It would just be Donny, and Amy, and me, or some of the other guys, and Kate would talk about her relationship. It didn't sound good, but then one night Donny and Amy had plans, and it was just me and Kate. That's when she told me about Mike, and how he worked a lot, and didn't pay her any attention. When he did, it was always to tear her down, and make her feel small. She's smart, and so much fun, but she can't be that way around him. That's why she was always pretending to have something wrong with her. She was just trying to get his attention."

"When did this happen?"

"When did what happen?" he asks, confused.

"When was this night when you were alone with her at the bar?"

"Oh jeez, I don't know, maybe February?"

Sarah counts in her head, "Nine months ago?" She can't believe this has been going on for so long.

"I guess, yeah."

"And, you don't think that this counts as an affair? Ha! Give me a break."

"Look Sarah, like I said, I never wanted to hurt you. I would be gone whether Kate was in the picture or not, I swear. Don't be mad at her. Our relationship has nothing to do with her."

"Wow. It's just amazing to me how good you are at compartmentalizing your life into these neat little boxes. First, I have nothing to do with you leaving, and now Kate has nothing to do with our relationship. You seriously might want to see a therapist, because that is messed up."

"I'm not going to argue with you. Is there anything else you want before I hang up?"

Sarah can't believe he is ending the conversation, just like that! Suddenly, a sense of clarity comes over her, and she realizes that he isn't hers anymore. She can't yell at him, or berate him, because he can just walk away, right back into his life with Kate. Perhaps they will sit down to watch a movie together right now, and Jeff will be thankful that he is with Kate, who won't tell him that he needs a shrink. *Great.*

"Um, no," she replies. There's nothing else to say.

"Okay. I'll see you then." He hangs up.

"Okay, bye." Sarah stares at the phone in her hand. She wonders how Bethany will react to the news that her father is now living with Kate Marsh. She opens her laptop, looking for something else to focus on, so she won't go crazy. On Facebook there is a new friend request from Ginnie Pavelka. *Who is this?* Sarah clicks on the name and smiles, as Sister Ginnie's Facebook page comes up, and she can see the larger profile picture. She immediately accepts her friend request, and browses through her page. A picture of a sky with the sun's rays catches her eye, and the words that are written on it say, "Until you turn your attention away from your cares, and attend to the cares of another, you will never be healed." Sarah's eyes fill with tears. *I have no one else to take care of. How can I ever recover from this?* She grabs a tissue from the box on the desk, and closes her eyes. In a few moments, she opens them to the sound of her email notifier. In the inbox is an email from her cousin, Carol. Clicking on it, she begins to read:

> Hi Sarah,
>
> I don't know if you received my Facebook message. I'm leaving for a mission in West

Virginia on Saturday, and I wondered if you might want to tag along. My friend runs it, and they are desperate for help down there. Let me know either way. Call me if you want to know more. Thanks, Cousin! Hope to hear from you soon!

Xo, Carol

Sarah shakes her head at the thought that this may be another sign from God. Wasn't she just thinking that she doesn't have anyone to take care of? *Wow, I really need to be careful what I put out there!* It only takes a second before she hits the reply button and starts typing:

Hi Carol!

Count me in! This is by far the craziest thing I have ever done, and we need to talk so that you can prepare me for this, but I want to go. What would I do there, though? I don't have any skills. Anyway, if you think they can use me, I'm up for the challenge. Talk to you soon!

Love, Sarah

After Sarah taps the send button, she leans back in her chair, and says to Click, "I'm going on a mission! How wild is this?" But, she's excited, and for the minute it took to write that email, she didn't think about her problems once.

In the morning, Sarah realizes that she hasn't spoken with her mother since prior to the convent, so she picks up the phone and dials her number. Sal answers in his best mafia voice, "Yeah. Dis is Sal."

"Hi Sal, dis is Sarah." She tries to imitate him, but it doesn't work.

His tone changes instantly to the loving teddy-bear that she knows him to be. "Oh. Hi, honey! How's my girl? How was your trip?"

"It was great," she replies, "how was yours?"

"Oh, you know how it is, sunshine, pool service, and more food than you can ever eat. Those boats are like a floating city. It's amazing. You know, they even have rock climbing walls on there now? Here these kids are, hundreds of feet off the ocean, and they gotta climb even higher. You believe this? It's crazy. But we had a wonderful time. Maria sends her love, of course. Says to tell you she's sorry to hear about everything, and that if you need anything, you should call her. You could go visit her, you know. She's got a pretty nice place down there in Sarasota."

"Maybe I'll have to do that. I'm glad you had a good time. Is my mother around, by chance?"

"Sure, honey. Let me grab her for you. Louise!" he yells. "Sarah's on the phone." Louise picks up the extension.

"I got it!" she screams, not realizing that they can both hear her through the phone.

"Okay, honey, you take care of yourself," says Sal.

"I will. Bye, Sal."

"Bye now," says Sal, and he is gone.

"Sarah? Are you there?" asks Louise.

"I'm here, Ma. How are you?"

"I'm just peachy! How was the convent? How's Theresa? Was she happy to see you?"

"One question at a time Ma, please. The convent was fine. Everybody there was really nice to me, and I think I even made a friend."

"A nun friend, or a man friend?"

"A man friend, Ma? It's a convent for God's sake."

"Well, I don't know, it was family weekend and all that. You could have met somebody."

"Well, I didn't. I'm talking about Sister Ginnie. Do you know her?" asks Sarah.

"Oh, Ginnie, sure! She's a nice girl, that one. Pretty, too. I'm not sure how she ever ended up in the convent, if you know what I mean." Sarah doesn't know what she means, and she's afraid to ask. Her mother continues, clearing any doubt, "It's usually the ugly ones that go into the convent; the ones who have no chance of getting married. I think she could've done okay for herself, don't you think?"

Sarah takes a deep breath, and releases it. Her mother can be so exhausting. "What I think, is that Sister Ginnie is perfectly happy where she is, and that even if the richest, most wonderful man were to wander into her life, she would still choose God. It's just a guess, though."

"Honey, you can still choose God without locking yourself up with a bunch of women. After all, I did." Barely able to say this without laughing, her mother brushes some imaginary lint from her sleeve.

"What? When did you choose God?" Sarah sounds incredulous.

"I beg your pardon! I raised you all by myself, and it was only by the grace of God that we didn't starve to death. Some people have to go to church to prove that they keep God in their lives, but believe me honey, I spent my whole life praying, until the day I married Sal, and I've spent every minute since then thanking

God for all the blessings in my life. I chose God a long time ago. He didn't always give me what I wanted, but he certainly gave me what I needed."

Sarah nods silently. Sometimes you just never know about somebody. It's refreshing, this conversation with her mother. Sarah feels closer to her somehow, as if she suddenly sees who her mother is on the inside. Sarah realizes they always talk about the little things, like the weather, and their health. Very rarely do they touch on their beliefs. In the confines of religion, she was told what to believe, and there wasn't any room for discussion. Outside of those confines, she didn't want to come across as an atheist, or religious zealot. Sarah was taught not to talk about religion or politics at all. Without this conversation, though, Louise would still be the woman Sarah always imagined her to be: a happy, carefree, and opinionated woman who is mainly concerned with her own comfort and joy. Now Sarah feels as though she's been given a glimpse of her mother's soul, and she likes what she sees there.

"Sarah?"

"Yeah, I'm here. Sorry, I was spacing-out there for a second. I'm wondering if you could do me a favor. Is there any chance you could watch Click for two weeks while I go away with Carol? We'll be leaving on Saturday, so I would bring him by on Friday night."

"You mean my niece, Carol? Sure, honey, Sal would love that. Where are you going? Someplace exciting, I hope!"

"We're going to West Virginia—" Sarah begins, before Louise cuts her off.

"West Virginia? Two weeks in West Virginia? Honey, you should pick a better place. Sal and I drove through those mountains, and seriously, after you take in the view you are going to die of boredom there! Why don't you go up to Mystic, Connecticut? I hear it's really nice up there."

"I was just in Connecticut. Carol asked me to go on a mission trip with her. They're in need of some volunteers, so they asked her to go." Sarah waits for her mother's response.

"You're going on a mission trip? Are you kidding me? I should have known, with that Carol. All that money she has, and she wants to take you on a mission trip? Did you tell her that your husband just left you? Honey, you need palm trees and ocean waves, not shacks and toothless, inbred people. Oh my God, what are you thinking? I'm telling you, this is going to be a disaster. Do they even give you a bed down there? You should reconsider this. Go see Maria. The both of you could go. Her place is beautiful, and you would love it. Do you want me to call her?"

"No, Mom, we are not going to see Maria. Maybe someday, but right now I need to do this. It just feels right, so please, enough with the grief. I'm excited about this." Sarah knows her mother is rolling her eyes on the other end of the line.

"Fine, you do what you have to do. Just don't come crying to me when you come home, because I'll tell you that I told you so."

Her mother is so predictable. "I'll keep that in mind. In the meantime, I'll see you on Friday."

"Okay, honey. Have a good day. I love you."

"Love you, too, Ma. Bye."

Sarah hangs up and shakes her head. Her mother is something else.

That night she calls Carol, who gives her the whole rundown. They'll have to meet at the mission, since they're coming from two different directions. Carol recommends that she leave at six-thirty in the morning, so that they can both arrive around three-thirty. Sarah is relieved, as she is nervous about arriving before her cousin. Carol is more concerned about being on the desolate and unlit West Virginia roads after dark. She tells Sarah to pack lightly, and after mentioning a few items that she should be sure to remember, they hang up with the promise of seeing each other in a few days. Sarah is confident she'll be ready.

Over the next forty-eight hours, Sarah runs some errands, has lunch with Des, and goes to the bank. Jeff always handles the banking, but based on the balance receipts from the ATM, it doesn't seem as though his checks are being deposited. He should have been paid on Thursday, which was yesterday, so Sarah stops at the bank.

"May I help you?" Sarah doesn't recognize the woman behind the counter. In her late fifties, she appears to be having a bad day so far, and acts as though Sarah is interrupting her misery.

"Hi," says Sarah. "I want to check the balance on my account, and see if the direct-deposit was made yesterday."

"Account number?" she peers up at Sarah over her half glasses.

Sarah slides her checkbook across the counter. The woman looks down at it, and then back up at Sarah. "You're Jeff's wife! I don't think I've ever met you!"

Sarah smiles, "No, I don't believe we have met. What's your name?"

The woman's attitude turns around completely. "I'm Pat. Gosh, Jeff has been my customer for years. I used to joke with him that I didn't believe he was actually married, and now here you are, in the flesh. I can't believe it!"

"Here I am," agrees Sarah.

"Okay. So it looks as though there hasn't been a deposit in over a month. The direct-deposit has been going into Jeff's new account, ending in zero-four-five-seven. The balance in here is one-thousand, four-hundred twenty-seven dollars, and sixty-three cents. Is there anything else I can help you with today, Mrs. Jackson?"

"Um, can I make another checking account with just my name on it?"

"You want three checking accounts?" Pat inquires curiously.

"Yes, if you wouldn't mind. Can you just transfer one-thousand from that account, and put it in a new one?"

"No, I'm sorry, it doesn't work that way." Sarah's face falls in disappointment. A thousand dollars isn't a lot, but it might be all she has, so she feels the need to secure it. "What you would need to do is withdraw the thousand-dollars and then see Penny over at the desk, and she'll get you set up with the new account. You could also just write her a check. It's up to you."

"Perfect. I can write the check."

"Wonderful, you can go right over and have a seat in the chairs. It was nice meeting you, Mrs. Jackson. You tell Jeff I said hello."

"I will tell him, thank you." *Just not in this lifetime.* Sarah makes her way over to the chairs and finds a seat.

As she steps out of the bank with her new checkbook in hand, Sarah feels relieved. This is the first official step in separating herself from Jeff, and it's a boost to her confidence. If he can do this, she can, too. She will need to find work when she returns from West Virginia, so she knows what the topic of her prayers will be until she finds a job. God hasn't let her down yet, and hopefully, he will come through again.

That night, after dropping Click off at her mom's, Sarah pulls out her red notebook, and climbs onto the bed. She opens to the next clean page and begins to write. "Today, I love my mother, my cousin Carol, and unexpected trips that appear in my life. I'm hopeful that I'll learn something, and have a great time in West Virginia. Opening my own checking account brought me joy, even though I thought it would make me sad. I expect that West Virginia is going to change my life for the better. I expect that God has a reason for sending me there. I'm excited to find out what that might be. I also expect that God will find me a job." Sarah closes the book, shuts her eyes and falls asleep.

———◦◦◦❈◦◦◦———

Six-thirty comes quickly, and Sarah is on the road on time. The gas tank is filled, and she has a Dr. Pepper and some trail mix for the drive. Sarah isn't a soda drinker, but there is just something about a Dr. Pepper on a long car ride that makes her happy. She also buys a medium coffee, figuring that a little caffeine at this hour can't hurt. It isn't bright out yet, but it looks like the sun will make an appearance.

As she pulls onto I-78, the drone of the tires, and the easy flow of the early morning traffic has Sarah's mind wandering. Will Jeff be angry that she moved the thousand-dollars? She still needs him to pay for the house, and transfer the car title into her name. Imagining him going back to Kate's well furnished apartment, and telling her about the money, makes her cringe. *Ugh! How can Kate be living with my husband?* It makes no sense to Sarah.

Kate never once implied that she knew Jeff outside of the bowling alley. All that while, she just sat there listening to Sarah go on about Jeff, pretending she didn't already know the things that Sarah was sharing with the group. She remembers the conversation that Kate had initiated about sex, and the dry spell that she was experiencing with Mike. Was the whole thing just a ploy to find out if Sarah was still intimate with Jeff? While Sarah remembers what some of the other women contributed to that conversation, she can't for the life of her remember if she had said anything. Usually not one to kiss and tell, she hopes this was the case that night.

The robotic voice of Sarah's GPS distracts her from day-dreaming, as it tells her to turn onto the exit for I-81 south. The longest stretch of her trip is ahead of her, and she knows she shouldn't dwell on Kate and Jeff for the whole ride. Sarah pops in a *They Might Be Giants* CD and sings along to the upbeat and nonsensical music. The next CD in the changer is the soundtrack for *Les Miserables*, and once again, Sarah sings with gusto; especially the song Stars, where Javert is singing about catching Jean Valjean. She imagines Jeff falling, as Lucifer fell. Instead of feeling sad, it gives her strength.

The rest of the trip is uneventful. Sarah stops to use the bathroom and eat. She also listens to *Tuesdays with Morrie*, by Mitch Albom, which she borrowed from the library yesterday. The eight hour trip would have seemed much longer without something to occupy her mind. She wishes the librarian warned her to bring along tissues, though. There are times when Sarah can barely see the road through her tears. While sobbing at one point, an older lady, a passenger in a beat-up Chevy sedan, actually mouths the words, "Are you okay?" Sarah gives her a weak smile, and the thumbs-up sign. It brings her comfort that there are still some kind people left in the world.

Sarah exits onto I-77 north, which brings her through the Appalachian Mountains. With only an hour-and-a-half left, she feels the urge to talk to God. Based on the information in *Life's Little Energy Book*, it's important to spell out for the universe what it is that you want in your life, and then leave it up to God to present opportunities.

The last few weeks have strengthened her relationship, and she is now comfortable treating God casually. "So, God," Sarah begins. "You sent me on this mission, and I'm feeling a little nervous. I'm not sure what to expect, and I'm afraid that I will feel out of place. I haven't been around people this poor. Please make this successful for me. I want to help these people in some way. I hope you have some ideas about this, because I'm clueless. What if they make me build a house? I've used a hammer to hang up a picture, but that's about it. Help me to feel useful. I am trusting that you won't put me in any situation I can't handle. So far, you've done okay. I mean, I was nervous about going to the convent, too, but that worked out. Please don't forget about me over the next two weeks. Help me to do your work. I guess that's all I can ask. Thanks."

The Mission

SARAH PULLS INTO THE LONG driveway of her destination at three thirty-five in the afternoon. She finds a small house, with a large front deck, surrounded by two-by-four railing. It isn't fancy, but it is well kept. Parked near the house is a white van, with the green mission logo on the side, as well as four other cars. The blue one has Pennsylvania plates, and she hopes it belongs to Carol.

Placing her GPS in the glove compartment, Sarah checks her phone, and realizes she doesn't have any service. Tossing the phone in with the GPS, she takes a deep breath and says, "Here we go." Sarah walks up the porch steps, and knocks on the screen door. There doesn't seem to be a doorbell, and it is deadly quiet inside. After a few moments, a tall, friendly looking man opens the door. "Hello there," he looks at her inquisitively. "How may I help you?"

"Hi, my name is Sarah. I'm supposed..." he cuts her off and pushes open the screen door.

"Sarah, of course, we have been waiting for you! Welcome to Revelations, come in! I'm Bob. Let me get that for you." He takes the suitcase from her hand, and asks, "How was your trip?"

"It was long, but other than that it was fine, thank you." Sarah replies.

"Cousin, you made it!" Carol screeches. "Give me a hug." Sarah drops her sleeping bag, and welcomes Carol's embrace. She hasn't seen her cousin since a family wedding in Pittsburgh, two years ago. Unfortunately, it seems that their extended family only comes together for weddings and funerals these days. It's wonderful to have this time to relax, and focus on each other. Sarah is already feeling confirmation about her decision to come here.

"You look amazing!" exclaims Sarah. Carol looks as though she has lost at least thirty pounds since the wedding.

"I know! Isn't it fantastic? Finally, something is working for me." Carol sounds exhilarated and proud. It's been tough for her since she had the kids. Being overweight is especially awkward for a doctor. She felt uncomfortable about giving out health advice, when it appeared that she couldn't manage her own health.

"What are you doing differently?" Sarah asks.

"Oh, honey, the question is what am I not doing differently? My whole life has changed. I developed adult onset diabetes, so I started working with a nutritionist friend. That woman, she has no mercy, but I'll tell you, she knows what she's talking about. Did you know that we are not designed to eat grains?" Sarah looks confused. "I know! Who knew, right? No grains, no dairy, except for some occasional raw cheese, and green smoothies in the morning."

"Sounds gross," says Sarah.

"They're not that bad, once you get used to them. It took me a while, though. Anyway, that's enough about me. Let me show you our room, so you can put your stuff away." Sarah follows Carol down the hall to a bedroom with two sets of bunk-beds. "They weren't able to recruit those last two people, so we'll have the room to ourselves until next Saturday, when two other women will join us." Carol's sleeping bag is already spread out on one of the lower bunks.

"Can I take this one?" Sarah asks, pointing to the other bottom bunk.

"Sure. Can you imagine climbing up there every night? Or climbing down, when you have to pee in the middle of the night? Forget that. Sleep on the bottom, that's my logic! Come on, and I'll introduce you to Bob's wife Shirley." They make their way back down the hall, and turn left into the bright farmhouse kitchen. The focal point is a large wooden table, with benches on both sides, and chairs at each end. A round, glass vase containing pine boughs sits in the middle, looking very rustic. A stocky woman, wearing a white floral apron turns toward them as they enter.

"Ah, Carol, this must be your cousin!"

"Shirley, this is Sarah. Sarah, meet Shirley. She and Bob have been running Revelations for five years."

"Welcome, Sarah! I'm thrilled that you could join us. Carol tells us you're a virgin. It's so exciting to have you here!"

Sarah looks at Carol, unsure how to respond. "It's your first mission, silly," explains Carol. "Get your mind out of the gutter. They don't sacrifice virgins here, so you're safe." Carol and Shirley burst out laughing.

Sarah grimaces at the thought of being sacrificed. "Well, I'm certainly glad to hear that. It smells good in here."

"Oh, thank you, dear. That's Bob's favorite dinner: chicken and broccoli casserole. He left to pick up the rest of the crew, and soon you'll be able to meet everyone. We have a really nice group here this week, and some old favorites heading in next week, so you picked a good time to join us. While I have you here, do you have any food allergies?" asks Shirley.

"No, none that I know of," replies Sarah.

"That's wonderful. I have to ask. Back when I was a child, nobody ever had allergies. We ate whatever we were given, and my own children grew up on peanut-butter-and-jelly sandwiches. These days, things are different, that's for sure. Would you believe, I had a woman here a few weeks back who was allergic to strawberries? Can you imagine not being able to eat a strawberry? It's heartbreaking, really." Shirley lets out a big sigh. "Anyway, if you girls wouldn't mind getting out the plates, silverware, and glasses, then perhaps you could help me set the table for dinner."

When Bob returns with the missionaries, the house immediately fills with voices and laughter. Everyone goes to their rooms, washes up, and makes their way to the kitchen. Shirley introduces Sarah and Carol, and a beautiful blonde-haired girl reaches out and gives Sarah a hug. "Welcome to Revelations!" She hugs Carol as well. "Where are ya'll from?"

Carol explains that she's from Pittsburgh, and that her cousin is from Allentown. "Oh, like the Billy Joel song?" The blonde asks.

Sarah gets that a lot. The girl introduces herself as Lauren. She's eighteen years old, and has decided to do six months of mission work before starting college in the spring. From Annapolis, Maryland, Lauren grew up on the water. Her father is a sail maker in his retirement. Her great-grandfather was a shipbuilding magnate, and he taught his children the principles of philanthropy. Lauren's mother feels that she's taking it too far with hands-on mission work, but her father supports her and finances her travels. She'll be leaving for Africa in just a few weeks, and she's thrilled to find out that Carol has already been there. While the two women exchange details, Sarah moves on to introduce herself to the others.

There are fourteen people at Revelations. Sarah shakes hands with a group of middle-aged women from a Baptist church in Richmond, Virginia. Two of them are named Kathy, and then there is Sue, Arleen, and Robin. Sarah is not holding out hope that she'll remember their names, but she figures that remembering the two Kathy's might be possible. One of the Kathy's acts like the leader of their group, and Sarah discovers that they are all part of the women's group in their church. Each woman had to write down a way in which their group could contribute to society, and apparently, Kathy's slip was drawn from the bowl, and that's how they ended up on this mission.

A bearded young man named Len puts his hand on her shoulder, and asks the ladies if he might steal her away for a minute. They all giggle and agree. The young man takes Sarah's hand, and leads her away from the group. "Hi. I'm Lenny, Lenny Goodman. It's nice to meet you, Sarah." His smile is genuine, and he looks into her eyes as if he can read her mind. Far from leaving her uncomfortable, Sarah's initial reaction to Lenny Goodman is that he seems like he would be a great listener.

"It's a pleasure to meet you," Sarah responds. "What made you decide to come to the mission?"

"That's a good question. Let's see...I guess the main reason I came here is my work. I'm a freelance writer, and I'm writing an article on infiltrating Christian missions."

"Is that true?" It seems to contradict Sarah's first impression.

Lenny smiles at her. "It's partly true. I'm a writer, but I'm not infiltrating anything. It would make a great article, though, don't you think?"

"I don't know," replies Sarah. "Honestly, I'm a little confused. Are you a Christian?"

"Wow, you're not letting me get away with anything, huh? She's going right for the big questions, folks. The non-Christian, exposed! Hang him!" Lenny pretends to tie a noose around his neck and hang himself.

"No, I didn't mean that! It's okay if you're not a Christian, I guess." Sarah feels like she is digging herself deeper and deeper.

"Unsure, the lady takes a guess! Perhaps God will not damn me after all, she proclaims. Perhaps it's okay if I am not a Christian."

Sarah is pretty sure that Lenny is playing around with her, but it's been a long day. While she really wants to get to know him, she isn't up for defending herself, and decides to change the direction of the conversation. "I'm not judging you, I was just wondering about your story. It's fine with me if you don't want to share the truth. It was nice meeting you." Sarah starts to turn away, but Lenny touches her arm.

"Hey, Sarah, wait. I'm sorry. I'm not good at the whole small talk thing. I apologize. Don't go." His expression is pleading, and Sarah decides to give him another chance.

Sarah shares his pain. She isn't a fan of small talk, either. "Why don't you just tell me your story?" Sarah offers.

Shirley bangs two wooden-spoons together. "Okay everybody, dinner is served! Take a seat, please."

"Sit by me." Lenny's eyes sparkle as he takes Sarah's hand and leads her to the table.

Bob clears his throat, closes his eyes and says, "Let us pray." Everyone holds hands and lowers their heads. "Heavenly Father, we thank you for your bounty which we are about to receive, in Jesus' name. Amen."

Everyone responds with a resounding, "Amen!" and they begin to pass the plates around. The woman across the table from Sarah gives her a shy smile.

"Hi," she says. "I'm Dawn and this is my husband, Joseph." She points to the tall, balding man to her left.

"Hello," says Sarah. "Where are you from?"

"We're from Boston," replies Dawn.

"It's not actually Boston," Joseph interjects, "It's Waltham. We live in Waltham." He looks at Sarah, and apologizes, "I'm sorry. She's always telling people that we live in Boston. It's just not correct." Dawn looks down at her hands.

Sarah feels uncomfortable watching Dawn shrink back inside of herself. "I'm not familiar with Waltham. Is that near Boston?" Sarah asks.

Dawn looks up and shakes her head up and down, while Joseph says, "Waltham is west of Boston, even west of Cambridge. People always just assume that if you live outside of Boston, you can just as easily be clumped in with the people who live there, but it's simply not true." Sarah is scrambling to think of a response. Every cell of her body wants to run from this man, and she understands why Dawn is such a shrinking violet.

Lenny comes to her rescue. "So Sarah, you asked me earlier about my story, but you never did tell us yours."

"I'm not so sure that you told me yours, either." Sarah smiles at him.

"I'm saving it for dessert, so you first." Lenny scoops another serving of casserole onto his plate and smiles back at Sarah.

"Okay. Me first then, let's see. I have a daughter, Bethany. She actually just started her freshman year at Boston University."

"I went to Boston University!" Dawn's face lights up for the first time, and Sarah gets to see a glimpse of the woman inside of her cowering shell.

"Big deal," says Joseph. "I went to Harvard. Let her speak, would you?"

All of the hairs on the back of Sarah's neck stand on end. This is so awkward. She can't believe everyone is just sitting here at this mission table, and allowing this man to bully his wife. Granted, it's only the people in the immediate area who are paying attention, but Sarah can't continue to watch Dawn suffer.

"That is a big deal," Sarah smiles at Dawn. "How did you like it?"

"Oh," replies Dawn, "I loved it. My friends…"

"What are you talking about?" interrupts Joseph. "You don't have any friends. You didn't even graduate! She married me in her junior year. She didn't even finish."

Sarah's appetite is gone. She doesn't want to cause a scene, but she can't sit across from this man for another second. She looks around and notices sliding glass doors which lead to a deck. "Will you excuse me for a moment?" she asks the others, and she climbs over the bench, and walks out the doors into the crisp night air. Sarah closes the door behind her, walks to the rail, and grabbing it she tries to squeeze out her frustration on the old, worn wood. She hears the door slide open, and her whole body tenses and then releases, as she sees Lenny walking toward her.

"Are you okay?" he asks. He meanders over to her side, and leans on the railing with his forearms.

"Oh my God, what is wrong with that man?" she tries to keep her voice down, but she wants to scream.

"Yeah, he has some issues, right?" he rolls his eyes.

"You think? How can he treat his own wife like that in front of everybody? And he's so damn cocky that he doesn't even realize he's being an ass. Wow, the poor girl. How can she stay with him?" Sarah wonders.

"We all have our demons, I suppose," replies Lenny. "For some of us, those demons are memories. For others, they are as real as someone like Joseph. And yet for others, the demons are imaginary. I think those are worst type, the imaginary ones. Which ones are you running from?"

"What makes you think I am running from anything?" she asks.

"Come on, Sarah, I thought you said that you wanted us to speak the truth. We're all running from something, right?

"So then, what are you running from?" she asks.

"You do know how to turn a conversation around, don't you?"

"I'm an expert." She smiles at him knowing she's won.

"Alright then, you want honesty, here you go. My father committed suicide when I was fourteen years old. I should be over it by now, eighteen years later, but I'm not. I was a good kid, but my father was hard to please, you know? I was always trying, though. I earned my black belt in karate when I was only eleven. I was on the honor roll without fail, and I was the quarterback of the high-school football team. Not once did my dad ever tell me that I did a good job. My mom, she's great, but all of her love couldn't fill what I needed from my father. When he killed himself, it just got worse for me. Everybody keeps telling me that my dad is an angel, and that he is watching over me. It doesn't help. I just want to be able to make my own decisions, and do things because they make me happy. I'm still looking for his approval, and I don't know why. It's why I'm here on this mission trip. Before he died, his church helped to found Revelations. He was so proud of this place, so I wanted to see it. I wanted to see this thing that was so worthy of his praise compared to me."

Sarah leans to the right, and bumps his shoulder with her own. "I'm sorry. That sucks."

"Yeah, what can you do, right? It is what it is. So, it's your turn. Which kind of demons are you running from?" he asks.

The sliding door opens, and a boy around the age of twelve sticks his head out. "Hey you guys, we're starting debriefing now."

"Thanks, Justin, we'll be right in," Lenny says, and Justin closes the door. Lenny looks at Sarah, "Well, it seems like you're saved by the bell. I'm not letting you off the hook, though. After debriefing, it's your turn."

"What is debriefing?" asks Sarah.

"Come on, it's easier to show you." Lenny takes her hand again, and leads her through the kitchen and into the living area, which is filled with mismatched furniture. They take a seat next to each other on Lenny's favorite floral couch, which faces the picture window. Three of the church ladies are sitting on the couch facing them, and the light from the window causes them to appear as shadows with glowing auras surrounding their heads. Lenny likes the affect and finds it peaceful, and he hopes Sarah will feel the same way. Carol smiles at Sarah from the rocker to her right and gives her a wink, as Bob begins to speak.

"If everyone will hold hands, we can begin. Let's just take a moment to reflect silently on today's events." Grasping hands, Sarah is disappointed to have an unobstructed view of Joseph. How unfortunate that she should start her trip with him. Lenny seems interesting, though, and Sarah is looking forward to knowing the others, as well. She asks God to help her to tolerate Joseph, and pave a smooth path for the rest of her relationships here on the mission. "Heavenly Father," Bob begins, "thank you for returning us safely back into this community of love. Help us to feel inspired to share, so that others may witness the power of your work, through the Holy Spirit." After a moment, Bob looks around the room and asks, "Who would like to begin?" Bossy Kathy raises her hand.

"I chose to go over to Mrs. O'Grady's home to help with her roof repair. I spent some time speaking with her, and it seems that she has an open sore on her foot. She showed it to me, and I believe she's in need of some medical attention. She also mentioned that she hasn't been able to write to her daughter in a while due to arthritis, so I told her that I would come back tomorrow, to help with the writing. She was very grateful."

"Thank you, Kathy," said Bob. Is there anyone else who was at the O'Grady place that would like to speak next?" A tall, thin man, sitting in the club chair next to Carol, raises his hand.

"I will. I got most of the roof done today. Tomorrow, I need to go back to put the gutters up. If I have another person to clean up on the ground, we can probably finish by noon and head to another job."

"That's great, Shawn, thank you. Wasn't someone working on the railing there, as well?" asks Bob.

"That was us," answers Robin. "It's all finished, though. We even stained it before we left. Mrs. O'Grady told Sue that her faucet was leaking. I don't know if we can do anything about that."

"Dawn and I can start out at Mrs. O'Grady's in the morning. I can fix a leaky faucet, no problem," offers Joseph. "We were on an evangelizing walk this afternoon. Mr. Minnick could use a ramp. He took us in his yard to see his chickens, and it was downright scary watching him walk down those steps in the back of his house with that walking stick. He said he doesn't use the front door, so the back is probably the best place for a ramp. Also, I don't know if you have access to those canes with four legs, but he could use one of those, too."

"He was really proud of the way he carved that walking stick. I don't know if he would want a cane," adds Dawn.

Joseph's eyes narrow. "Don't be a moron. Of course he would want the cane. He only has that stupid stick because he can't afford a cane. You should use your head sometime."

Dawn drops her eyes to her lap, and Shirley places her hand on her chest and says, "Oh my." Everyone looks as uncomfortable as they feel. Everyone that is, except Joseph.

Bob speaks first. "We'll see what we can do about finding one of those canes. Who would like to go next?"

"I'll go," says Sarah. They all look over at her in surprise, and she has to admit, she feels the same way. She is especially shocked by what comes out of her mouth. "Hi. I'm Sarah." She makes eye contact with the few people that she doesn't yet know, and says, "I haven't met some of you, and I hope you won't take this the wrong way. I have only been here since four o' clock, but already I have been made to feel so uncomfortable by Joseph's treatment of Dawn, that I have to say something. I-"

"Excuse me!" exclaims Joseph. "I will not stand for this kind of treatment!" Bob puts his palm up toward Joseph.

"Please, Joseph, let her finish, and then you may speak." Bob requests.

Sarah takes a deep breath, and continues, "I just want to say that we are supposed to be here to help people who are so much less fortunate. This behavior, it isn't loving behavior. It's not kind. I don't see how we can claim to be Christians and then condone this type of behavior. I can't do it. I don't know much about the Bible, but-"

"No, obviously you don't," fumes Joseph, "because if you did, then you would know that a woman is supposed to cleave to the man and obey him! Dawn is a good person, and you have no right to attack her like this!"

"What are you talking about?" responds Sarah. "Dawn is clearly a good person. What I do know about the Bible is that somewhere in there it says something about defending the weak, and I am not going to sit here while you speak to her like that in front of us. Have some respect for your wife, and if you can't do that, at least try to respect all of us."

Joseph crosses his arms over his chest, leans back on the couch, smirks and shakes his head slowly back and forth. "You're really something, you know that? I do respect my wife. I'm not the one who called her weak, that was you. Let me tell you something, lady, I'm not going to let you talk about my wife that way. If you want to question anybody's Christianity here, you should go take a look in the mirror first."

Sarah's head is buzzing with anger and frustration. *Poor Dawn!* She can't imagine living with a man like this, or trying to have a reasonable conversation with him. In a moment of clarity, Sarah realizes that she can't change a man like Joseph. If she is going to help Dawn, she will have to talk to her alone. She hopes she might have that opportunity. She looks over at Bob and Shirley, "I'm sorry," she says, "maybe I'm out of line." Bob pinches his lips together in a firm line. Sarah can see that he doesn't want to continue the conversation and aggravate Joseph further, but he is clearly on Sarah's side. Shirley surprises her by speaking.

"Please, Sarah is right. This is a Christian mission, and our job is to demonstrate, through the grace of the Holy Spirit, Christ's love in action. Joseph, if you could please refrain from calling your wife insulting names like moron, I would see it as a personal favor. Now, who would like to go next?"

They all finish check-in, and the evening proceeds without incident. Joseph excuses himself and goes to his room, and Dawn follows along like a reluctant puppy. She does make eye contact with Sarah right before she turns the corner, and Sarah believes she can see a flicker of gratitude in the young woman's eyes. Gratitude mixed with fear, which breaks Sarah's heart.

That evening, Sarah, Carol, Lenny, Sue, Robin, Theresa, and her son Justin, are sitting around the farm table playing a game of five-hundred rummy, which has been going on for over an hour. "I'm out!" shouts Carol.

"Add them up everyone, this might be the final round," says Lenny, as he examines the score sheet. They all tally their points, and Lenny commences with the totals. "And the winner is Theresa, with five-hundred-and-thirty points!"

"Yay, Mom!" shouts Justin. "Good job!"

"Thanks, honey, why don't you go get ready for bed, and I'll be there in a minute."

"Okay, goodnight everybody."

"Later, Justin," says Lenny.

"Good-night, Justin," everyone else sings in chorus. Lenny looks at Theresa, "He's a great kid."

"Thanks," says Theresa, "I'm a fan of him myself. He's got a good head on his shoulders for a kid, you know? He's very compassionate, too, which makes these mission trips a perfect fit for him."

"That's nice," says Sue. "How many missions has he been on?"

"This is our sixth. His first was right here with Shirley and Bob during their first season here. His favorite was Australia, although we both agree that the flight was a nightmare, and now we try to stay closer to home. My husband and younger son will probably join us next year in Louisiana, but for now Josh is too young, and my husband would prefer to stay home with him.

"It's such a great educational opportunity," says Sue. "I wish my kids had opportunities like this. I'm surprised you don't go in the summer, though. Does he have a hard time catching up with school work?"

"Not at all. Justin is homeschooled, so we just schedule the trips so his workload is lower while we are away. He does a lot of projects based on the trips, though, so it works out well."

"So, you're a teacher then?" asks Robin.

"I'm Justin's teacher, yes, but I was a nurse before I had Justin," replies Theresa.

"What about friends? Isn't it very lonely for him?" asks Sue.

"I was afraid it might be, but it didn't turn out that way. We have a bunch of kids in the neighborhood, and he is involved in Boy Scouts, and sports. Justin is smart. It works well for him because he can work at his own pace, and he usually finishes the curriculum well ahead of schedule. I like it because we can provide opportunities like this for the boys, which they wouldn't be able to take advantage of, otherwise."

"Interesting," remarks Robin, "I would have gone crazy if my kids were home all the time."

"Well, I can see how it's possible, but the kids know what I expect from them, and our family works well together. It actually makes me sad when I send him off to camp in the summer. He loves it, though. Anyway, thank you everyone. It was a fun night. I will see you all in the morning. Good night!"

As Lenny cleans up the cards, the rest of the ladies beg off to bed, and leave Carol, Lenny, and Sarah at the table. Lenny looks at Sarah, and says, "Well?"

Sarah feigns ignorance. "Well, what?" she asks.

Right then, Dawn walks quietly into the kitchen. "Sarah," she whispers, "may I speak with you for a minute?"

Sarah is happy Dawn has found an opportunity. "Sure." She glances at Lenny and Carol, and excuses herself. The two women make their way to the empty living room, and sit on the sofa furthest from the doorway. Dawn keeps glancing up nervously, obviously fearful that Joseph will discover her deception.

"Is Joseph sleeping?" Sarah asks.

"Yes. Sarah, please, I can't stay long. Please, I am begging you. I know you are trying to help me, but I need you to ignore him." Sarah twists her face in disbelief. "Please, Sarah, you don't know him like I do!"

"No offense, Dawn, but I don't want to know him." Sarah starts to raise her voice, and Dawn puts her finger to her lips and glances at the doorway. Sarah lowers her voice immediately, "I'm sorry. I just don't know how you can stand it! He's so cruel to you. You shouldn't put up with that."

"I know. I know you think I'm stupid, and maybe you're right. He is my husband, though, Sarah, and my job is to deal with him. That's what God wants me to do. It's what I have to do."

"Dawn, that's not true! God doesn't want this for you!"

"Don't say that." Dawn looks down at her hands, "We're married."

"I was married, too! My husband left me, but before he did he was kind! You can find someone who will respect you. You don't have to tolerate this."

Dawn rings her hands, as tears run down her cheeks. "Please, Sarah. Nobody would want me. I am ruined.

I have no education. I need him, so please don't make him angry. It doesn't make it easier for me." She looks right into Sarah's eyes and pleads, "Please."

Sarah grabs Dawns hands and squeezes them. "I can help you. You don't have to stay with him!"

Dawn grips her hands in return. "You are a good person, Sarah. I have to go. Remember what I said, please." With that, she wipes her cheeks with her shirt sleeve, and leaves the room.

Sarah walks back into the kitchen, stunned by her conversation. She had assumed that Dawn would thank her for intervening, not ask her to retreat. Part of her is disappointed in Dawn. If she's being honest, another small part is even disgusted.

A dim light burns over the sink, but otherwise the kitchen is dark. Lenny and Carol assumed that Sarah and Dawn might be gone for a while, so they decided to turn in for the night. Sarah pours herself a glass of water, and walks down the hall to her room. Carol is in bed reading by the light of a small book lamp. "How did it go?" she asks.

"It wasn't good."

"No? What happened?" Carol inquires.

"Oh, I don't even know. She doesn't want me to interfere. She said it will make it worse for her, and I should ignore him. Can you imagine?"

"I'm not surprised."

"You're not? I can't believe that girl. What is she thinking?" The frustration is still swirling through Sarah's body.

"Face it Sarah, Dawn doesn't have one shred of self-esteem. How could she possibly muster the courage to rebel against Joseph if she doesn't feel worthy of anyone, but for the likes of him? Nobody wants to end up alone."

"Yeah, tell me about it," agrees Sarah.

"What does that mean? Are you having problems with Jeff? Is that why you are acting so sensitive about this whole situation?" Carol looks curious.

"Sensitive? Are you kidding? That guy is a jerk, Carol. I don't understand why everyone isn't rebelling and kicking his ass out of here. He doesn't even deserve to step foot in any place that associates itself with Jesus Christ. Jesus would be appalled if he met that man."

"That may be true," replies Carol, "but we have no right to judge him. He is a child of God, just like the rest of us, as flawed as he may be. You can do more for Dawn by befriending the poor girl. Be a bright light in her week, maybe in her life, but don't push her into a situation that she's not prepared to handle. That will just stress her even more."

Sarah stares at Carol for a second, "My God, you're right. I have gone about this the wrong way, haven't I?

"Don't beat yourself up," offers Carol. "Your intentions are in the right place. I'm sure she knows that."

"My heart, it was my heart that was in the right place. She needs love. She deserves it, you know. I'm going to make sure that she gets it."

"Good for you, Cousin. Now, I have to get some sleep, because I can't keep my eyes open for another second."

Carol switches off her book light, and is sleeping in minutes. Sarah isn't so lucky.

After a fitful night, Sarah doesn't feel her best in the morning. Her head is a little achy, and it seems as though she's pulled a muscle in her neck, which prevents her from turning her head completely toward the left. When she and Carol join everyone in the kitchen at seven-thirty, she learns that breakfast is a much more casual affair than dinner. There are some dry cereals on the counter. Sarah sees a box of Special K and a few sweetened ones which don't interest her. There is instant oatmeal, a bowl of apples and bananas, and the makings for toast. Some people are eating, while others are busy preparing their lunches.

Shirley appears from amongst the crowd, and says, "Good morning! I hope you both slept well. We have cereal, oatmeal, fruit, yogurt, and toast for breakfast. Please help yourselves. In the refrigerator, you will find some sandwich fixings. There should be turkey, bologna, ham and cheese, and there is also a bowl of tuna salad, or peanut butter and jelly for lunch. Go ahead and pack your own lunch now, and you'll take those with you. Make sure you fill your water bottles, and bring them along, as well. Did you bring water bottles?" she asks.

"Yes," they both reply.

"Excellent! If you have any questions at all, please just ask me."

Sarah picks up a brown paper bag, and begins to fill it with a banana and an apple. She puts together a tuna salad sandwich, fills her water bottle, and sits down to eat a bowl of maple-and-brown-sugar oatmeal. Carol sits down across from her with a banana, picks up Sarah's empty oatmeal packet, and reads from the back, "Thirteen grams of sugar. Wow, that's half of your day's sugar right there in that bowl."

"I didn't put any sugar in it." Sarah defends herself.

"Good thing that you didn't, or it would be even worse. You're supposed to limit your sugar to twenty-four grams per day," volunteers Carol.

"Says who?" asks Sarah.

"Says me, I'm a doctor, remember?"

"I remember. Did you just make up that number?" Sarah inquires. She never considered sugar grams before.

"No, I didn't make it up! It's about the amount of sugar your pancreas can handle before it becomes overworked and stressed. It's especially important, since we have diabetes in the family."

"We do? Who has diabetes?" Sarah asks.

"Hello? Our great-grandmother had no legs, Sarah!" Carol can't believe what she's hearing. *Have you been living under a rock?*

"That was because of diabetes?" asks Sarah, surprised.

"Yes! What did you think happened to her legs?" Carol can't wait to hear the answer.

"I don't know. I knew she was in a wheel-chair because she had no legs. I guess I never really thought about it."

"Well, now you know," says Carol. "One of our aunts has it pretty bad, too. Aunt Marjorie, remember her?"

"Yes, from when I was little. I haven't seen her in a long time, though," replies Sarah.

"Well, she's nearly blind, and is missing some toes, as well."

"Oh," Sarah looks down at her bowl of oatmeal, which looks far less appealing, "I guess I'll just have a banana."

"It doesn't matter. A banana can have eighteen grams of sugar, so you may as well just finish your oatmeal." Carol shrugs, and takes another bite of banana.

Sarah, more confused than ever, finishes her oatmeal, washes the bowl, and follows the others into the living room for devotions. After prayer, Bob begins to explain the options for the day. "Some people will need to head back to Mrs. O'Grady's this morning, including Shawn for the gutters, and Kathy to help her write to her daughter. Carol, I'd like you to take a look at her foot. Joseph, you said you would fix her faucet, and then we'll need one more volunteer to help Shawn with the gutters. Anyone interested?"

"I'll go with Shawn," offers Justin.

"Great. That will work perfectly. Thank you, Justin." Bob writes everything down on a notepad.

Joseph speaks up, "Dawn would like to come with us, too. She can clean the lady's house or something."

Bob looks over at Dawn, and sees her eyes drop immediately to her hands. "You can clean if you would like to, Dawn, but I could really use your help in the evangelizing group today. I have a list with a few female shut-ins, and I think they may appreciate your gentle spirit. Would you be willing to do that instead? Carol and Kathy can help Mrs. Grady if she needs any cleaning."

Without lifting her eyes, probably because she is afraid to see Joseph glaring down at her, Dawn shakes her head to convey her willingness.

"Thank you," says Bob. He writes her name on the list. "Lenny, Sarah and Theresa, would the three of you be willing to evangelize, as well?" Sarah isn't sure how she feels about evangelizing, but she likes the idea of working with Lenny and Theresa, so she agrees, along with the rest of them.

"That just leaves the laundry and cleaning, over at Mrs. Ritter's home. I received a call from the agency, and apparently this woman is a hoarder. They have dropped a dumpster outside her home, and we need to get that house back in living order." He looks over at Robin, Sue, Arleen, the second Kathy, and Lauren, "I need all of you to start working over there, and then I'll pick up everyone from Mrs. Grady's after lunch, and bring them over to help. Are there any questions?" Nobody responds. "In that case, I'll give this evangelizing list to you, Lenny, and you can drive the car for your team. The rest of you can follow me out to the van."

Just like that, Sarah is headed out on her first mission, without her cousin, and without a clue as to how to evangelize. She is nervous, horrified, and excited, all at once. Theresa sits in the front with Lenny, while Sarah and Dawn climb into the back. Lenny enters the first address into the GPS. It looks like their first visit will be with a Mrs. Dorothy Leary. They follow the winding mountain road, and when the GPS announces that their destination is ahead on the right, Lenny slows the car and they look for signs of a residence. Finally, Theresa notices what appears to be the remains of a mailbox post, fallen to the ground, with the mailbox lying on its side a few feet away. Sure enough, there is a driveway through all of the weeds, and Lenny turns the car onto the dirt and gravel path. The pot holes are like craters, and with no sign of a house in sight, Sarah would be lying if she said she wasn't hesitant. If someone were to offer her a way out of this right now, she would take it and run.

Eventually, they pull up in front of a trailer. Aside from being rusty and ancient, the place is neat, and there are signs of life. A plant in the flowerpot on the porch looks taken care of, and there is a half-empty glass of iced-tea on the small table next to an old wooden rocker. Lenny looks at the others, lifts his hand and knocks on the door. He calls out, "Mrs. Leary? We're here from the mission."

"Come in!" a small voice calls from inside. The four make their way in to find a petite woman sitting on a faded brocade sofa. She removes her reading glasses, replaces them with another set, and says, "That's better. Now I can see you!" Mrs. Leary examines each one, and invites them to come in and sit down. "Young man, if you would grab one of those chairs from the kitchen, then there will be enough seats. I wasn't expecting so many! Usually only two people come, but this is lovely! It's like a party, don't you think?" They all agree, and Theresa speaks first.

"It is so nice to meet you Mrs. Leary. My name is Theresa, and this is Dawn, Sarah and Len. How are you feeling?"

"Oh, I'm just fine, just fine. There's no use complaining when it won't change anything, am I right? That's what my husband always used to say, bless his soul. My Jimmy is gone twenty years now, but I'm still here, watching the sun rise every morning."

"You must miss him terribly," says Dawn.

"It's a funny story, that," replies Mrs. Leary. "My Jimmy, he was an angry man. What I miss most is that he would drive me places, to visit our friends and such. Now, I don't get out much. Well, that's not true. Now, I really just don't get out at all. I'm ninety-three, though, ninety-three or ninety-four, somewhere around there. I don't really expect too much. I had a cat for a while, and that was nice." She looks at the others, and smiles a toothless grin.

Looking around the room, Sarah sees there's no television. In fact, there isn't even a lamp in this room, other than a small oil lamp that looks more like a decoration. "Do you have electricity here?" she asks.

"Oh, sure, sure," replies Mrs. Leary. I don't need to use it much. Sometimes in the kitchen I will, but I wake up with the sun and go to sleep when the sun goes down. Seems how nature intended, wouldn't you agree?"

"Yes, I would agree. I wish I could do that myself!" says Sarah.

"Well, I reckon you could if you want it badly enough. It's very simple, really. You know what? I just thought of something you nice, young people could do for me. Follow me." Mrs. Leary practically leaps from the couch, and makes her way to the kitchen, and then into a small hallway which leads to the bedroom. She opens a closet in the hall, and points to the high shelf.

"See that shoe-box? That brown one?" Lenny steps forward and points to the only shoe-box on the shelf.

"This one here?" he asks.

"Yes, yes, take that down. Put it over there on the kitchen table, would you?" Lenny follows her directions.

"Come, come," Mrs. Leary beckons everyone to the kitchen table, "sit down." Lenny hustles back to the living room, and returns with the missing chair. Everyone watches expectantly, as Mrs. Leary slowly opens the box.

"These are my treasures." She holds her hand over her heart, and looks over the contents of the box. Slowly she reaches in, and retrieves a picture. "This is my son, Charlie. He's been gone for over fifty years now. He died from the drugs, which near broke my heart. You're not supposed to bury your children, but that's what me and my Jimmy had to do." She passes the picture, so everyone can see it.

"He was so handsome," comments Dawn. "Was he married?"

"He was married, but his wife left him. She was right, too. Charlie brought everyone heartache." Mrs. Leary wipes a tear from her cheek. She reaches back into the box, and pulls out a black and white picture of a young couple. "This is me and my Jimmy." Again, she passes the photo. Picking up another, she says, "I haven't looked at these pictures for years. I've been too afraid to climb on the chair, to get the box. This is very nice of you. Thank you."

"Maybe you can find somewhere else to keep the box, so that you can get to it easily," offers Lenny.

"Yes, that's a good idea," she agrees.

"Mrs. Leary," says Dawn, "you have been through so much in your life. I was wondering, do you accept Jesus as your Lord and savior?" Sarah cringes. It seems like such a personal question to ask a total stranger. She looks to Mrs. Leary, curious to see her response.

"Sure I do, dear. Sure I do. Would anyone like some tea?" she asks.

Dawn looks disappointed. Sarah isn't sure if Dawn was hoping to be able to save Mrs. Leary, but it certainly appears that way. Everyone declines the woman's offer of tea.

Lenny says, "If there is nothing else we can do for you today, Mrs. Leary, we should probably be on our way."

Dawn puts her hand on his arm, "Wait," she says, "Mrs. Leary, are you willing to proclaim Jesus Christ as your Lord and savior right now?"

Mrs. Leary looks down at her hands, and then she looks Dawn right in the eye, and says, "I'm suddenly feeling very tired, dear. I think I'm going to lie down

for a while. It was nice of you to visit me, though."
Mrs. Leary walks toward the front door, and everyone
follows. Lenny seems to be lingering, and as she glances
back to look for him, Sarah notices that he retrieves
something from his wallet, and places it on Mrs. Leary's
kitchen counter. They say their goodbyes, and make
their way back to the car, as Mrs. Leary closes the door
behind them. Sarah falls behind the other two women,
and waits for Lenny to catch up to her.

"What did you put on her counter?" she asks him.

"What do you mean?" He sees her inquiring look,
and realizes he's been caught. "I'll tell you later."

Sarah says, "Okay," but she's puzzled. Why won't
he just tell her? It looked like money, but she's not sure.
They all climb into the car. The other two women are
already in the back, so she sits in the front with Lenny.
Their next house is only down the road, and they don't
need to bother with the GPS. Fortunately, the driveway
belonging to Mr. Peter Reilly is clearly marked, and not
nearly as long as Mrs. Leary's.

"Before we go into the house," begins Theresa,
"how do you guys think it went over at Mrs. Leary's?"

"I had a good time there," offers Sarah. "I was
nervous going in, but she was very nice."

"She was nice, but you could tell that she isn't saved,"
sulks Dawn.

"You don't know that for sure," says Lenny. "She said she accepts Jesus as her savior."

"She didn't actually say it," whines Dawn. "I think she was just agreeing because she knows why we were there. That's how it seemed to me."

"It's my belief, and this is only my opinion," offers Theresa, "that our job is to talk with these people, and build relationships with them. I know that we are here to evangelize, but we can do that by spreading the word of God, and showing them Christ's love through our consideration for their needs and feelings. I don't think it's imperative that we get them to expose or admit their beliefs, unless they want that."

"Well, what is the point of this then?" asks Dawn. "I thought the whole reason for these visits is to tell people that their life can be so much better if they are willing to admit that Jesus is their savior."

Lenny feels compelled to speak up, "I think that God would want us to be kind and loving. It's our job to try to find as many ways to do that for these people. For whatever reason, fate has not smiled on them, and we have the opportunity to bring a little bit of happiness into their lives. We are happy people, because we know our own value in the eyes of God, and in the eyes of each other and ourselves. When we meet these people, our happiness can be contagious, and maybe they will ask why we are so happy, and we will have an opportunity to tell them about God's love. I think it should flow easily, and it doesn't have to happen on the first visit."

"Are you happy, Dawn?" Sarah can't resist asking.

"Of course I'm happy. Can we go in now?" Dawn opens the car door and steps out. It takes all of Sarah's will to leave it at that.

The mission works closely with social services, as well as a few contacts throughout the region that let them know of shut-ins who might appreciate a visit. That is how Sarah's group ends up at Peter Reilly's home this morning. When they pull into the driveway, Peter rolls his wheelchair around the side of the house to meet them, with a shotgun across his lap. Lenny tells the women to stay in the car, and steps out with his hands in the air.

"What do you want?" Peter asks.

"We're from the mission," replies Lenny.

"Oh! Come on in! Sorry about the gun," says Peter. "You can't be too careful when you're in a chair. I don't think I'd stand a chance in a brawl!" He laughs out loud, and instantly puts Lenny at ease. Lenny motions to the women to join him in the front yard, and they all introduce themselves. "Listen," says Peter, "I have to go up the ramp in the back, so if you don't mind, we can all walk around the house together. So, who else have you visited this morning?"

"You're only our second stop. We were at Mrs. Leary's place before this. Can I push you up?" Lenny offers.

"That would be great." Peter allows Lenny to push his wheel-chair up the ramp. "How is old Mrs. Leary? That lady just keeps on ticking. Did she try to feed you?"

"No," says Theresa, "but she did offer us some tea."

"Oh no, did you drink it?" Lenny asks, sounding concerned.

"No, we didn't," Theresa replies.

"Good thing. That woman is crazy with the herbs. When I was younger, she was always trying to get my mother to force me to drink her awful concoctions. She said it would make my legs work again. I drank some of them, because I tried everything back then, but eventually, we figured out that she didn't know what she was talking about. She's a trip."

"I don't think she accepts Jesus as her Lord and savior, though," says Dawn. Sarah can't believe she has brought this up again.

"Oh, I don't know, she is a good person, just a little bit of a witch-doctor is all," replies Peter.

"And that doesn't bother you? Why would you want to associate with someone who is a witch?" asks Dawn.

"Well, first of all, I don't really associate with her. I don't get out much, as I'm sure you can imagine. Secondly, who am I to judge her? I don't think she is really a witch, but even if she is, that would be her problem. I knew her grandson, Mark. He and I would play when I was a kid. My legs worked back then, and Mrs. Leary was always nice to me."

"What happened to your legs, if you don't mind my asking?" Sarah inquires.

"I was hit by a falling tree, about twenty-two years ago now. I was only a kid, sixteen years old, and I was helping my Pa and my Uncle Joe with the cutting. It was a freak thing. The tree started to fall, and when I turned around to grab the chainsaw off the ground, it bounced off another tree and swung over in my direction. I never saw it coming. All of a sudden there was this blow to my back and I was pinned to the ground. I never walked again after that day."

"I'm so sorry. That must be so hard for you," says Sarah.

"It was at first. I had a girl back then, and I always thought we would end up together. It was too much for her, though, trying to imagine how I could be a proper husband or father. I couldn't even imagine it at that time, so I wasn't able to convince her to stay. I should've tried harder. I heard that her husband beats her, so I'm sure I could have done better than that. Can I get you anything, tea maybe?" Peter winks and smiles. Once again, everyone declines the offer.

"Is there anything we can help you with while we are here?" asks Lenny.

"Not really. At this point I have everything down to a science. If there's not a tool to help a short person reach and grab something, then I have invented it. Come look at my collection." He rolls over to the other side of the living room and picks up a long pole with pinchers on one end, and a squeezable grip handle at the other end. "Check this out. I made it myself." Lenny uses the pinchers to grab a book on the mantle and bring it down to his lap.

"What's this?" asks Theresa, as she picks up a fifteen inch piece of wood that is about one inch in diameter with a handle across the top, so that it looks like a letter T. On the bottom is a rubber foot, attached with duct tape.

"I call that my short cane, watch this." Lenny takes the cane from her, and then drops the book on the floor. Using his left hand to balance on the floor with the cane, he is able to lean out of the chair, and grab the book. "That move is just too risky without the cane. If I fall out of the chair, I'll spend the rest of the day on the floor."

"That must be awful. Who takes care of you?" asks Dawn.

"I like to think that I take care of myself, but truth is, there's a woman who comes at night and in the morning, to get me in and out of bed."

"What if something were to happen to her? Would you just be stuck there?" asks Dawn.

"I do have a phone, and I keep it near me all the time. My uncle lives right on the other side of the mountain, so he can come if needed," replies Peter.

"Can't you just go live with him?" asks Theresa.

"I don't know whether I could or not, but I do know that I don't want to. This is my home. It was my parents, and my grandparents before that. This is where I belong. So that's enough about me. Tell me, what do you folks do for fun?" Peter asks.

"What do I do for fun?" asks Theresa. "Goodness, let's see. We go bike riding a lot with the kids. Lately that's been our go to activity when we get some free time together. On my own, I like to read, play volleyball, and bird watch. I crochet like a mad woman. Last year, I donated thirty-seven blankets to the nursing home in our town, so I am trying to beat that number this year. I started painting a few years back, with oil paint, and I'm actually pretty good. So, last winter, a friend of mine paid me to paint a portrait of her dog's head, on a human body. It turned out so well that I've done seven for other people since then. That's about it, really, other than spending time with my boys and husband."

"Wow," exclaims Sarah, "I'm impressed! Your life sounds so interesting compared to mine, and I know you've also been on five other missions, right?"

"Yes," confirms Theresa, "this is our sixth mission. What do you do for fun, Sarah?"

"Let's see," says Sarah, "I have a labradoodle named Click, and we go for long walks every day."

"What's a labradoodle?" Peter asks.

"It's a dog," answers Sarah, "and it is part Labrador retriever, and part poodle. He's great. We got him because he doesn't shed, but it turns out he's a friendly guy, too."

"Okay, so what else?" asks Peter.

"What else do I do for fun?" Sarah scrunches her brow in thought. "I don't know. On Tuesday nights, my best friend sings karaoke at the pub near our house. That's fun, I guess."

Lenny laughs out loud, "You sound convinced! Do you sing, too?"

"Oh, God no, that would just be cruelty to others," laughs Sarah.

"You should sing," says Peter. "Life is too short not to sing. Who cares what other people think, right?" He looks around to the others for support.

"Absolutely," agrees Lenny. "You should sing right now."

"What?" screeches Sarah, "Are you out of your mind?"

"No, seriously," adds Theresa, "we should all sing. Do you guys know *The Lion Sleeps Tonight?*" Everyone nods, and Theresa becomes the conductor, assigning parts, and explaining how it will all play out. On the count of three, she points to Dawn, and begins to sing with her, "Wee-ee-ee-e-he-he-ee-ee-ee-e-ee-um-um-buway," then she points to Lenny, who chimes in with, "a-wimoweh-a-wimoweh-a-wimoweh-a-wimoweh." Before long, everyone is singing and laughing. Peter covers the main part of the song, and Theresa sings the wailing part in the background exceptionally well. They aren't ready to start their own band, but the song is certainly recognizable, with all the parts included. Most importantly, it is fun! They do it one more time for good measure, and then Peter asks Dawn what she does for fun.

"Well," begins Dawn, her smile vanishing in an instant, "I...we..." They are all focused on her, wondering what she will say. She starts to feel really warm, and knows that her cheeks must be turning pink. Joseph always yells at her when she blushes, but she can't help it. It always happens when she is nervous, and, unfortunately, she is usually nervous. Her mother wouldn't be surprised, either. According to her, Dawn can't do anything right. She had tried to talk to her mother when Joseph began to berate her on a regular basis, but her mother accused her of trying to ruin any chance she had of ever getting married. At the time, Dawn couldn't imagine that anything could be worse than living with her mother, who was constantly insulting her, so Joseph seemed like the best opportunity to escape. Sadly, it seems that Dawn jumped from the frying pan into the fire. Joseph is cruel. He isn't like any other man she's ever met. *Peter is so full of life, and optimistic, even though he's in a wheelchair. Lenny is so kind, and cheerful. It just isn't fair.*

"Dawn?" asks Theresa. "Are you okay?"

"What? I'm sorry. Yes, I'm fine. I just got a little distracted."

"That's okay," says Lenny, "It happens to all of us. Peter asked what you do for fun."

"Right, so, Joseph likes to play golf, and he owns racehorses, too. We watch them race."

"That must be interesting," offers Peter. "Do you have to travel around to race them?"

"We take them to New Jersey, and Kentucky," replies Dawn. Everyone waits for her to expand on that, but it seems as though she is finished, so Theresa rescues her.

"So, Lenny, it's your turn. What do you do for fun?" Theresa asks.

"Probably about ten years ago, I decided that I was only going to do fun things. I play guitar and ukulele. I like to skateboard and rollerblade, and I travel, a lot."

"Where have you been?" asks Sarah.

"Oh, gosh, let's see. I've been all over Europe, my favorites there are Scotland, Switzerland, Sweden, and Vienna. I loved Peru, Ecuador, and Costa Rica. If you can ever go to Thailand, you should. It's so beautiful there, and the people are so kind. It's a magical place, and very spiritual."

"Wow," says Peter. "I can't even imagine being able to travel like that. What kind of job do you have?"

"I'm a writer, for the most part. I also play music in bars and restaurants. That's mainly for fun, but it does provide some spending money, so it's a good hobby." Lenny smiles, "When I was in France, I actually posed as a nude model."

"No, you did not!" exclaims Dawn with wide eyes.

"Yes, I did!" Lenny's face lights up like a little kid at Christmas. "It was fun. It was daring. I was so nervous the first time, I almost chickened-out, but it really wasn't that bad. The artists are concentrating on what they're doing, so I didn't feel self-conscious at all. There was one time, though, that I made the mistake of looking at one of the artists eyes because they were so pretty. It was fine for a while, until she started painting my face, and then it felt like we were staring at each other. If you decide to do it, just remember not to look at their eyes."

"I'll keep that in mind," says Theresa, and everyone bursts into laughter.

"You should come back, and bring your guitar," suggests Peter.

"I would like that, but only if everybody agrees to be my backup singers," says Lenny.

"That would be fun!" exclaims Dawn. Sarah and Lenny look at each other, and smile.

Sarah feels so good about this visit that she doesn't want it to end, but they need to get moving so they can see the others on the list.

Lenny spots an area near the creek where they can pull over and eat their lunch before they head over to the next stop. Dawn and Theresa decide to walk along the water while they eat their sandwiches, and Sarah and Lenny sit down on a fallen tree trunk, not far from the water's edge.

"Whatcha got there? Anything good?" he asks.

"Tuna," Sarah holds up her sandwich, "you want some?"

"No thanks. Tuna's not really my thing. I have peanut-butter-and-jelly."

"Ah, a big boy sandwich," Sarah smiles.

"Hey, how do you think I got this big?" he asks while patting his belly.

"So," Sarah begins, sounding more serious, "Tell me what you left on Mrs. Leary's counter. Was it money?"

"It wasn't just any money, it was lucky money," replies Lenny.

Sarah turns to face him, straddling the log like a horse. "Why is it lucky?" she asks.

"It's not really as lucky for her, as it is for me. It's something that I learned from my grandmother. She would always write little notes that said, "It's your lucky day," and then she would fold them up in one-dollar bills, and leave them all over the place, for people to find. When I was little, she used to let me stick them places when we went to the store or the movies. One time, when we were at a restaurant, I had to go to the bathroom, so she gave me a dollar with a note, and told me to leave it on the sink. I was probably about seven at the time, and I was trying to save my money to buy a Star Trek shirt, like Captain Kirk used to wear. After I went to the bathroom, I stuck the dollar in my pocket, and when I got home that night I threw away the note, and put the dollar in my Scooby-Doo bank. The next morning, I went downstairs and my mom was crying. Apparently, she thought the dog was sleeping in front of the refrigerator, but when she went to get the cream for her coffee, he didn't move."

"That's terrible," says Sarah.

"I know. I thought I had killed my dog because I stole the lucky money. I promised God that day that I would never steal again, and that when I got some money of my own, I would give it away."

"That's interesting. Did you ever ask your grandmother why she started giving her money away?"

"You know, I never did. She did tell me that it was how she made good things happen, and I believe that's true."

"Because of your dog?" asks Sarah.

"No, it's not just because of the dog. I think it makes me feel better to do it. I like knowing that every day, somebody is finding those dollars and feeling lucky. No matter how crappy their life is at that moment, they might think that because it's their lucky day, good things can happen for them. And then, because they are thinking that way, good things will happen. Or at least, they'll be more aware of the good things."

"That's really sweet. I like it," Sarah says.

"Good, I'm glad. You should try it, because I really believe that we should spend the majority of our energy being happy, doing things that make us happy, and making other people happy. People always seem to be on an eternal quest for happiness, as if it's this elusive thing, like the holy grail. In all that searching, though, they're missing the truth which is right there inside of them the whole time."

"And what is that truth?" asks Sarah.

Lenny smiles at her. He's seen so many people like Sarah. They're good people who want to do the right thing. They know that there has to be something more to this life and they feel so close to the answer that they can almost taste it, yet they're just not ready for the truth yet. They can hear it physically, but it just doesn't compute. He wonders why that is. Why are some people ready to awaken from the drudgery that they've created, in order to start creating something amazing, while others aren't? He wonders if Sarah is ready.

"We create our own happiness. It's the truth. It's the reason some people come through tragedy unscathed, while others go as far as suicide, in order to escape the pain. It's the pain, Sarah, it's not real. We create it ourselves, all of it, and in an instant, we can decide to create something else instead. Isn't it incredible?" asks Lenny.

Sarah thinks about her life, and about Bethany leaving, and Jeff being with Kate. This pain is not real? How can that be true? Sometimes, even when Sarah isn't thinking about them, she has this terrible feeling inside, and then she remembers her situation. She thinks about telling Bethany about the separation, and it breaks her heart all over again. Sarah looks at Lenny, and he's looking back at her with such exuberance. She doesn't have the heart to tell him that some problems are just too big for his little theory. "It is incredibly unbelievable," she says.

The sparkle literally fades from Lenny's eyes. Sarah isn't ready. Deep inside he knew that, but he didn't want to believe it. Eventually, she'll catch on, but how much of her life will she waste, before she figures it out? His grandmother's words ring out in his head, "When the student is ready, the teacher will come." It seems he isn't going to be that teacher for Sarah, and that is disappointing.

"So, when are you going to tell me your story? Who is the real Sarah?" he asks.

"Who am I?" repeats Sarah. "This is as real as I get. No makeup, really bad hair, eating lunch in the woods. It's just me." Lenny watches her silently. Sarah looks around, avoiding his gaze until she can stand it no longer. "What?" she asks. "I feel like you are waiting for me to say something else. What is it?"

"I'm just curious, I'm sorry. I feel like you are holding out on me, and I'm not sure why. I can't help but wonder, it's just the way I am," he replies.

"You are reading too much into this. I am not holding out on you, it's just that I don't know where to begin. There's so much that you don't know about me."

"I know that you have a daughter, and that she's a freshman at Boston University. Why don't you start there?" Lenny suggests.

"Okay, let's see..." Sarah begins.

"Hey, are you guys ready to head out?" asks Dawn. The two women are walking toward them and stop in front of the fallen tree.

"Sure," replies Sarah. She swings her leg over the log and stands. Lenny looks up at her, smiles, and shakes his head. She is saved again.

After visiting a Mrs. Murray, the four of them head over to Mrs. Ritter's crowded home, where everyone is loading up a dumpster in the front yard. The property is swarming with activity. Apparently the others who were over at Mrs. O'Grady's this morning have already arrived to help. Sarah walks up the three steps, onto the porch. At least she assumes that there must be a porch under all of the stuff. It appears that Mrs. Ritter's hoarding isn't just contained to the inside of the house. It looks like a flea market gone wild. An old refrigerator with a missing door is filled with stuffed-animals, tools, some purple silk-hydrangea flowers and other miscellaneous things. The porch swing is covered with a blanket that has seen better days. A fat, grey, tiger-striped cat is curled up on it, her head resting on the strings of an old tennis racket. There are five gallon buckets filled with things that have no reason to be clumped together. As Sarah nears the door, she inhales a strong aroma of must, dust, and something that must have been dead for longer than she has been alive. She instinctively covers her nose and mouth with her hand, and ducks inside. Immediately, she has to step aside, so that workers can walk past with laundry baskets filled and headed to the dumpster.

"Do you need a basket?" asks Bob.

"Oh, sure," responds Sarah. "Where do I start?"

"Wherever you'd like, just keep an eye out for Mrs. Ritter. She's in the kitchen right now, and she gets rather upset and resistant when she sees her things going into the baskets. Just avoid her as much as you can if you're cleaning. When you are talking to her, try to distract her as much as you can. It's been working well so far. You should've seen this place this morning!" Bob hands her a basket, and heads back outside.

Sarah can't even begin to imagine what it must have looked like this morning. It's still the most cluttered house she has ever seen, by far.

"Oh, hi Sarah," says Carol, carrying a laundry basket from the kitchen.

"Hey Cousin, how's it going? Can you believe this place?" asks Sarah.

"It's really something, huh? I feel bad for her. She's pretty stressed about losing all her stuff. We need to have this done by Friday, or they'll condemn the house, and she'll have no place else to go."

"Who's going to condemn it, the health department?" asks Sarah.

"I'm not sure. I'm just telling you what Bob told me earlier," Carol responds.

"You wouldn't think they have a health department down here." It's so remote, and these people seem all but forgotten. Sarah can understand why it's the perfect location for a mission. She places her basket on the floor, and picks a pink shirt off of a pile of stuff in the living area. Looking to Carol, she asks, "Do I just throw this away?" The shirt is a wrinkled mess, but it's in good condition, and it looks clean enough.

"Put all the clothes in a pile. In the end, if she has too many, they'll donate some to a charity. Just throw away the garbage and the things that have no value, like this, for example." Carol holds up a bobble-head figure of President George W. Bush. Sarah watches as she throws the toy into her laundry basket, and wonders if Mrs. Ritter paid money for that thing, or if someone had given it to her. Sarah can't stop wondering about the psychology of hoarding.

"Why do you think she lives like this?" asks Sarah.

"Well, I don't know her, but from what I know about hoarding, it's classified as an obsessive compulsive disorder. Most hoarders don't really care about collecting things, but they get extreme anxiety about throwing things away. Ironically, it's because they are perfectionists."

"Perfectionists, are you kidding?" questions Sarah, as she looks around. "No perfectionist in her right mind would live like this!"

"Well, it would seem that way," offers Carol, "but in fact, perfectionists are afraid of making the wrong decision when it's time to get rid of things, so instead, they just hold on to everything. It's very difficult to help someone like that. We'll clean out her house today, but she still won't be able to throw anything away tomorrow. Someone like Mrs. Ritter won't be able to get the therapy she needs to have any hope of living without hoarding. It's unfortunate."

"It's still so weird to think of her as a perfectionist. It just goes to show you that you just can't judge people." "It's true. You should go talk to her. I had a conversation with her earlier, and she is a very organized woman, in her own way." With that, Carol picks up her laundry basket and heads outside.

Sarah finds her way into the kitchen, stepping over piles and walking through narrow paths along the way. Mrs. Ritter is sitting in a chair next to the kitchen table, which is piled high with stuff. She has her hand over her mouth and seems to be staring at the white porcelain sink.

"Mrs. Ritter? Are you okay?" Sarah asks. The woman lifts her gaze to look into Sarah's eyes. There's so much fear in her eyes that it makes Sarah's heart clench. How can she help this woman? She closes her own eyes, and sends up a quick prayer, asking for some guidance in this situation. Immediately she is overwhelmed with such a feeling of love for this disheveled woman, whom she has never met. Sarah kneels down on the floor in front of her, and takes her hands in her own. "Look at me Mrs. Ritter. I'm not going to leave you. My name is Sarah."

"Sarah," repeats Mrs. Ritter in a whisper, "are you an angel, Sarah?"

Sarah squeezes Mrs. Ritter's hands tighter. She has never been called an angel before. Just as she is about to say no, she has a thought, or perhaps it is a feeling. In fact, it's both at once. Sarah knows that this is an opportunity to do God's work, and that she should not let it pass. She feels the need to step into the role of an angel for Mrs. Ritter, and that somehow it is the right thing to do. Taking a deep breath, Sarah looks into Mrs. Ritter's eyes and says, "I am an earth-angel Mrs. Ritter. Everything is just fine. Is there something you need to tell God right now? He is always listening, and I am listening, too."

The corners of Mrs. Ritter's mouth turn up, and she starts to cry. "God sent me an angel? Oh Sarah, I am so scared, all of these people..." she looks around the kitchen in fright, and Sarah places her hand on the woman's cheek, and redirects her gaze back to Sarah's eyes.

"Stay with me. Look at me. What is your first name, Mrs. Ritter?" asks Sarah.

"My name is Aggie."

"Aggie, look at me Aggie," says Sarah. "I want you to tell me about something, or someone, that you love. Can you do that for me?"

"Someone that I love, like my sister?" asks Aggie.

"Yes, tell me about your sister. What is her name?" Sarah inquires.

"Her name is Martha. She is so wonderful. I wish you could meet her."

"Where does she live?" asks Sarah.

"Oh, she moved out to Blacksburg, in Virginia. She comes to visit sometimes, though. She doesn't like to stay here because she says the house is a mess, but maybe now she will be happy. Oh Sarah…" Aggie squeezes her hands again.

"How long does it take to get to Blacksburg?" asks Sarah.

"About two and a half hours, I think. I've never been there myself. Martha always comes to visit me because I don't drive. She always says that I should come out and stay with her, but I hate to make her drive both ways, it's just too much." Looking over at Lauren, who is placing some boxes of Saltines in the laundry basket, Mrs. Ritter says, "Oh please, don't take the crackers. Those are still good!"

"But, they expired three years ago," replies Lauren.

"They are still good. They aren't even opened. Please, please, put them back," begs Mrs. Ritter. Lauren looks to Sarah for help, and Sarah nods toward the shelf, indicating that Lauren return the crackers where she found them. As she does, Mrs. Ritter loosens her grip on Sarah's poor hands.

"Aggie, do you have a phone number for your sister?" asks Sarah.

"Yes, I have Martha's phone number, but I don't have a telephone. If something were to happen, I have to walk up to Johnny North's house, to use his phone. He's not nice about it either, so I only did it once. It would be nice to talk to Martha, though. It's been a few months since I've seen her, and now with all of this happening, she has no idea."

Sarah's wheels are spinning. She wonders if she would be allowed to drive Aggie to her sister's house, so that she could stay there for a while. This is so traumatic for her, and Sarah just thinks that if she can get the woman out of her house, it might help her peace of mind. "Aggie, I was thinking. How would you like it if I drive you out to your sister's house, so that you can stay with her for a while, and then she would only have to drive you back? Would that make you happy?" Sarah isn't even sure that she can get permission to do such a thing, but it seems harmless enough. Certainly, the mission can go on without her for the five hours that it would take for her to make the round trip. She wants to run and ask Bob right now, but she promised Aggie that she wouldn't leave her.

Mrs. Ritter's hands fly to her chest, "Oh, Sarah! That would be wonderful! But it's too much! I couldn't ask you to do such a thing for me."

Sarah feels a warmth spreading in her heart. "That's what angels are for, right? Come walk with me. I want to find the person in charge, to ask him if it's okay for us to use his phone, so that you can call your sister. Can you find her number?"

"Really, you are truly going to do this for me?" Aggie asks, her eyes brimming with tears.

"I am really going to try," responds Sarah. She stands up, and reaches out for Aggie's hand. "Let's go find Bob," and she leads the woman out the kitchen door and down the steps, into the yard. Carol is standing with the five women from the church. "Have you seen Bob?" Sarah asks, and they let her know that he is in the front. "Carol, will you do me a favor, and get him for me?"

Carol makes eye-contact with Mrs. Ritter. She has no idea what Sarah is up to, but she's smart enough to realize that Mrs. Ritter might have a heart attack if she catches sight of everyone tossing her things into the dumpster. "Sure, I can. Excuse me ladies, I'll be right back," and she wanders around the side of the house.

"Why don't we sit over here at the picnic table while we wait?" Sarah can see that Aggie is tired, and needs to rest her legs. Moments later, Bob seats himself across from Sarah.

"How can I help you, Sarah?" he asks.

"Bob, Mrs. Ritter has a sister who lives in Blacksburg, Virginia. Do you know how far away that is?"

"Oh, I'd say Blacksburg is a little over two hours away by car; maybe two hours and fifteen minutes."

Sarah is happy about this. It would take even less time than Aggie had estimated. "I am wondering if Mrs. Ritter might use the phone at the mission to call her sister, to see if she may be able to visit with her for a while. If she agrees, then I would like to know if I may drive her out there tomorrow morning. I could use my own car, if it's not a problem."

Sarah is certainly one of Bob's favorite guests. She impressed him yesterday when she defended Dawn during circle time. Joseph is not an easy man to love, but Sarah managed to put him in his place by condemning his actions, and not his person. It is something that even he had been struggling with, and yet she managed to come in and see what needed to be done for the integrity of the group. Bob has seen a number of people talking with Mrs. Ritter today, but Sarah was able to quickly determine a way to bring her some happiness during this time of stress. Aggie Ritter appears more peaceful than he has seen her look all day.

"It is an unusual request, but if you can make the arrangements with Mrs. Ritter's sister, then I think it's a fine idea. Let me drive you back to the house, so that you can use the phone."

Sarah and Aggie smile at each other like two six-year-old-girls who are given permission to have a sleepover. "Let me go get Martha's number. I'll be right back!" exclaims Mrs. Ritter.

After Aggie returns to the house, Bob reaches across the table and clasps Sarah's hand in his own. "That is a fine thing you're doing, Sarah. I hope it all works out for her. Thank you for suggesting it."

Sarah smiles, looks down in her lap and then back up at Bob. "When I was driving down here, I worried that I wasn't going to be able to help these people. I'm not a doctor like Carol, or a construction worker. I don't know anything about building anything. What they need though, is love. Everybody just needs love, you know? And by loving them, it has just filled my own heart so much. I feel like I don't need anything else, like I am complete. It feels good."

"Now you know why I do what I do," he replies. "Sure, Shirley and I could live in a nicer house. At one time, we did. Our relatives come to visit, and they can't figure out why we want to live in one of the poorest areas of West Virginia, with neighbors who all depend on welfare to survive. But, we aren't poor, Sarah. Shirley and I feel rich and very blessed. We meet kind and caring people like you, who visit us over and over, in order to make a difference in the lives of others. It's when we finally recognize Christ in ourselves that we have the ability to create miracles. You are creating a miracle for Aggie Ritter today. That's what it's all about." He gives her hand a final squeeze and stands up, as Aggie comes down the steps with her purse. "Shall we go, ladies?"

Martha is thrilled that Aggie will be coming to stay, and the two women make arrangements for Sarah to pick up Aggie at nine-thirty the next morning. Bob returns Mrs. Ritter home, picks up the others, and after dinner they all gather in the family room, once again. Sarah finds a seat next to Carol on the sofa, and Lenny joins them there. Everyone holds hands, and Bob opens with a prayer.

"Heavenly Father, we thank you for the opportunities that you have provided for us to do your work here on Earth. We ask you to bless us as we share our testimonies, so that we may be witness to the work of the Holy Spirit, through us, and in us. Who would like to begin?"

Dawn raises her hand half way. "Can I...may I start?" she asks. Joseph looks over at her, but he doesn't speak. "By all means, please do!" offers Bob.

"Today, when I was out evangelizing, I had this revelation. I just want to thank Theresa, because of something she said that made this connection for me. I think before today, I felt as though I was a better person than people who haven't been saved. I felt like my job here was to convert as many people as I could. Now though, I realize that my job is just to get to know these people, and find out who they are and what they need. Not to say that Jesus can't be a part of what they need, but that if they aren't willing to accept him yet, I can still be of service to them. I don't know. Does that even make sense?" Dawn asks. Everyone else nods and agrees.

"It's true," says Bob. "Believe me when I tell you that there are people here who want nothing to do with Jesus. But that doesn't mean that they aren't good people, or that we shouldn't help them. We need to treat them with dignity and respect, just like Jesus would have done."

"Anyway," Dawn continues, "I just wanted to say thank you, Theresa."

"You're welcome," Theresa replies. "I think today was a really good day. I feel great about the interactions that we had."

"Thank you, Theresa," offers Bob. "How did things go at Mrs. O'Grady's this morning?"

"The gutters are finished," volunteers Shawn. "Justin was a big help there, so thanks, Justin." Justin smiles, and nods his appreciation.

Carol speaks up next. "I dealt with the wound on Mrs. O'Grady's foot. Her blood sugar levels were high, and she should be on diabetes pills, so I wrote her a script. I left some clean bandages, and instructed her on how to change them, but you're going to want to keep somebody on that. I can go every other day to change them while I'm down here, and hopefully, we can get it healing by the time I have to leave."

"Thank you, Carol. Anyone else?" asks Bob.

"I'll go," volunteers Lauren. She twirls her long blond hair in her fingers, as she thinks and speaks. "I felt really bad for Mrs. Ritter today. I wanted to help her, but at the same time it was hard for me to relate to her. I just don't understand what she is thinking. Like, this one time, I was cleaning up the kitchen and there were these crackers that were expired for years, and she was begging me not to throw them away. Why would you want to keep old crackers?"

"Can I answer that?" asks Carol, and Bob nods his head. "I was telling Sarah that hoarders are usually perfectionists. Mrs. Ritter is afraid that by deciding to throw away the crackers, she will one day learn that she could have used them, which would thereby make her decision to throw them away a bad decision. Perfectionists have a lot of trouble making decisions, for fear of getting it wrong, so they tend to put off decision making. Procrastination is a trait that goes hand in hand with perfectionism."

"That's interesting," responds Lauren. "It almost makes it sound like being a perfectionist is a bad thing."

"Well," replies Carol, "it is a bad thing if it keeps you from trying new things, and growing. It's much more important to do a thing, than to do it perfectly. We only become perfect through practice, but if we are afraid to do something until we can do it perfectly, then nothing will ever get done."

"That's a good point, Carol," says Bob. "Would anyone else like to share?" No one raises a hand. "In that case, I would like to tell you about something that happened today, while we were over at Mrs. Ritter's home. Sarah was talking with Mrs. Ritter, and she offered to drive her to her sister's house in Blacksburg,

Virginia, which is little over two hours away. Sarah saw that Aggie Ritter was having a hard time of it, and she found a way to help her, which seems both simple and obvious.

I encourage all of you to remember this story as you are dealing with these people here. What is it that you can do for them that they can't do for themselves? What is it that they need? Sometimes all it takes is to be a presence for them. Hold their hand, listen to them, and be in the moment with them. Other times, there is more to be done. Now is your opportunity to stretch yourself, or what my Shirley here likes to call *giving until you feel good*. Seize this opportunity while you are here, and then take the lesson back into your own lives. Right where you live, in your neighborhoods, and at your jobs, there are people who need help. Be that light for them. Fill yourself with the Holy Spirit, and then let your light shine. People who need you will find you, and you will find them. You don't need money, or special skills, or lots of time. You just need to open your heart, and let the love pour out. Let's join hands. Heavenly Father, thank you for the lessons we have learned today, and for allowing us to be beacons of light for those who are lost in the dark. We ask that you guide us in Jesus' name. Amen."

The group responds with a cheerful, "Amen," and they disperse for a slice of Shirley's famous apple pie, and then break into smaller groups for conversation. Lenny grabs Sarah's hand as she starts to get up.

"Wait, Sarah," he begins, as she lowers herself back onto the couch. "I would like to go with you tomorrow, to Virginia. Is that okay with you? I didn't want to ask Bob without talking to you first." Sarah is caught off guard. She was hoping to bring Carol along, so the two of them could spend time alone on the ride back.

"That's really kind of you, Lenny. I was hoping that my cousin and I would get to spend some time together. We don't see each other very often, and even though we've been here for two days, I still haven't really had an opportunity to talk with her."

"Please, you don't have to explain. I understand completely. You should definitely take Carol." Lenny has this way of staring at Sarah that makes her feel so vulnerable. His eyes are so warm, and kind. She feels she could gaze into them forever. She isn't attracted to him, and yet something inside of her longs to curl up next to him on this couch and lean her head against his shoulder. He seems so steady and grounded. She also has this mad desire to touch his beard. *Is it soft?* "Shall we get some pie?" he asks, and holds out his hand to help her up.

"What? Pie? Oh, right. Yes, please. It smells so good, doesn't it?" she sniffs the air, and Lenny agrees.

———◦◦◦)◉(◦◦◦———

The next morning, Sarah packs lunch for herself and Aggie, and then finds a seat on the loveseat in the living room. Carol plops down in the spot next to her, excited about making the trip to Virginia with Sarah.

Bob completes the opening prayer, and then lifts his legal pad. "Okay, let's see what's going on today. It looks like Shawn will be heading up a crew at Mr. Minnick's to build his wheel-chair ramp. We will need another group at Mrs. Ritter's to continue emptying her house. Can someone volunteer to be the lead over there?"

"I can," offers bossy Kathy.

"Thank you, Kathy. Carol, I'm hoping you will take the lead on the evangelizing group today. There are three people on the list who can use a doctor, so that will work out well."

Carol looks at Sarah, and then back to Bob. There is silence for a moment, as she struggles with her decision. Finally, she says, "That's fine," and then looks at Sarah once more, and mouths the words, "I'm sorry." Sarah shrugs her shoulders. It's the right thing to do, and Sarah would have made the same choice.

"Bob," interrupts Lenny, "would it be alright with you if I ride to Virginia with Sarah?"

Bob's eyes latch onto Sarah's, and he asks, "Is that okay with you?"

"Sure," Sarah agrees. "That would be great." Lenny grins and winks, and Sarah can't help but wonder if he had arranged it so that Carol wouldn't be able to go. Realistically, she can't imagine him doing such a thing, and she certainly doesn't see Bob going along with it.

Sarah is relieved. She is excited about the idea of spending time with Lenny, but she feels caught off-guard by the change in plans, and she wants a little time to herself to gather her thoughts. After she says goodbye to Carol, Sarah excuses herself and returns to her room, where she leans back against the pillows on her bed.

"God," Sarah begins, "why am I feeling so flustered?" She wonders about her feelings for Lenny. It seems like she knows him so well, as if they have some sort of connection. *This is crazy!* She hasn't even been here for two full days, but for some reason there is already something there. Sarah has been holding back, too. She knew as soon as she met Lenny that she would end up telling him everything, but she's also afraid that once she does, anything could happen. As far as Lenny knows, she could be happily married right now. After all, he knows about Bethany. *Why am I even thinking about any of this? It's not as if this can go anywhere, can it?* Lenny looks young, and that beard could be making him look even older than he actually is. *Wait, didn't he tell me his age? His father died when he was fourteen and now it is eighteen years later, so he's thirty-two.* Well, that's not as bad as she thought, but he's still over ten years younger. *Ugh! I need to stop thinking about this.* Instead, she turns her thoughts to Bethany, and how in two weeks she'll be telling her about Jeff. *It is much easier to think about Lenny.*

———◦◦◦)◉(◦◦◦———

At nine-fifteen Sarah slides into her jacket and heads down the hall. Seated in the rocking chair, Lenny strums his guitar. He stops when he sees her. "Are we ready?" he asks.

"I am, are you?"

"I am, yes. Do you play guitar?" he asks.

"No, I wish I did. I never had any kind of musical talent."

"You can sing," he offers.

"What? No, I can't, not in a good way, anyway."

"See, that's the great thing about singing. It doesn't have to be good for you to enjoy it. As long as it makes you feel good. You like to sing in the shower, right?" he inquires.

Sarah thinks about that. "I don't think I've ever sung in the shower."

"Really? You're kidding me. Do you sing in the car?"

Sarah smiles at the thought. "Yes, in the car, I definitely sing. As long as someone is singing much louder on the radio, it's usually safe."

"Awesome, then we can sing in the car," he replies.

"Wait, what? How did this just happen?" she laughs.

"You're going to love it. Let's go so we don't keep Mrs. Ritter waiting. Let me grab some CDs from my car and then we can hit the road."

Everyone is already hard at work when they arrive at Mrs. Ritter's. Aggie, wearing a red sweater, is sitting in the chair on the front porch, looking impatient, with her purse sitting at the ready on her lap and her suitcase at her feet. When Sarah pulls up in front of the house, Aggie lifts her suitcase, and slowly hauls herself down the steps. Lenny jumps out of the car to help her with her bag, pops the trunk and stows it away. He holds open the passenger's side door, offering Aggie the front seat.

"Do you mind very much if I sit in the back?" she asks. "Cars make me nervous, and I'll have more room if I sit in the back."

"By all means then, please, sit in the back." Lenny opens the back door, and hovers awkwardly, in an attempt to help Aggie lower herself onto the seat of the car. Once she is safely inside, he closes the door, and climbs in beside Sarah. "All right ladies, we're off!"

Sarah pulls out of the driveway, and directs the car toward Bartley Store Bottom Road. There aren't many roads in this part of West Virginia, so it appears that Sarah will be re- tracing much of the route she used to arrive at the mission. In the back seat, Aggie is rambling on about the work being done at her house, and how it's a waste to dispose of all those perfectly good things. Lenny tries to explain that the things that are in good shape will be donated to people who need them, but Aggie argues that she *is* one of those people. Furthermore, if that's the case, they should just leave it all where it is. Sarah doesn't want to argue with Aggie, so she tries to use some of her tactics from yesterday to distract the woman.

"So Aggie, tell me all about your plans once you get to Martha's house. What will you girls do there? Is Martha married?"

"Oh yes," replies Aggie. "Martha has a very nice husband named Jim. I haven't seen him in years, because Martha always comes to visit by herself. She has four children, you know, but none of them live at home anymore. Hopefully, they'll come to see me. I know her one daughter lives in Vermont now, and I reckon that's a bit too far for visiting, but I think the others live close enough." Sarah manages to keep Aggie talking about everything from raising children, to canning pickles. Apparently, she was quite the farmer in her day, and she grew and jarred enough food to help a good portion of her community eat throughout the winter. "Life in English wasn't always so bad," she says. "My Granpappy was a lumber man, and there was a time when the people who settled in English did alright for themselves. Eventually, though, the industry fell apart and everyone was left without a job. That's when things got real bad."

After exactly two hours and thirteen minutes, the GPS directed them onto Martha's street. Her husband Jim is a professor of entomology at Virginia Tech, which Aggie finds fascinating. The neighborhood is beautiful, and nothing like Sarah was expecting when they set out this morning.

"Would you look at this house? My goodness, you should come in, Sarah! I want you to meet Martha," says Aggie. "Also, Martha told me that Jim has a huge bug collection all over the house. I can't wait to see it!" Sarah wishes she could feel the same enthusiasm. Bugs aren't really her thing, but she's excited for Aggie.

Sarah wonders how it is that Martha is residing in such luxury, while her sister lives in squalor in English. Being an only child, Sarah always wanted a sister. She can't help but hope that she would be more generous than Martha appears.

The three of them climb up the porch steps, and before they can ring the bell, the front door swings open and a petite brunette in a navy pencil skirt, white silk-blouse, and red pumps shouts, "Baby sister! I can't believe you're really here! Come inside, and give me a hug!" Martha is so well coiffed, she looks like a president's wife. Aggie introduces Sarah and Lenny, and the three of them are ushered over to the seating area. "Please, make yourselves comfortable. Can I get you a drink? If you need to use the powder room, it's right down this hall, on the left. Oh my goodness! I just can't believe you're here, Aggie!" gushes Martha.

"I know," agrees Aggie, "Sarah is my angel, aren't you Sarah?" The compliment makes Sarah feeling slightly uncomfortable, but Aggie gazes at her with such adoring eyes, Sarah continues to play along.

"That's right, Aggie. You deserve only good things. I'm glad that we were able to help you come here and see your sister." Aggie squeezes Sarah's hand.

"I am so grateful, Sarah. I'll never forget what you've done for me. Your kindness has been a lesson to me. My mother always used to ask us if we were willing to love enough. Do you remember that, Martha? Whenever we were having a problem, or complaining, Mama would slam her hand on the table and say, 'Tell me Agatha, are you willing to love enough? Are you?' And, you know what? I don't think I ever knew what that meant until today. It's easy to love when things are good in your life, but to be able to fill your heart with love when times are trying, that's another story, or to love someone who is making you crazy, that's a true test. What you've done, though, Sarah, showing me such love and kindness, when you don't even know me, I believe Mama would say that you are willing to love enough to make a difference. Thank you." Sarah leans into Aggie's open arms. She is a good woman, and Sarah is glad that she made the effort to make a difference for her.

Martha is a gracious hostess. Her home is magnificent, and she treats Sarah and Lenny as if they are honored guests. Unfortunately, Jim isn't home to provide a narrated tour of the bugs, but Martha does her best to make sure that they're able to see all of the specimens, before they leave for West Virginia. After they all exchange hugs, Sarah and Lenny finally wave goodbye, and drive away.

"What are you grinning about over there?" Lenny asks, as a huge smile stretches across Sarah's face.

"I don't know, it just feels good, you know? We made a difference for her."

"You made a difference. This was you're idea. I'm just along for the ride, so thank you for allowing me to tag along with you. Tell me, how are you feeling about the whole mission experience?"

"It's like nothing I've ever experienced before, that's for sure. You're catching me at a really good moment, after this whole day with Aggie, but overall, I don't know. I don't think I want to do it again if that tells you anything. Is that terrible of me?" she asks.

"No, it's not terrible, if it's your honest opinion. What is it specifically that you don't like?" Lenny is curious.

Sarah glances over, trying to find the right words so as not to offend him. She isn't sure of his beliefs, and in no way does she want to insult his religion. "I was raised Catholic, not that I have been a good one, by any measure. There's something about the language of being saved that just doesn't resonate with me. The idea of going out, and trying to recruit people to be saved is so foreign to me. It feels uncomfortable. I'm sorry."

"Please, don't apologize, I can understand that. Because of my dad's heavy involvement with the church, and the mission, I pushed it all away. At this point, it feels foreign to me, too. That whole thing with Dawn..."

"Oh, I know, right?" Sarah interrupts. "That was so uncomfortable. I felt so bad for Mrs. Leary, and I would hate if someone put me on the spot like that. I feel at any moment someone might ask, 'So, Sarah, do you accept Jesus Christ as your Lord and Savior?' I don't want to have to answer that! Don't get me wrong, I think Jesus was an amazing teacher. I'm in complete agreement with him that we should love one another, and that we shouldn't judge each other. He said that the Kingdom of Heaven is within us, and I believe that, too. I just feel that religion has turned the tables on Jesus, you know? Deep down I just can't believe that he would want to be worshipped. He wanted us to be examples of love, and act like him, so that's what I try to do."

"I agree," says Lenny. "I also find it very frustrating when the people who are making a point of advertising their Christianity are the very people who are the most judgmental and hateful. It's as if they feel that since they have accepted Jesus as their Lord and Savior, he's going to give them a free pass to break all of his rules."

"Exactly. Anyway, I think that's why I wouldn't do it again. I do like meeting the people and hearing their stories, though. I could have stayed at Peter's all day, and I hope that we can all go back and sing with him."

"He is a great guy," agrees Lenny. "So, Sarah, tell me about you. I'm not letting you out of this car until I hear your story. There's no one here to interrupt us, so you should be able to get it all out this time."

This is it, they'll be no going back after this. But in another week-and-a-half, she'll never have to see Lenny again, so why not just lay it all out there? "Okay, I'm not sure where to begin." Sarah pauses for a few moments to gather her thoughts, and Lenny remains silent and patient. "My husband and my daughter, they were my life. It got to a point where I never thought about myself. It was all about what they wanted to do, and I fit myself into that. My husband is a big bowler. I was never very good at it, but I sat at that bowling alley for more nights than I could ever count supporting him, and talking with his friends and their wives. I already told you that on Tuesdays, I sit and watch my best friend while she sings karaoke. Before I dropped my daughter off at college, I sat through rehearsals, plays, and recitals, and chauffeured her around to wherever she needed to be. In doing all of that, I somehow forgot about me. I was no longer a writer, or an artist, or a dancer; all things that I once considered myself to be. I was just a mother, a wife, a daughter, and a friend. The day after we dropped my daughter off at Boston University, my husband told me that he doesn't want to be married to me anymore."

"Wow, I'm sorry," says Lenny.

"Yeah, thanks. I didn't expect it. I mean, some marriages are rough, but mine wasn't like that. My daughter still doesn't know, and she's going to be in shock when we tell her over Thanksgiving break. It's the main reason that I don't want this mission trip to end. I can't even imagine what that conversation will be like. Isn't that strange? I keep rehearsing it in my head, but it's never the same way twice, and it may still turn out nothing like I've imagined."

"You seem like a great mom. Your daughter is lucky to have you," offers Lenny. Sarah smiles half-heartedly.

"Thanks, that's nice of you to say. I wish it didn't have to be this way, but there's nothing I can do."

"Can I ask what made you come to the mission? I know now that it's not because you were determined to save some lost souls." Sarah chokes on a laugh.

"No, I'm afraid it is much more selfish than that. I was visiting my aunt in Connecticut after Jeff left. When I came home there was an email from Carol, asking me if I wanted to come with her, now that my daughter is away at school. I didn't even consider it at first, but then I got a call from the wife of one of my husband's bowling friends. She left a message on my answering machine, telling me that Jeff was having an affair with another one of the bowling wives."

"Oh no, so you decided to run away to the mission."

"Wow, you're good," says Sarah. She glances over at him for a moment.

"Not really. I told you that everybody has demons. Now I know that yours are real, like Dawn's."

"I don't think you can really compare Jeff to Joseph," she replies.

"I'm not. But as far as demons go, he's not imaginary."

"You said the demons could be memories, too. I think that's what my demons are. I'm constantly looking back, and remembering all of the things that we'll never experience again, as a couple, and as a family. It's killing me."

"It takes time," offers Lenny. "I was the same way when my father died. It changed holidays, my relationship with my mother, and even our relationship with the extended family. I can tell you what helped me, if you want to know. I don't want to be that guy who shoves advice down your throat, when you're not ready to hear it."

"No, I want to know. What is it?" asks Sarah.

"You have to live in the moment, as much as you can. This moment is the only thing that's real. You can worry about what's going to happen with your daughter, but that won't change what actually happens. You can also dwell on the past, and what you should have said or done, but it'll never change anything. The only moment that matters is this one right now, and right now you're on this awesome road trip with me. In a few minutes, I'm going to whip out my guitar and we're going to sing all the way back to the mission, and laugh until our cheeks hurt, what do you think of that?" Lenny sounds excited and happy, and Sarah decides right then to join him in this moment of bliss. It is a good moment, and if she can keep creating good moments, than maybe she can expand it to a good day, and then a good week. *Hell, I might even have a good life.* In this moment, anything seems possible, and Sarah feels at peace.

Back at the mission, Sarah and Carol decide to lock themselves in their room for some girl time after dinner. They make some tea, grab a bag of chips, and close the door. Sarah fluffs up her pillow, props it against the side of the bed, and settles herself on the floor facing Carol.

It's been too long since the heart-to-heart conversations of their youth. Carol's mother Margaret, and Louise, were close siblings, so Carol and Sarah were together frequently as children. Sarah tagged along on more than a few of Carol's family vacations. Two of her summers were even spent living with her Aunt Margaret, so that her mother could continue working while Sarah was not in school.

"How are your parents?" asks Sarah.

"They're doing okay. Mom's legs have been bothering her a bit, so she's not walking as well as she used to. It has slowed her down some, but she still gardens, cooks, and plays bingo at the church. Dad is exactly the same, watching horse racing and Nascar. His hair is completely grey, and he's lost some muscle, but overall, his health is good. How about Louise and Sal, how are they?"

"My mother is as crazy as ever," replies Sarah. "She's still running those trips to Atlantic City, and she and Sal just got back from a cruise with his sister and her husband. Mom thinks I'm crazy for coming down here. She told me that we should have gone someplace with palm trees and beaches."

"Palm trees and beaches would be nice, but you can do that with Jeff. If you want to go someplace exotic, you stick with me," Carol winks at her cousin. Sarah's smile fades, and she lowers her eyes to her hands. She would have to tell the story of Jeff for the second time in one day, and she hates how retelling the story makes her feel pain like she felt on the day it happened.

"So, there's something I need to tell you. Jeff left me the day after we dropped Bethany off in Boston." Carol stares at Sarah with her mouth half open, trying to process what she's just heard.

"Wow, I don't even know what to say. How do you feel about this?" asks Carol.

"How do I feel? Let's see. I feel like a fool, mainly," she wraps her arms around her shins, and shrugs. "I thought everything was fine, and then he told me that he's been planning this for two years. All I can think of is that nothing has been real for the past two years, and I had no idea. How is that even possible? Seriously, how stupid do I have to be in order to have believed that everything was fine, while he was counting down the days until his escape?"

"Sarah, don't do this to yourself. Now that you are looking back on it, does it make any sense at all?"

"No! That's the thing, it doesn't. We still had sex. Well, maybe not as much, but we did. We talked and went on vacations. It just doesn't make any sense to me. It's just crap. My life was planned, Carol. I wasn't supposed to have to worry about big decisions anymore." Sarah's eyes start to well up, even though she's determined not to cry about this again.

"Did he tell you why he was leaving?" Carol asks.

"I had to drag it out of him. He said it was best for the both of us, and acts like I should be relieved that we can both finally start living again; as if I've been dead for the past twenty-four years. It gets worse, though. I went up to the convent to visit Aunt Theresa, and when I came home there was a message on my machine. It was from a friend who told me that he was having an affair with someone I know."

"Was he seeing her before he left you?"

"Even if they weren't sleeping together, he was definitely having an emotional affair. He claims that he decided to leave me before she was in the picture, though, as if that's supposed to make me feel better."

"Oh, Sarah, I'm so sorry," Carol wonders how she can help. *Louise was probably right about the beaches and palm trees.* "And here I drag you here to do missionary work. It's probably the last thing you need right now."

"Well, one might think that," agrees Sarah, "but in fact, it's helped to take my mind off my problems. These people have so many dilemmas that go far beyond what they can do for themselves. At least my issues are only emotional, for now."

"What does that mean, for now?" she asks.

"Only that I am living in limbo. I have a thousand dollars to my name, and I am depending on Jeff to keep the roof over my head and the car in my driveway. The very man who I can't trust at all has the power to leave me homeless, and stranded."

"Did you get a lawyer yet?" asks Carol.

"I have the number for one, but I haven't called her," Sarah shrugs.

"What are you waiting for? You should call her. You'll be able to sleep easier once you know that everything is going to be alright."

"That's the thing, Carol, what if it's not alright? What if we have to sell the house, and I have to get a place of my own? How am I going to afford that? I need to get a job."

"Well," says Carol, "a job is an option. It'll give you something to do with yourself, too. If you have to sell the house, then you'll get half of the proceeds. You'll also get alimony from Jeff. After all, you've devoted yourself to raising his child, and now you don't have the necessary skills to maintain your lifestyle. I'm sure any judge will see it that way."

"You think? I have no idea how this works. I just can't stop wondering what I am going to do for money. Click is going to need dog food when I get back, and one bag of his food is literally one-twentieth of my savings. That no longer seems practical."

"Honestly, Sarah, it's all going to work out. I want to pay for your lawyer, so I'll call her and tell her to send any invoices to me," offers Carol.

"What? Carol, I can't let you do that! No, thank you, but I have to say no."

"Come on, Sarah, that's total crap. You just told me that you have enough money for twenty bags of dog food. I'm a doctor! I have plenty of money, and I spend my free time volunteering at places like this, so I have no time to spend it. Grandma always used to say that charity begins at home, remember? I want to pay for this so that you don't have to worry about it. Please, Sarah, don't say no. You know you would do it for me in a heartbeat, if you had the means." Carol looks pleadingly into Sarah's eyes. She knows that her cousin will give in after that last comment. The two are like sisters, and nothing is too much to ask. Sarah's eyes well up again. She leans across the floor and throws her arms around Carol.

"Thank you, so much. I will pay you back, I promise. I can't believe you are doing this for me. Thank you, Carol." Sarah is amazed by her cousin's generosity.

"Your thanks are payment enough. I don't need the money, and I don't want you to think about it again.

And, if you happen to need anything down the road, I hope you won't hesitate to ask me. Well, I know you will, but I want you to think about this conversation and know that I am going to give the money away to someone, so it may as well be you. Do you understand what I'm saying?"

Sarah did understand. Her love for her cousin is deep, and clearly, the feeling is mutual. It occurs to Sarah that the main reason she hasn't called the lawyer yet is because she was afraid that she wouldn't be able to pay her. With this burden lifted, she's anxious to get the process started and receive the answers to the questions that are occupying her darkest thoughts.

That night, as Sarah is lying in bed, once again she has that feeling of peace wash over her. She thanks God for helping her to find her way, and for carrying her burden while it's too heavy. Mulling over the course of events which have brought her on this mission, so that she could receive Carol's generous offer, she can't help but think of Des. Sarah wonders what her friend will think about all of this, and whether or not she'll believe that God has had a hand in any of it. Regardless of what Des believes, Sarah can't help but feel that listening to God has been beneficial. She looks forward to seeing just how far he can take her, because she has a feeling the possibilities are endless.

———◦◦◦❧◦◦◦———

The next few days are a blur of activity. Sarah decides to try something different, and opts to join Shawn on a building project. Three generations are living in a small, one bedroom house, and Bob has raised funds to add a two bedroom addition onto the back of the residence. Sarah knows nothing about building, but when Bob announces the project, she has an epiphany. She can either keep making excuses for the things she doesn't know how to do, or she can start learning. A number of other women have volunteered for the build, including young Lauren, so if they can be of help, so can she. No one arrives on this earth as an expert. Many times in her life, Sarah has held back, afraid that she wasn't as good as someone else. In this moment, she realizes that the combination of practice and time creates experts, and she's determined that her practice will begin now, in all aspects of her life.

There are a number of things that Sarah really likes about the building project. First, the manual labor feels great. Her body is exhausted by the end of the day, after long hours of lifting, hauling, drilling, and hammering, and she easily falls into a deep sleep at night. More than that, though, Sarah finds satisfaction in watching the project develop. To create on such a large scale is fascinating, and she finds herself constantly repeating, "I can't believe that we built this!" Sarah realizes that it's this sense of creation that's missing from her life. When she was younger, she loved to write, but devoting herself to her family left little time for such an outlet, and she hasn't written a thing in almost twenty years. Once she returns home, she'll try her hand at writing again, and hopefully, it can help to pay the bills.

Sarah takes a break on the front porch of the house where they're building. Charlene, the matriarch of the family that lives in the home, rocks back and forth in a wooden rocker beside her, knitting a hat for her granddaughter, Emily. It's unusually warm on this day, and feels more like spring, than late fall. The smell of dying leaves, warmed by the sun, won't let Sarah forget the season, though. It reminds her of Thanksgiving, and Bethany.

"Why such a long face, Sarah?" asks Charlene. Sarah is confused for a moment, not realizing that her face must be like an open book. She smiles at Charlene, not wanting to ruin this beautiful day with her own concerns.

"I'm just fine. It's almost too beautiful to work today, isn't it? It makes me want to walk by the stream, with my shoes off."

"Do you want to go down there? I'm sure Sandy and the girls would be happy to go with you." Charlene nods toward her two granddaughters, who are playing circle games with Lauren and the neighbor children.

"Oh, no," says Sarah, "they're having too much fun to be disturbed." Sarah watches them, admiring Lauren's good looks and her natural ability with the children. "Have you seen the addition today? We hung the drywall, and it actually looks like a room now. The girls are going to be so happy in there."

"I imagine they will be. They're always happy, playing and making a ruckus," adds Charlene.

"Do you like living here, Charlene?" Sarah asks.

"Do I like it? It sure beats dying, so I like it well enough. Do you like living where you live?"

"I do," replies Sarah, thinking about the Lehigh Valley of Pennsylvania and all that it has to offer. "There's a lot to do there."

"Really, tell me about where you live, Sarah. What do you do there?"

"Well, I live right near an amusement park, and we're also very close to some mountains for skiing.

There are many colleges and universities nearby, so there are a lot of cultural opportunities."

"And what is a cultural opportunity, exactly?" asks Charlene.

"Well, it's something that teaches you what you might not know about another person, or a group of people. It might be an artist's exhibit, or a jazz concert, something like that." Charlene smiles and continues knitting.

"And do you do those things often, skiing and cultural opportunities?" she asks.

"No," Sarah is surprised by her own answer, "actually, I don't." She can't believe it. If you were to ask Sarah what she liked about living in Allentown, she would tell you all about the wine trails, the new arts center, and the wonderful festivals held in the Valley, celebrating everything from music, and Celtic heritage, to Christmas. Ironically, Sarah doesn't participate in any of those things. Clearly, she has a long to-do list when she returns to Pennsylvania.

Once they return to the mission, Sarah enjoys a shower and joins the others in the kitchen. Shirley is making lasagna, and it smells like heaven after a hard day of work. Sarah is busy setting the table, when the room falls silent, and she immediately looks up from her task. Standing in the doorway is Lauren, her long blonde hair freshly shaven, her head bald and shining like the sun. "Hi!" she says to everyone in her typical chipper cadence. They all mumble hello in return, wondering what on earth has possessed her to do such a thing.

"Okay, everyone," announces Shirley, "let's all take a seat before it gets cold." Bob says grace and then they all look over at Lauren.

"Lauren," Bob offers, "is there anything that you would like to share with the group?" Sarah smiles at his diplomacy and the graceful way he allows Lauren to choose whether or not to share.

"Sure. Some of you have met the little girl at the build named Hannah. She has the long dark hair and the purple shirt, do you remember?" Some nod, while the others just wait on the edge of their seats. "All of the girls are really affectionate, but there is something different about Hannah. She's so desperate for attention. The lady that owns the house, Elizabeth, she told me to stay away from Hannah, because she has lice. As soon as she mentioned it, I became aware of the white spots in her hair, and this might have all been in my head, but I swear I could see them moving. If you could have seen her though, with those big brown eyes, just begging for affection, you would know why I had to do this. I didn't want to bring the lice back to the mission, so I avoided her, but tomorrow I'm going to bring extra clothes and give that girl the attention she deserves."

"Good for you, dear," says Shirley. "That's very kind of you. I'm sure it will mean everything to that little girl that someone would do something so special for her."

"Oh, I'm not going to tell her!" cries Lauren. "I would never want her to feel badly about herself. Maybe she will think my head is cool though, and she'll want to shave her head, too. I don't know if it will really play out that way, but maybe it will. I know any of you would have done the same thing once you got to know her."

Sarah thinks about that for the rest of dinner. Lauren's hair was so beautiful. Sarah never considered herself a vain person, but at the same time, could she handle everyone staring at her bald head? She would always be wondering if people thought she had cancer or alopecia. Either way, she's so impressed by Lauren's kind heart, and it makes her realize that she has a long way to go to truly open herself up to loving enough. Helping Mrs. Ritter get to her sister's house was an act of kindness on her part, but Lauren taught her that she can do so much more.

———∘∘○-❧-○∘∘———

The next morning is Saturday, and while some of the group will be leaving, more new people will be arriving in the afternoon. Unfortunately, Lenny is one of the people finishing up his mission trip, and this leaves Sarah feeling blue. Sure, the other people are great, but there's something about Lenny that just lights up the room. He is so easy to talk to, now that they've moved past the awkward stage, and he has a lot of wisdom for someone his age. They sit on the front porch swing that morning with their coffee and reminisce about their week together.

"I feel badly that we never made it back to Peter's," says Sarah.

"You're right!" Lenny exclaims. "I totally forgot about that. We should go. Would you like to go there this morning?" he offers.

"I don't know," Sarah is excited by the sudden possibility that her day might be more entertaining than she expected. "What time are you planning on leaving?"

"Well, I was going to leave after circle, but we could head over to Peter's and then I could drop you off at the build. That would work, don't you think?"

"I think that should be fine. We can ask Bob. Should we invite Theresa and Dawn to come along?" Sarah asks.

"Sure, let's go do that now," Lenny replies. He stands up from the swing, and with the hand that isn't holding his coffee, he reaches for Sarah. Like a butterfly landing on a delicate flower, she places her fingers in his hand. She can't help but think about how warm he is and how good he smells. Lifting herself from the swing, she realizes that this could be the last time he holds her hand, and it makes her heart sink. "You look really pretty today," he says quietly. Sarah breaths deeply and looks into his caring eyes.

"Thank you," is all she can manage in the moment, and they move inside.

Unfortunately, Joseph is anxious to leave, so he makes it clear to Dawn that joining Lenny and Sarah for a trip to Peter's is out of the question. Theresa has already promised Justin that they can stop by Elizabeth's, to say goodbye to the kids he's met while working there, so she declines as well, sending her best wishes to Peter.

"It looks like it's just us," says Lenny. He smiles at Sarah, not looking the least bit disappointed.

Sarah smiles in return. She isn't sure that it's a good idea to be alone with Lenny. She's drawn to him physically, but she knows there's no point in pursuing him that way. After all, he's leaving this morning, and she'll probably never see him again. At the same time, the fact that she may never see him again makes it especially urgent to find out about the texture of his beard, before he disappears from her life leaving her to wonder forever.

Sarah concludes that Saturday morning circles are the worst. All of the hugging and tears provide her with a preview of how she'll feel next Saturday, when she's the one leaving. Bob and Shirley are so wonderful at creating a welcoming place, where everyone is honored for their strengths and supported in their weakness. Sarah felt *seen* this week, for the first time in a long while; not just in a physical way, but at a long-dormant soul level. She's been able to catch glimpses of her own desires, and to see the person that she really is on the inside. More importantly, she's caught glimpses of the person that she wants herself to be. Sarah recognizes the infinite possibility that is her life. She can be anyone that she wants to be! No longer tied to the confines of mother or wife, Sarah is free to make choices. As she sits next to Lenny on the faded floral sofa, she realizes that these choices were always available to her. She alone let herself be defined strictly by her roles as wife and mother. How many years she had wasted, forgetting that she was a writer and an artist. She forgot to feed her curious soul and instead made sure that her daughter and husband did not want for anything. She put so much effort into Jeff's happiness, as he watched her wither away to someone who depended on him for money, entertainment, and comfort. No wonder he couldn't wait to get away.

"Are you ready?" asks Lenny.

Sarah looks up, startled. She smiles as he holds out his hand. "It wasn't the last time," she says out loud.

"The last time for what?" Lenny asks, and Sarah blushes a deep shade of scarlet.

"It's silly," says Sarah, as she takes his hand and he pulls her up to standing. "I was just thinking when we were on the swing, that it might be the last time I held your hand, but it wasn't." Lenny squeezes her fingers, and wraps his arm around her shoulder.

"Let's go," he says, and turns her toward the door.

Grabbing his guitar, Lenny and Sarah walk around to the back of Peter's house. Surprised when he doesn't meet them with a gun in his lap, Sarah knocks on the metal rim of the sliding door. The two wait for five minutes, giving Peter a chance to get to the door, before Sarah wonders aloud if he is home.

"He told us that he never leaves," says Lenny. "He must be here." This time he knocks on the glass, a bit harder than Sarah had before.

"What if he's in the shower? Maybe we should leave," suggests Sarah.

"I just want to make sure he's okay." Lenny peers into the glass and sees Peter rolling toward him, wearing what looks like red flannel-pajamas.

"Hey ya'll," says Peter, "I didn't know ya'll were coming today."

"We weren't scheduled, but Lenny is leaving today, and we wanted to stop by and sing with you for a little bit, if that's okay with you," offers Sarah.

"That sounds great. Come on in," he rolls back and out of the way, and Sarah and Lenny step inside. "I've gotta be honest with ya'll, and tell you that I'm not feelin' too well this morning."

"Oh, no!" says Sarah. "Do you want us to go?"

"Not yet," says Peter, "please, come sit with me a while." He rolls into the living room, and Sarah and Lenny take a seat next to each other on the sofa.

"So, what's wrong Peter? Do you have a cold?" asks Sarah.

"No, every now and then, it gets hard for me to breathe. It makes me pretty dizzy, so I just lay around, and then I really feel like shit." Peter flashes them a half-hearted smile. "I try to be positive as much as I can, but when it gets like this, I can feel myself slipping into a funk, and it's just hard to get out of it."

Sarah thinks about how she's been feeling since Jeff told her that he was leaving. There are times when she wants more than anything to feel happy, but something just holds her back. She knows what Peter means about the funk, and she wants desperately to escape the grasp that it has on her mind. She wishes she could offer him some advice, but she has none. If anything, Sarah realizes that, like Peter, she needs help. Being with everyone this week, and turning the focus away from herself, made Sarah realize that life is easier when you make room for other people. She doesn't want to go back to a lonely life.

"There must be some way that you can socialize more, Peter. Are there any groups or meetings that you can attend?" asks Sarah.

"Are there groups for thirty-year-old paraplegics? I don't think so. Not that I would want to attend a meeting like that, anyway."

"It wouldn't have to be a group of paraplegics. I meant that there may be some groups of people that you can join, like a Lion's club or something, a place where you can socialize with other people. You're such a nice person and so much fun. I just wish there were more for you here," says Sarah.

"Yeah, I know what you mean," agrees Peter. "I wish that, too, but wishing isn't going to make it happen. So, Lenny, you've been all over the world. Tell me, where's the best place for me to live, if I could go anywhere?"

"If you could go anywhere, you should go to Vienna," says Lenny. "There's so much to do there, day and night. There are museums and music everywhere. Most importantly, though, they value people in that society. If you're able to do something to give back to the community, then they encourage you. They say that people never retire in Vienna, because there's always something to be done. Older people work with young children, teaching values and skills, or they sweep the streets, or care for the roses in the park. They're revered for their wisdom and taken care of by their families and the community. I never had a hard time meeting people in Vienna."

Peter looks around the room as if seeing the contents of his home through new eyes. The furnishings are from the time of his great-grandparents. The tapestry on the sofa is long faded and the old carpet worn thin. Leaving isn't really an option, but it feels good to dream of something new. Not just new furnishings, but new possibilities. Peter always thought it was good that he accepted his lot in life. There's never anything to be disappointed about if you don't have any expectations, but there's nothing to be excited about either. Now, Lenny and Sarah have him thinking, what if there is a way to have more?

"Should I play a few songs?" asks Lenny, when Peter glances over at the guitar case.

"I'd like that," replies Peter, "a lot. Thank you." Lenny begins with *Imagine* by John Lennon, and it feels just right.

The ride over to the build site is quiet. Lenny pulls the car over, parks in the abandoned service station just up the road from Charlene's, and cuts the engine. He looks over at Sarah, takes a deep breath, and groans.

"This is so weird," says Sarah. "I've only known you for a week, but it feels like forever, and I don't want you to go." She looks down at her hands, because she's afraid that if she looks at him she'll cry. "Thank you for listening to me. Thank you for being my friend here."

"Sarah," Lenny reaches over and entwines his fingers with hers, "we're still going to be friends. Technology is crazy these days. I can Skype you and see your beautiful face tomorrow." Sarah grins at the thought.

"Not tomorrow," she finally says. "I won't get any reception here. You'll have to wait until next week."

"You're right," he laughs. "I can't imagine living in a place without any cell reception. That annoying Verizon guy needs to get his butt down here."

"I know, right?" Sarah laughs. "Seriously, though, thank you." She squeezes his hand, and he squeezes back.

"You're so funny," says Lenny. "You act like I've been this incredible blessing in your week, and yet you have absolutely no idea how you've saved me here. All of my good memories include you. In fact, if it weren't for you, waking up in the morning would have been a real struggle for me, so thank you."

"Give me a break," says Sarah, "you had no problem waking up. You're this big world traveler, so this is probably easy for you."

"That's not true! Sure, I'm used to being away from home, but my travels are selfish. I do what I want, when I want, with the people that I choose to be with. Being here, thrust into this group of people who are nothing like me, this was a challenge. My faith, it's not something my life revolves around. I don't advertise it, or try to push my beliefs on others. What I believe is personal to me. It's who I am. It is how I behave toward others and myself. I was nervous to be here, but it was something that I had to do, so that I could slay my demons and move on with my life."

"Have you slayed them, do you think?" asks Sarah.

"Time will tell. I think so, though. I have to forgive my Dad for devoting so much time to the church and to this mission. Obviously, he had issues, and maybe by focusing his energy on saving others, he thought he could save himself. I'll never know the truth about his motives, but at least I know what this place is about. It's our imagination that will drive us crazy. The mission is real to me now, so hopefully I can put it to rest...put him to rest." After a long pause, he adds, "So, thank you. I would not have enjoyed this nearly as much if you weren't here with me."

"I feel the same way," she says.

"Give me a hug," he leans over, and they wrap their arms around each other. Sarah rests her cheek on his shoulder, her nose nuzzling his neck and inhaling that incredible scent that's his alone. Lenny brushes the hair away from her face, and Sarah is sure he's going to kiss her. Not wanting to tear herself away, she sits up anyway.

"Hey," she says, "can I touch your beard?" her face breaks into a huge grin.

"Sure," he says, staring into her eyes, as she tentatively reaches for his beard and runs her fingers through the length of it. Sarah is surprised by the silkiness, as she expected it to be much scratchier, like her grandfather's moustache. "Can I kiss your lips?" he asks.

"I..." Sarah immediately averts her eyes and presses her lips together. She thinks of Jeff, and the fact that they aren't even divorced yet. In a flash, she pictures Bethany and remembers that her daughter has no idea that her parents are separated. Lenny brushes the hair away from her face and runs his thumb over her lips. It feels so good to Sarah. She wants to kiss him, and no one would ever have to know. "I can't. I'm sorry, Lenny. I want to, but..."

"Shh, don't apologize," he says, and he pulls her close and holds her there. She melts back into his chest and breathes him in. "I never should have asked," he says, and she hugs him a little harder. The truth is that she's glad he has asked. It feels good to know that her feelings are reciprocated, even if she isn't ready to act on them.

"It's okay, really," she whispers. "We should probably go, though." Sarah doesn't know how long she can stand to be so close to him without crossing the line.

Lenny pulls the car up in front of Charlene's and says, "Stay there." He runs around the car, opens her door, and reaches out with his left hand. Sarah smiles and places her hand in his.

"Thank you, kind sir," she says, as he pulls her from the car and into a hug.

"I'll never forget you, Sarah," he whispers into her ear.

"I don't want you to," she replies. "Don't forget to friend me on Facebook."

"As soon as I get reception," he winks at her, and kisses her on the cheek.

"Bye, Lenny," she says, and she touches her cheek and waves as he climbs back into the car and drives away.

The rest of the day is a blur of activity. They finish painting the trim, and move the furniture into the new room to make it ready for the girls to sleep in that night. Charlene and her daughter Elizabeth throw a party for everyone to celebrate the completion of the project, and they're all in high spirits when they return to the mission. The barbeque that Elizabeth made is the best that Sarah has ever tasted, but she didn't eat much, and now her stomach is rumbling like thunder. Deciding to see what she can scrounge up in Shirley's kitchen, she makes herself a sandwich and then heads off to her room to eat it before evening circle. Walking down the hall, she's looking forward to some alone time and secretly hopes that Carol won't decide to come looking for her. The door is closed, and when Sarah opens it, she's shocked to find a spritely little gray-haired woman sitting in the lotus position on the top bunk of Carol's bed.

"Oh," says Sarah, "I'm sorry, I just wasn't expecting anyone to be in here. Should I go?" she asks.

"No, please come in!" invites the woman with a smile. She leans over, grabs the headboard, and before Sarah can even figure out what's happening, she flips herself out of the bunk and lands on her feet with her hand out in front of Sarah. "I'm Alice. You are...?" she inquires. Sarah takes her hand and shakes it, realizing that Alice is much younger than her gray hair implies.

"I'm impressed!" says Sarah. "My name is Sarah. Wow, I can't believe you just did that!"

Alice laughs out loud. "It is impressive, isn't it? Don't try that one at home, by the way. I had a top bunk all my life, so it was essential to develop some short cuts if I wanted to beat my siblings to the shower, and to dinner. Survival of the fittest, if you will. Needless to say, I survived! So, Sarah, tell me why you look like your puppy just died? And please, if your puppy did just die, don't tell me. My head is big enough already without walking around thinking that I am psychic."

"Do I look sad?" asks Sarah.

"Oh, honey, have you looked in a mirror? Yes. You look very sad. Let's just get it off your chest, so you can move on. Tell me everything. Here, sit down." She seats herself on Sarah's bed, and pats the spot beside her.

Sarah can't help but to smile. *This Alice is a hoot!* They haven't even known each other for five minutes and she already expects Sarah to tell her everything. Ironically, Sarah is ready to spill.

"There was this guy here last week named Lenny. He left this morning, and I've been bummed ever since. We even had a party at the build site that we were at today, and while I was really happy for the family, I mean, I am really happy for them, I just can't seem to shake the blues."

"What are you afraid of?" asks Alice.

"What am I afraid of? I don't think I'm afraid of anything. I am just feeling a little sad, that's all."

"Oh honey, you're afraid, let me assure you. Think about it. This guy Lenny left. What is it that you're afraid will happen now that he's gone?"

Sarah ponders this question. Is there something that makes her feel afraid? Right away she considers that she's afraid she'll never see him again. That doesn't seem scary, though. She's disappointed that their time together is over, and she does wish that they could have had more time. She's nervous that they might lose contact, but he promised that he will friend her on Facebook.

"I guess if I have to say that I am afraid of anything, it would be that I don't know what it's going to be like here without him. I mean, I'm not really afraid, but I just don't know."

"Won't you be here?" asks Alice.

"Me? Yes, I'm staying until Saturday." Sarah doesn't understand why Alice would ask, as the answer seems obvious.

"So, if you are going to be here, what's the problem?" Alice sits next to her with her eyebrows raised and waits for an answer. Sarah has no idea what she's supposed to say. "Here's the thing chickadee, you're looking for happiness outside of yourself, and you're setting yourself up for disappointment. Happiness comes from within! This is the secret to life that no one manages to teach us through thirteen years of school!" Alice's hands are flying and she's thrilled to have found a new student. "Honey, only two beings are going to love you unconditionally in this life, and those beings are God and yourself. If you aren't feeling loved, then you need to get on that! God already loves you more than anything, regardless of what you perceive as your sins and disappointments. There's nothing that you can do on this earth that will destroy God's love for you. But you, that's a whole other story. I can tell that you doubt your own perfection, and you are hard on yourself. Am I right?"

Sarah's mind is spinning. *Is Alice right? Am I hard on myself? What does that even mean? Sometimes I do stupid things, it's just a fact. The whole thing with Jeff, well, the more that time passes, the less I feel responsible. Initially, I was definitely hard on myself, though.* "I'm sorry, can you ask me the question again?" asks Sarah.

"Sure," Alice replies in a kind and supportive voice, "do you doubt your own perfection, and are you hard on yourself?"

"Okay," begins Sarah, "as for my perfection, nobody is perfect, right? So that would imply that I'm not perfect, either."

"And who told you this?" asks Alice.

"Who told me that nobody is perfect? My mother, teachers maybe, I'm not sure, but I've definitely heard it plenty of times before."

"And in what context would someone tell you such a thing?" asks Alice.

"Hmm, I suppose that if I had tried to do something, and it didn't work out, then my Mom would tell me not to worry about it, because nobody's perfect."

"Okay, now we're getting somewhere!" exclaims Alice. "You see, Sarah, it's not actually you that your mother is referring to in that story, it's your actions. The thing about your actions that wasn't perfect was that they didn't produce the result you were looking for, so they were perceived to be imperfect. But, let's imagine for a moment that you want to pull a lever that you run across in your travels, and you pull. You pull, and you pull, until you literally turn blue in the face, but the lever will not budge. Feeling like a failure, you wander away, and your failed attempt can be perceived as imperfect. In reality, though, the lever that you were trying to pull would have released a dam, and flooded a whole city. Well! Now what do you think of your failed attempt? Is it still imperfect? No! You see, all of our actions are the same, Sarah. Everything that happens is perceived to be good or bad, perfect or imperfect. You, on the other hand, you are perfect in every way. A true reflection of the creator, you are! We all are! Isn't it fabulous?" *Wow.* The implications of this are huge, and Sarah's head is spinning once again.

"It sounds fabulous, but does that mean there are no such things as good and bad?" she asks.

"Exactly, oh honey, you are quick! I love it! Yes, good and bad are perceptions, or illusions. Think about a fresh-baked loaf of Italian bread. See it, with its golden-brown crust from the wood-burning oven, the smell of it filling the whole room and flooding your nostrils. Mmm, I love bread! But, alas, I'm gluten intolerant, so that bread will wreak havoc on my insides. So, is the bread good or bad? It's neither! It's just bread, and we have the opportunity to perceive it however we chose. Everything is like that Sarah, and you're in control of your thoughts. You can allow yourself to think that Lenny's leaving is a sad affair, or, you can be so thankful that you spent a week with such an amazing person, and you can look forward to the day when you decide that your paths will cross again. Which do you chose?"

"I choose that one!" says Sarah, bubbling with joy. She doesn't know who this Alice is, or where she came from, but Sarah is hooked. Alice has such powerful energy about her, and Sarah feels exuberant in her presence. She wishes Lenny could have met her, but then realizes that perhaps it's better that he isn't here to distract her from her new-found friend.

Just then, Shirley sticks her head through the doorway. "Are you ladies planning to join us for debriefing? We're about to begin."

"Yes, I'm sorry." Sarah jumps off the bed and turns to see Alice, who's looking at her with her head tilted to the side and a confused expression on her face.

"Why are you sorry?" Alice asks.

"Excuse me?" replies Sarah. "I don't understand."

"You apologized to Shirley and I'm wondering why you felt the need to do that."

"Oh, I guess I just feel badly for holding them up. We should really go," replies Sarah, glancing nervously toward the door. Alice smiles and stands up.

"We can go, sure. Just remember Sarah, your words matter. They affect you in ways of which you are not aware, so choose them carefully."

"What should I have said, then?" asks Sarah.

"Thank you. Just, thank you," Alice replies.

It's an exciting debriefing session. Shawn, Lauren, Carol, and Sarah remain from the previous week, but there are nine new people to meet, aside from Alice. Sarah is thrilled to learn that Alice owns a metaphysical bookstore in Allentown, only fifteen minutes from Sarah's home. She makes a mental note to stop by once she returns to Pennsylvania.

A new woman named Eunice questions Alice about the store, while they're in the circle. "Doesn't metaphysical mean psychics and all that stuff?" she asks.

Alice smiles, but hesitates before she responds. "There are a number of psychics who come into the shop, yes. Mainly, the store focuses on books and objects that remind people of the infinite love of God and the presence of angels. Have you ever been in a metaphysical shop?" asks Alice.

"Me? Of course not! I am a church-going woman." replies Eunice

"That's what I love about going to church," interrupts Shirley, "it constantly reminds us that we're not here to pass judgment on one another. Wouldn't you agree, Eunice?" Sarah admires how Shirley is so good at re-directing a conversation.

"Absolutely," agrees Eunice, although her face exposes her true feelings. Shirley smiles and asks the petite woman seated next to Eunice to tell everyone a little about herself. The woman shifts, looking nervous to say the least, but she begins speaking with a clear voice and a confident tone.

"My name is Mary and this is my first mission. For years, it has been something that I've wanted to do, but I always thought you had to go to Africa, or someplace remote or exotic, and while I did look into it, there was just no way I could afford something like that. Then, my sister-in-law, Terry," she glances at the woman seated beside her, "she told me about this place, and I decided to give it a try. I miss my dog already, but I'm excited to be here." Everyone chuckles, and some nod in agreement.

"Thank you, Mary. We're glad to have you here. Terry?" Bob nods toward the buxom blond seated in the recliner, next to Mary. Terry is meticulous from head to toe, and not the type you might expect to find in an old farmhouse, on a mission in West Virginia. Her nails are freshly manicured and her fashionable outfit belongs on Fifth Avenue, as opposed to Bartley Store Bottom Road.

"Hi everyone," gushes Terry as she smiles warmly at each person in the circle. "It's so nice to be surrounded by such beautiful people, on such a wonderful mission. I fell in love with Bob and Shirley when I came down for the first time three years ago, and since then I just can't seem to stay away! I've thought about trying something else, but then I think about how I would miss out on Shirley's cooking and Bob's kind hospitality, and I just can't imagine being anywhere else. I hope you all will love it here as much as I do." With that, she blesses herself, touches her hands to her heart, and then holds them out to Bob and Shirley, and says, "Thank you."

"That's very kind of you to say, Terry. Shirley and I both enjoy having you here, as well, so you just keep coming back. Our home is your home."

Terry appears incredibly touched. "Thank you, Bob," she says.

"James, why don't you go next," suggests Bob.

"Okay. My name is James and I'm from Newport News, Virginia. This is my wife Kelli, and next to her are our two sons, Tucker and Mason. We decided to do this for the boys, mostly," he smiles at his wife for confirmation and she squeezes his hand as it rests on her shoulder.

"James is in the Air Force," Kelli begins, "and he's away a lot. Our boys are great," she smiles at them as she continues, "and I want them to know how fortunate they are. I think it's hard these days to teach our kids about good fortune. We live in a middle class neighborhood, and the kids there have everything they could want. I don't want them taking things for granted, or thinking that material things are more important than family."

"I don't think that," expresses Tucker, the older of the two boys.

"I know that, honey. I just think this will be a good experience for our family," replies Kelli.

"Tucker, why don't you tell us about yourself," offers Bob.

"I'm Tucker. I'm fourteen years old and I'm in eighth grade. I am in a band, and I like to skateboard." He looks toward Mason as if to pass the platform to his brother.

"Um, my name is Mason. I'm twelve, and I'm in sixth grade. I train seeing-eye dogs, but I don't have one right now, because the one I had just went to live with her new owner. So, hopefully I will be getting a new puppy soon."

"That's very impressive, Mason," says Shirley. "Is the dog you had before living with a blind person now?"

"Yes. Well, she's legally blind, so that means that she can see a little, I think, but mostly she's blind. Is that right, Mom?"

"Yes, honey, that's correct," replies Kelli.

"Well, I think that's just wonderful. Who's next?" asks Shirley. The big man sitting next to Mason folds his hands across his ample belly and speaks in a warm, soothing voice.

"That would be me. How is everyone this evening?" He looks around the circle, making eye contact with each person as if exchanging a personal greeting. "My friends call me Joe, and I consider all of you to be my friends. I've been hoping to come down here for a few years now, but something would always manage to come up instead. This time it all worked out, and I am very happy to be here with all of you." He folds his hands in a prayer position in front of his chest and gives a slight nod with his eyes closed. Sarah is intrigued by his soothing tones and his gentle disposition. She hopes to get to know Joe better over the course of the week.

"Where are you from, Joe?" asks Bob.

"Ah, yes," replies Joe, "I forgot to mention that I'm from Stowe, Vermont. Thank you." Again, he folds his hands in front of him and gives the little nod.

"Oh! Are you a ski instructor?" asks Shirley. Joe laughs a hearty, warm laugh and slaps his thighs with his hands.

"No, I don't think my knees would appreciate that at all. I'm a sculptor, an artist by trade. I also teach djembe drumming and lead drum circles. I brought a load of drums in my truck, if anyone is interested in participating. It's a ton of fun and can be very stress relieving. Just let me know!"

"Count me in!" requests Alice. "I love drumming!"

"That sounds like fun," agrees Shirley. "I would love to join you."

"I'm interested, too," offers Sarah. She's excited at the thought of trying something new. The slight panicky feeling that she won't be able to do it lasts only for a moment. It seems that the more she tests herself by placing herself in unknown territory, the less she's afraid.

"Excellent," says Joe, "I've enough drums for everyone."

The last two women sit together on the loveseat. Sisters from New Jersey, Karen and Maureen decided to do some good while reaping the benefits of "sister time." Karen is an aesthetician and Maureen a nutritionist. The two own a popular wellness center, and since their daily work is so fulfilling, it feels like they're on vacation every day. Now that they're beginning to experience success, the urge to give back is becoming stronger. They're both hoping that this mission will be the beginning of something wonderful in their lives.

After everyone chats for a while, people begin to slowly disperse to their rooms. Many of them have travelled long distances and are anxious to get some sleep. Sarah is thinking that Alice might feel the same, but it seems that the woman has endless energy. Even after they're all in their beds, Alice continues with her questions.

"So, Sarah," she begins, "what's your story? We already know that you like that character from last week. What is his name? Lenny?"

"What?" shouts Carol, "You like Lenny? When did this happen?"

"No, stop," explains Sarah. "It's not like that."

"It's not?" asks Alice. "I thought you said you liked him."

"I didn't! I never said that I liked him. What I told you was that I was sad that he left. That's all. I'm sad, still. I don't think I would've enjoyed myself as much if he weren't here last week, and I'm just a little nervous about this week. I do feel somewhat better after the debriefing session, though. The new people seem nice, and you and Joe are really interesting. I'm looking forward to getting to know you both. I think it's going to be a good week."

"It's always like that," offers Carol. "When you get to know people, it's sad to see them go, but at the same time, there are always new and interesting people to meet, once they're gone."

"It's like life, girls," says Alice. "Over the course of our lives, we meet so many people. Some of them we allow into our inner circle, and some stay out on the perimeter. The ones inside often have the greatest impact on our hearts, but it's interesting that sometimes the turnover in the inner circle is far greater. Some see this as a bad thing, in the cases of death, divorce, or the loss of a good friend for whatever reason. I view it differently, though. For me, those people have finished the job that they came into our lives to complete. Once they're gone, it's time to send them off with blessings and allow new folks into our circle, so that we can keep learning and experiencing. That's what keeps life interesting."

"But your heart," whispers Sarah. She can't help but to think about Jeff. Not only does she have to forgive him, but now she needs to send him off with blessings, too? That's *not* going to happen. Allowing others in will just set her up for heartbreak once again. "How much heartbreak can one person take? It doesn't seem safe."

"Honey," chirps Alice, "safety is an illusion. We're always safe, because we're a part of God. Nothing can happen to us that can take us away from God. It's only our minds that allow for the separation from source. Our souls know that we can't ever be separated. So when we live from our souls, instead of our egos, we never need to fear. Our hearts have the capacity to love endlessly! The more we love, the more we connect ourselves to source. The more connected we are, the more we feel the love, and not the fear."

"Can we talk more about this tomorrow?" requests Sarah. "I'm fascinated, but my brain is too tired for new concepts, and I don't want to miss anything because I think this is really important."

"Sure," replies Alice. "Have a wonderful sleep."

Sarah closes her eyes and thinks about everything they've just discussed. She feels closer to God than she has in her whole life. So far, he's given her signs to go to the convent and on this mission, and both experiences have made her want to be a better person. She can feel her heart stretching and her capacity to love growing. Sarah feels more alive, and happier. There's still something missing, though. For some reason, Sarah still feels afraid. While she wants to believe that God has her back and will keep her safe, her new-found faith is shaky at best. She's willing to listen to God and do what he tells her to do, but will that always be in her best interest? Of that, Sarah is unsure.

The next three days of work are grueling. In order to prepare for a build, the condemned home that already stands on the property must be torn down and removed. Sarah feels like a member of a prison chain gang by day, but thankfully the nights are filled with lively conversation and spirited gatherings. Unlike the week before, there's no tension in the house, and the fourteen guests quickly become a family. There's much to be done at the build site, so almost everyone except Shirley spends their days in the same location.

Sarah gravitates naturally toward Joe. In his early sixties, he is worldly, educated, and kind. The two spend hours carrying boards back and forth to the dumpster, while discussing art, politics, and religion. The more taboo the subject, the more likely it is to become a topic.

"What about you?" asks Joe. "You know that I love drumming, sculpting, and Kirtan singing, but how do you feed your spirit?"

"Hmm," Sarah ponders, "that's a good question. You see, Joe, I don't exactly have much experience with that. My life before my divorce was more like an existence. I didn't realize it at the time, of course, but I see now that it's true. It makes me kind of sick when I consider how much time I've wasted just coursing through life with no enthusiasm. I didn't know, though, that there could be more. I thought my life was fine the way it was. I was so stupid."

"That's a little harsh, Sarah. There's quite a difference between being ignorant and being stupid. You just didn't know. What clued you in, if you don't mind my asking?"

"What do you mean?" Sarah asks.

"You know, what was it that made you realize that there's something more?"

"Well, after Jeff left, I read something in a book that I found in my step-father's library. It inspired me to start listening to God, which was something that I never really made an effort to do before. My best friend thought it was ridiculous, the idea that God could make better decisions for me than I could make for myself. She flat out dared me to listen to God and do what he tells me to do, so I accepted. The next thing I knew, I was in a convent!"

"You're kidding me!" Joe's eyes are wide with interest, and this encourages her to continue.

"It's not all that shocking, as my Aunt is a nun there, and I was only visiting. While I was at the convent, though, I met some amazing women who really seem to have their lives figured out, even though they are completely deprived of physical love. It made me understand that I could have that, too."

"You are considering becoming a nun?" Joe questions her.

"No, nothing that extreme, but it occurred to me that I could have that sense of fulfillment with myself, or with God. If I find someone compatible along my path that will be great, but I want that sense of completeness, before I go losing myself in another relationship."

"It doesn't have to be like that, you know," offers Joe.

"No, I know that. I guess I just want to know myself better, before I meet someone, so that I will have the confidence to maintain my sense of self."

"How do you think that happens, maintaining your sense of self?" asks Joe.

"Well, I pray a lot," replies Sarah. "I learned in the convent. Prayer and meditation, they all bring you to that same spiritual place. I like that place."

"It is a good place, I have to agree," says Joe.

"The best," affirms Sarah. "I'd like to learn how to get there more often."

"You only need to ask!" exclaims Joe.

"You know how to do it?" inquires Sarah, amazed that she has found another teacher on her path.

"I mean ask God, Sarah." Sarah grins sheepishly.

"Right, God," she replies. How easy it is to forget.

That next night after dinner, Sarah, Carol, Alice, Joe, Eunice, Terry, and Mary are sitting on the deck around the fire pit. The conversation flows freely, and it isn't long before Eunice raises the subject of Jesus.

"You can't possibly be a follower of Jesus and own a metaphysical bookstore at the same time," she says to Alice.

"Why do you believe that?" asks Alice.

"Followers of Jesus only need one book and that's the Bible. So, the very fact that you encourage people to buy any book that's not the Bible proves my point."

Eunice looks proud of herself. Obviously, she's sure that Alice has a thing or two to learn about Jesus.

"Well, Eunice, you're right. I am not a follower of Jesus in the traditional sense," replies Alice.

"I knew it!" Eunice puffs up, proud in her successful exposure of Alice to the group.

"I should really expand on that, though, so you can better understand," explains Alice. "You see, for me, it isn't enough to worship Jesus. He was such a brilliant teacher, and I believe he was demanding far more from us than to worship him. For example, in John 14:6, Jesus says, 'I am the way and the truth and the life. No one comes to the Father except through me.' I think most people assume Jesus means that if you know him well and you get on his good side by praising him, then he will let you into Heaven. For me, though, I believe that the way Jesus behaved was the way he wanted us to behave so that we could know the Father like he knew him. So, I love everyone, regardless of race, religion, or sexual orientation, because they are my brothers and sisters and they are part of God, just like me. Jesus never judged anyone, so I won't do it either. In Matthew 25:40, Jesus says to the people, 'Truly I tell you, whatever you did for one of the least of these brothers and sisters of mine, you did for me.' Jesus wants us to help everyone we can, regardless of whether we see them as worthy or not. Our job is to love. My job is to love, and that is what I do."

Eunice stares at Alice, speechless for once. She shrugs her shoulders and says, "Some people will never understand. You're always going to figure out some way to twist words around and justify your heathen behavior. That's the work of the devil himself, and you've bought into it, hook, line, and sinker."

"That's not nice, Eunice," offers Mary. Eunice turns quickly toward her as she rises out of her chair.

"Careful, Miss Mary, or you'll be drawn in by her charm just like the rest of them. I know the work of the devil when I see it." With that, Eunice steps through the sliding door, and slams it closed behind her.

"I know evil when I scc it, too," says Sarah, with a nervous laugh. The whole situation is so awkward, and the tension is thick like fog. Everyone else giggles uncomfortably.

Alice closes her eyes, draws in a deep, cleansing breath, exhales, and looks kindly toward Sarah. "We have to be vigilant not to judge others during our time here on Earth. Eunice is a good person, Sarah. She was raised to believe that Jesus Christ is her savior, and that she must worship him, defend him, and cast out 'evil.' She came on this Christian mission, in all her innocence, never expecting to encounter a 'heathen' like me.'"

"But she's not being very Christ-like in judging you and calling you the devil!" exclaims Mary.

"You're right," replies Alice, "she's not. But these are lessons that Eunice still needs to learn. If she doesn't, she'll just keep coming back until she does."

"Back to the mission?" asks Terry.

"No Terry, not back to the mission. I was talking about coming back to Earth, in another lifetime." Alice notices everyone staring at her as if she has two heads. "I suppose you don't believe in reincarnation, and that's okay. Based on my experience, I believe that we live many lives. I think that while we are spirits, we decide to come back again, to learn some things that we didn't get to experience before. If we don't learn those things, when we die, we'll want to return again for the same reasons. So, as I see it, it's best to embrace your problems and really experience them fully now, so that we can clear those issues and move forward in this lifetime, and the next one." There's silence for a few moments when Alice finishes speaking as everyone tries to absorb what she had said.

"I think that's really beautiful," offers Carol. "Even if it isn't true, and I'm not saying that it's not, I think it's a really great way to approach life. Running from our problems and ignoring our issues never seems to work."

"I agree," adds Terry. "I used to be so insecure. I worried about what other people were thinking about me, and it caused me to be afraid to speak my truth. I always thought that other people were talking about me, and I was overly obsessed with my appearance for the same reason. One weekend I became very sick. My husband was away on business, and I was home all alone, thinking that I was possibly going to die. This is going to sound crazy, but I swear to you that it's true. I had a dream that the archangel Raphael came to me. He told me that he could heal me, and I was so grateful that I cried. He told me that he needed to heal my mind, because I had forgotten that I was one with God. So, he put his hands on my head, and the whole room was lit up in the most beautiful green and glowing light. While his hands were on my head, I had visions of all the pain I had caused myself, because I didn't remember that I was part of God. All of my fears were created in my own mind, and they weren't real or true! I know it seems silly now, but honestly, at the time I was so shocked that I'd been torturing myself all those years. Ever since then, because I know myself to be worthy in the eyes of God, literally a part of Him, I have no more fears. I am also able to see everyone else as the beautiful extensions of God that they are, too."

"Wow," says Mary. "I wish that angel would put his hands on my head!" Everyone laughs in agreement.

"Me, too," whispers Sarah.

"So here's a question for you, Terry," begins Carol. "Now that you're able to see everyone as the beautiful children of God that they are, what do you see when you look at Eunice?" Terry fidgets with her painted fingernails. Carol immediately regrets asking the question, although she's still curious. "You don't have to answer that, if you don't want," she offers.

"No, it's alright. Obviously, I don't want to talk about Eunice when she's not here, but I know I would've felt like all of you before my experience with Raphael. I think that knowing how I feel now will help you understand. The way I see it, Eunice doesn't like herself very much. As a result, she's projecting her feelings onto other people, and she assumes that they don't like her either. I don't think she has experienced God herself yet, and so she assumes that we've not had that experience, either. As a result, she's clinging to the idea of the God that she has heard about from others. God does not judge us, so the stories of a judgmental God come from people who haven't experienced God's love for themselves."

"How do you explain judgment day, then?" asks Joe. "I have some ideas about it myself, but I'm curious to hear what you have to say."

"I haven't really given that any thought," admits Terry. "I just know that God loves us, and he wants only the best for us."

Alice says, "I believe that judgment day isn't about God's judgment at all. I believe that when we die, we see all the good that we've done in this lifetime, as well as all of the bad. The judgment is our own. When we see where we could have done better, those are lessons that we still need to learn."

"With all due respect, Alice, what about Hell?" asks Mary. "Who decides that we're going to Hell, if God is not judging? I certainly won't send myself there!"

"See Mary, those are questions that you need to ask yourself, or God, and then listen for the answers. Nobody can tell you what's true for you. For me, I don't believe in Hell. I believe that being on earth and living in separation from God, by not remembering that we are God, creates a state of hell. To me, that's the message that Jesus was trying to bring to humanity. He often mentioned his father and that he was the son of God. He also said that we're his brothers and sisters, and yet, while we use the language of God as our heavenly father, we rarely refer to ourselves as the sons and daughters of

God. That relationship, to me, is empowering in such a beautiful way. We can do anything that Jesus could do, including perform miracles, if we just accept it as our birthright!"

"See, now that just seems a little extreme to me. Are you telling me that you can make a blind man see?" asks Mary.

"I don't know," replies Alice. "I've never tried. But, I do believe that the key to doing it would lie in not just believing that I could do it, but in firmly knowing that with God anything is possible." Everyone just nods until finally Mary stands up from her chair.

"Well, everyone, this has been a very enlightening evening. Thank you all for the wonderful conversation, but I have to get some sleep. Alice, I just want you to know that I don't think that you are the work of the devil, at all. Thank you for your wisdom. Goodnight all!" With that said, Mary turns toward the house, and disappears inside.

That night, Sarah lay in her bed thinking about the events of the evening. She can't get the vision of Archangel Rafael out of her mind, and she wonders about the ability to dream at will. Sarah decides to ask God to send her an angel in her dreams who will help her, so that she will no longer feel afraid. In the morning, the light that's shining through the windows wakes her from sleep. Sarah doesn't remember any angels, but she did dream of a small boy dressed in a burlap sack, who handed her a scroll of paper. He said, "It's all in your records, Sarah," and then he ran away. Sarah has no idea what it means, but the boy's eyes were so sincere, and so loving, that she feels as though she knows him. It all seems so real.

On Friday, Sarah's mind is on Bethany, and the fact that she will be coming home next week for Thanksgiving. Between the convent and the mission, so much has happened over the last month, that it makes Sarah's mind blur. She feels as though she is in a movie, traveling from place to place with no itinerary and not knowing what to expect. Sarah has to admit, though, that life is much more interesting this way. The spiritual and emotional growth that she's experienced in the last few weeks is more abundant than what has occurred over the course of her entire life. No wonder Jeff was so unhappy. Looking back now, she could cry at the stagnation that they experienced while living together. Sarah isn't sure what's next on her life's agenda, but she knows it'll be fresh and exciting. She can't go back to that time when she was sleep-walking through her existence.

That afternoon, Alice, Sarah, and Terry are sanding the dowels that will be used in the railings of the new home. Sarah shares the story of her pending divorce with the women, and her concerns about how she might finance the new life that's brewing in her mind. There are so many things that Sarah wants to experience and so many places that she hopes to see. Until she finds a job, though, everything seems just out of reach.

"What did you do before your daughter was born?" asks Terry.

"I was a writer. I mean, not a real writer. I worked for a teen magazine, so I wrote silly articles about make-up tips, and how to get boys to notice you."

"Oh my goodness, are you serious?" asks Terry. "I used to read those magazines from cover to cover! That's so fascinating!"

"You think?" asks Sarah. "It is not much of a resume, though. Do you think a real magazine would take me seriously? I'm not interested in writing about how to give the perfect kiss anymore. I don't even think I was interested then."

"So, what would you like to write about?" asks Alice.

"I'd like to learn. I'd love to be able to pick a topic that I know nothing about, and then experience it and write about it. I think that would be awesome," replies Sarah.

"Okay," says Alice, "What's stopping you?"

Sarah contemplates that question. "Nothing, I suppose." A few moments pass as Sarah considers those words. "Wow, nothing is stopping me, but me." Sarah smiles at the women, and a surprised little laugh rises up from her belly. "I can't believe I haven't thought of this before. Thank you!" Sarah drops her dowel and sanding block, and leans over to hug Alice and Terry. "This is awesome. I actually feel excited about the future, and I can't say that I have experienced that in a long time. I feel like a weight has been lifted off my shoulders."

"You are going to be a great writer, Sarah, I just know it," offers Terry. "You should see your eyes right now. They are sparkling with light and happiness."

"In the meantime, Sarah," begins Alice, "if you need some extra money while you're getting started with your writing, I'd love it if you would consider working in the bookshop. I've been hoping to get away more often, so it would be wonderful to have an extra set of hands around. I think you'll love the other women who work there. It really is a nice little community, and I know you would fit in perfectly. You'll have to stop by the shop when we get home and tell me what you think."

For a moment, Sarah is speechless. *How amazing is the Universe?* God sent her to this miniature hamlet in West Virginia, to meet an enlightened woman who would offer her a job. She reaches out her hand, and grasps Alice's tiny hand in her own. "Thank you, Alice. I can't thank you enough. I would love that."

Alice gives her hand a squeeze and says, "Please, Sarah, you'll be doing me a favor! I'm happy to help if I can. Like I said, you come by the shop and see what you think. I don't want to pressure you. The decision is yours, and I won't hold it against you if you decide it's not for you."

Sarah loves this little woman. Alice seems to have no concept of the hope that she has set free in Sarah's heart. Everything in Sarah is shouting 'Yes!' in response to Alice's offer. Even though she imagines that the money will be insignificant, she feels that the education she'll receive from being near Alice will be worth far more than any paycheck.

Friday night is hard for Sarah. It's been such a pleasurable two weeks with her cousin, and she's amazed by the bond that she's formed with Bob and Shirley. Joe sits next to her on the deck during the final drumming circle, and she beats her drum with abandon. Afterward, she promises him that she'll make a trip up to Stowe, Vermont, to visit and write about the area. With a new sense of purpose, she's eager to return home, see Bethany, settle the situation with Jeff and move on with her life.

The ride back to Pennsylvania is long, and Sarah has never been so happy to pull into her driveway. She should've stopped at her mother's to pick up Click, but she just wants to climb into her bed and sleep. Sarah slips under the covers, grabs her red notebook and a pen, and begins to write. "Today, I am thankful for new friends, new opportunities, and a safe ride home. God, if you can hear me, and I'm pretty sure that you can, please don't stop guiding me. I'm so thankful. Please help me figure out what I'm supposed to be doing here. Is there a purpose for me? Am I supposed to be a writer? If you could give me a sign, I'd appreciate it." With that, Sarah turns off the light and immediately falls asleep.

———◦◦◦◦———

In the morning, Sarah relishes in the feel of her soft sheets and comfortable mattress. If she ever comes into money, she promises right then that she'll purchase new mattresses for all the beds at the mission. Sarah can't remember the last time she went for two solid weeks in an uncomfortable bed, and it makes her feel extra grateful for the luxury that surrounds her.

In the kitchen, she pours herself a cup of tea, and climbs onto the stool at the counter. Breathing in the warm scent of the spiced tea, Sarah mulls over the phone calls she needs to make today. First on the list is Bethany. It's been a long time since Sarah has carried on a real conversation with her daughter. After Jeff left the house, Sarah was so afraid that she'd let something slip, or that she wouldn't be able to control her emotions. Bethany is her daughter, but somewhere between her sophomore and junior year of high school their relationship evolved into a friendship. It's extremely difficult for Sarah to hide the situation with Jeff from her. Sarah presses the speed dial and Bethany picks up on the third ring.

"Hi, Mom, I miss you!"

"Aw, I miss you, too, honey! How's everything there?" she asks.

"Oh my God, Mom, I have so much to tell you that I don't even know where to start. Lexi is great, but I can already tell that I want to live with Audrey sophomore year. She's majoring in music, too, so we have been playing together a lot, and we have so much in common! Lexi has been hanging out with Abby, and they are already talking about which building they want to live in next year, so I don't even have to feel guilty."

"Well, that's good news," says Sarah. "Have you finalized your plans for coming home yet?"

"Well, yeah…Dad bought me a train ticket on the fast train, so I'll get to the station on Wednesday at noon, remember?"

"Fantastic. Can I pick you up?" Sarah asks.

"Duh! Why are you even asking me? You better be there!" Bethany laughs, and Sarah remembers that Bethany has no idea that she and Jeff are no longer together. Sarah makes a mental note to text Jeff to let him know that she needs to ride along.

"So, how was the mission?" asks Bethany. "Was it gross?"

"No, it wasn't gross! You're so funny. Who asks that?"

"I don't know. I just figured that it's West Virginia, and I think of missions as places that have minimalist accommodations. The combination of West Virginia with a mission doesn't paint a pretty picture, that's all. So, what was it like?" asks Bethany.

Sarah remembers walking into the mission on her first day. The building is nicer than she had expected, although the furnishings look as though they have been donated from various people throughout the years.

"It wasn't bad," offers Sarah. "The volunteers at the mission were extremely nice, and the people we helped were incredibly grateful. I actually built an addition to a house!"

"Wow," Bethany sounds impressed, "that's cool. Was it really religious?"

"We did pray in a circle in the morning and evening, but it wasn't like we were just sitting there praying for hours. We would talk about the events of the day, and then pray for the health and safety of ourselves and the people we were helping."

"Sounds like a thrill a minute. Listen, Mom, I hate to cut you off, but Audrey is waiting for me to go to breakfast."

"I'm sorry, honey! Go! I'll see you on Wednesday."

"Yes! I can't wait! Love you, Mom."

"I love you, too, honey." Sarah hears the click signaling the end of the call and she stares at the phone. Bethany is a strong young woman, and hopefully that strength will serve her in the days to come.

Next on the list is the lawyer. Carol is so altruistic, and Sarah is overwhelmed with mixed emotions over her cousin's generosity. Unfortunately, she needs a lawyer so that she can gain some clarity on her financial situation, so she has no choice but to accept Carol's offer. From the depths of her purse, Sarah pulls out the business card that Des had given her last month. The corners are worn, but the writing is still perfect. With a shaking hand, Sarah dials the number.

"Feinstein and Feinstein, how may I direct your call?" a nasal voice answers.

"Hi," replies Sarah, "I am calling for Lauren Zator."

"Who may I say is calling, please?" replies the voice.

"My name is Sarah, Sarah Jackson. My friend gave me her number."

"And, who is your friend?" asks the secretary.

"Desiree Phillips." Sarah hopes that throwing Des' name out there will help, as opposed to hurt, her chances of speaking with Ms. Zator. When it comes to Des, one never knows.

"Please hold." Sarah waits for what seems like an eternity, when a smooth voice finally comes over the line.

"Ms. Jackson? This is Lauren Zator. How on earth is Desiree? You will have to tell me what that crazy girl has been up to lately." Sarah knows immediately that she's going to like this woman. Lauren is quick to flip the conversation to Sarah's story, and then says, "Sarah, I see this situation all the time. I can tell by the way you speak of Jeff that you have no intention of hurting him, but I'm telling you right now that I am going to make sure that you get what you need to feel comfortable and secure. In Pennsylvania, you're entitled to half of everything in the marriage, and that is exactly what you will have. Depending on your situation, we may be able to get you even more than that. If you can just fax my secretary, Joan, the information that she asks for, I'll put something together, and then contact your husband's attorney. We'll get this settled before you can say, 'Damn girl, you're good!' " Sarah feels as though she can finally breathe fully again. The invisible weight that's been pressing on her chest and crushing her lungs vanishes, and a sense of hope fills its place. Is it possible that she can support herself? Sarah knows that if she spends too much time trying to wrap her mind around the details of her financial situation she'll likely find a budget imbalance. She opts instead to spend the afternoon comfortable in the expectation that everything will work out perfectly.

Feeling exceedingly productive, Sarah decides to go for broke. She picks up her cell phone and dials Jeff's number. After the beep, she says, "Hi, Jeff. I want to pick up Bethany from the train station with you. Shoot me a text when you get a chance, and let me know what time you'll pick me up on Wednesday. Thanks."

Click is the only thing left on her list, so Sarah hops in the car and calls Des on the way to her mother's house. Her friend offers to meet her for dinner at Wannabee's, but Sarah wants something new and exciting. "How about Apollo Grille?" she suggests. Apollo is classy, with tempting tapas and tasty martinis. Des is simultaneously surprised and delighted, as it was less than a month ago that Sarah had balked at eating at the burger joint for fear of spending what little money she had left. The two women agree to meet at seven o'clock, just as Sarah is pulling into her mother's driveway.

Sarah walks in and Click goes wild, jumping, barking, and spinning in circles like a whirling dervish. "How have you been, baby?" Sarah plops herself on the floor and pulls the dog into her lap, and he immediately gives her his stomach to rub. "Who's my good boy?" she asks, using her best high-pitched doggie voice. Sarah is so thankful to have this giant ball of fur in her life. His need for a haircut leaves him looking extra fluffy, and he resembles a giant beige stuffed animal. Sarah pushes away his bangs, and gazes into his beautiful brown eyes filled with unconditional love. A wave of appreciation crashes over her, as she realizes the incredible loyalty of a dog. All these years she has catered to his needs, seeing him more as a responsibility than a joy. Suddenly, she's seeing his soul for the first time and she's awed by his devotion and love. She's trying to convey her love back to him with her eyes, when her mother comes toward her from the kitchen.

"Look who's here! Sal! Sarah's here, come out of your office." Louise reaches her hand out to Sarah to pull her daughter from the floor. "What are you doing down there? You'll get yourself all filthy. God knows, I haven't mopped that floor in years."

"You have a maid, Mom."

"Maritza?" Louise asked. "That woman is useless. She spends more time singing and dancing around than she ever does cleaning. I just keep her for Sal. She's easy on the eyes, if you know what I mean. And those gazoongas, can they possibly be real? Have you seen those things?" Louise laughs out loud. "I bet if you looked up perky in the dictionary, there would be a picture of those gazoongas. I'm not even kidding you."

"Please tell me that you did not just refer to Maritza's breasts as gazoongas. Seriously, Mom, who says something like that?"

"What are you talking about? Everyone says that. I bet they even say that down in West Virginia. How was your trip?" Louise asks.

"It exceeded my expectations. In fact, now that I think about it, it was actually pretty amazing."

"Really?" asks Louise, sounding somewhat dubious, "What did you do that was so amazing?"

"Well, it's not so much about what I did, although I did help build a house, which is pretty damn special. But, the people, they were just so interesting and unique. I had a really good time getting to know everyone."

"So, did they have any teeth?" Louise asks.

"Mom," Sarah frowns at her mother. "Did you really just ask me that?"

"What? I'm sorry. I just don't picture West Virginia people with teeth, okay? Is that such a crime? I mean, they're poor, right? So, I just figure that they don't get the proper nutrition to have nice teeth. That's all I meant." Louise reaches into the refrigerator and pulls out a pitcher of iced-tea. "You want some?"

"Sure, thanks." Sarah knows that her mother isn't mean spirited. Prior to her trip she would have felt the same way. Somehow, though, being there left her inclined to defend her new friends, even the ones with no teeth. "I also met some great missionaries."

"Oh yeah, tell me about them! Were they crazy, or what?" asks Louise. "Did they try to convert you?"

"Convert me to what?" asks Sarah.

"You know, crazy Bible thumpers, like them!"

"Seriously, Mom, it wasn't like that at all. Out of everyone there, even the people who came in church groups, there were only one or two people who were closed-minded in any way. Everyone else was very caring and loving. They were there because they want to make a difference in somebody's life, and this is a great opportunity to do that. Anyway, I had a fantastic time with Carol and everyone else, and I'm glad I went. How was Click?"

"Click is my buddy, aren't you boy?" boomed Sal, as he strolls into the kitchen and pulls Sarah into a bear hug. "How are you, sweetie? How is Carol?"

"She's great Sal, thanks for asking." Sarah shoots her mother a disapproving glance. These are the first questions she expected to hear, not questions about teeth. "I had a fabulous experience. I don't know how quickly I would volunteer to do it again, but that's only because the beds are uncomfortable, and there are just too many other things to see in the world."

"I agree. I'm thinking of taking your mother to Italy this summer."

"What?" Louise shouts, "You are out of your mind. Italy. What am I going to do in Italy? I can't even speak the language."

"Oh my God, Mom, it'll be incredible! You'll love it."

"We're not going to Italy. When would we go? Who would run the Atlantic City trip? It's not happening."

"Stop it, honey." Sal wraps his arms around his wife. "We are going to Italy. Atlantic City will wait until you get back, and besides, I speak enough Italian for both of us. It'll be fine, you'll see. You deserve tiramisu in Piazza di Trevi, and I'm going to be the one to feed it to you." He leans down, kisses her gently on the lips, and Louise melts.

"I do like tiramisu," she smiles.

"I know you do, baby. You'll love Trevi fountain even more than tiramisu." He gives her a little squeeze, and looks back up at Sarah. "Click was a pleasure. I don't know who is going to walk with me now. I don't think I can convince your mother to walk around the neighborhood for no good reason." He pinches Louise's behind and smiles.

"I don't know," says Louise, "If you keep offering me exotic vacations, who knows what I might be willing to do!" and she winks in his direction.

"Okay, lovebirds, I'm going to take Click, and leave you two alone," says Sarah.

"Oh no, honey, don't go on account of him! Stay for dinner," begs Louise.

"If Sal is cooking, I'd love to, but I already promised Des that I would meet her at the Apollo Grill. You'll have to give me a rain check, and we'll see each other next week."

"Fair enough, honey, you're always welcome here," offers Sal, and he leans over to hug her.

"So tell me more about this Trevi fountain..." Sarah hears her mother's voice trail off as she closes the door behind her. Sarah is so thankful for Sal. Louise is much less of a handful now that Sal is taking care of her.

Sarah drops off Click at home and makes her way to the parking garage in downtown Bethlehem. Walking along Broad Street, she's lost in her thoughts of Italy when her shoulder bumps a tall man and literally spins her body in the opposite direction. He gently grabs her by the upper arms to steady her. "I'm so sorry, are you okay?" he asks.

Sarah looks up into his handsome face. With dark brown hair and knowing eyes, he reminds her of a knight she had seen in a movie. "This is so embarrassing. I'm sorry, I was totally daydreaming." They lock eyes and neither can bring themselves to look away. Finally, he drops his hands from her arms.

"It's okay, as long as you're not hurt." He seems truly concerned.

"No," she says, "I'm fine, really."

"Okay. Have a good night then," he offers.

"Yes, you, too," Sarah holds his gaze for a moment longer, and then turns back toward her destination. With a little extra skip in her step, she burns the memory of the handsome stranger into her mind. He'll make excellent fodder for fantasy in the lonely nights ahead.

As Sarah enters the Apollo Grill, she spots Des at the far end of the bar. Laughing and entertaining those around her, as usual, she's the center of attention. Sarah admires the ease with which she handles every situation and secretly wishes that she could have some of those skills herself. When Des makes eye contact with Sarah, she screeches and runs toward her friend with outstretched arms.

"How are you? My God, you look fabulous! Did they not feed you at that place? You've lost at least ten pounds, so tell me all your secrets. Wait here, I'll be right back." Des snatches her drink and purse from the bar and with a big smile says, "Later, boys! Thanks for the drink!" She lifts it in salutation, links arms with Sarah, and gives the men no further notice. "Let's grab a table. I'm starving!"

Sarah orders a Bellini martini and moans as the peach perfection slides across her lips. Apollo is too far away to be a regular haunt, but Sarah believes there's only one other man in the Lehigh Valley who could rival the famed Bellini martini. Since Grille 3501 is so much closer and the bartender there is fantastic, Sarah has little reason to come out to Bethlehem. When she does though, she savors every calorie laden sip!

"So," Des questions her friend with raised eyebrows, "how's God been treating you? Was West Virginia everything you dreamed it would be?" She laughs at her joke and looks to Sarah for a response.

"You know, it was actually much better than I'd hoped. And, I think I might have found a job, too!" Sarah proceeds to tell Des all about her trip, and then she finishes up with Alice and the metaphysical shop.

Des just stares at her friend in disbelief. "Who are you?" she asks in bewilderment. "Are you seriously considering working for some nut job in a bookstore for witches? Sarah, have you lost your mind? Please, tell me that this is all some kind of joke gone wrong. I don't even know what to say." Des picks up her drink, and takes a long draw of the liquid.

Sarah's heart drops. For someone who didn't know what to say, Sarah thinks that Des has said plenty. In fact, it feels like far too much, and Sarah isn't sure how to recover the conversation. In one moment of time, she's able to see her friend in a different light, and it no longer shines quite as brightly as before. Yes, Des is fun to be with. She's absolutely the life of the party and there's never a dull moment. But, who is she? What does she want besides pedicures and purses? Sarah has no idea, and she knows that Des will never share at that level. Suddenly, everything that made Des glamorous to Sarah before, such as the wine, the singing, the sex talk, and the shopping, seem like a sorry way to cover up what's going on inside. Sarah is heartbroken as she realizes that this isn't the kind of person she wants as a best friend. Sarah wants someone who'll support and encourage her at the deepest levels.

"Honey," continues Des, "you are a writer! We're going to find you a great job and you're going to do what you love. I know you're panicking about money, but working in a little shop for seven dollars an hour is not going to keep a roof over your head. Now stop with this crazy talk!" She lifts her martini and holds it out to Sarah, "Let's drink to your career as a writer."

Picking up her drink, Sarah taps it against Des' glass. She's planning to write, so it's certainly worth some celebration. Something inside of her dies a little at this dinner, though, and as she drives home she has a scary thought. She had once read that sometimes things fall away to make space for new things to come together. After losing Bethany and Jeff, Sarah doesn't know if she's ready to lose Des yet. Deep in her heart, though, she knows what the future will hold for them.

The Metaphysical Shoppe

THE BOOKSTORE IS MUCH MORE than Sarah could have expected. From the outside it looks like a typical brownstone in Allentown. Just past 17th Street on Tilghman, the neighborhood is still cared for and safe, and Sarah is happy to find a parking lot on the side of the building. The indigo, wooden sign that hangs out front says Metaphysical Shoppe in hand carved letters, which are painted with metallic gold. Sarah turns the handle, and the blue door makes a wonderful squeaking sound as the bells hanging on the inside doorknob jingle like Santa's sleigh. The smell of frankincense wafts from a diffuser, and the sounds of harps, wind chimes, and flowing water fill the air. Immediately, she feels at peace, and at home.

Everywhere Sarah turns is an adventure for the eyes. Beautiful statues of dragons, fairies, and angels are scattered throughout the displays of books. Racks of essential oils and aura candles contribute to the wonderful aroma, and Sarah can't wait to smell them all. As she passes from the front of the store into the center room, a glass counter stands to the left. Its case is filled with jewelry made from gemstones, and baskets overflow with crystals. The wall behind it is covered with canisters that contain dried herbs and teas, while another wall houses compact discs and a sound station with headphones so that you can listen to the music before you buy.

Just as she's thinking that she'd like to stay and play all day, Alice emerges from the back room. "Sarah! What a wonderful surprise." Embracing Sarah, she says, "How very nice to see you. Welcome, I'm so glad you came. What do you think?"

"Oh Alice, it's just beautiful! It's so relaxing, and it smells so good in here."

"Doesn't it? I'm so glad you like it. Let me show you around." Alice takes Sarah's hand, and leads her back through the kitchen. Opening the refrigerator, she says, "Liz comes in on Monday, Wednesday, and Friday with wonderful green drinks and kombucha that she brews herself. You can help yourself to whatever you'd like. The cabinets are filled with mugs and teas, and there's an electric kettle right there for you. Do you like chocolate? Of course you do, I can tell just by looking at you! So, the pantry here is filled with chocolate, and it's all organic and fair trade. There are some cocoas and coffees in there as well." Leading Sarah through a hall and past the bathroom, she continues, "This is our yoga and meditation room. We don't let people back here unless there are classes going on. Beth should be in shortly for meditation if you'd like to stay and sit. She's a Buddhist priest, and I just know she would love to meet you."

"Sure, that sounds perfect," replies Sarah.

"Excellent! Now, come see the upstairs." As they proceed toward the front of the shop to ascend the staircase, Alice informs Sarah about the various treatment rooms upstairs and the practitioners who spend time at the Metaphysical Shoppe. "It's such a wonderful group," she continues. "I can't wait for you to meet them all." Just then the jingle bells on the front door signal an arrival, and Alice waves her hand toward the stairs. "Go on up and look around. No one is up there right now."

Sarah finds the rooms upstairs to be just as fascinating as the shop itself. Strict attention to detail makes them feel cozy, light, clean, and spiritual. Sarah imagines lying on the table while a faceless practitioner cleanses her of all her sorrow. She wonders if that is the kind of activity that goes on here. The tuning forks and singing bowls make her think there must be something more than just massage. Back in the hall, spread out on a glass table supported by two stone angels, Sarah finds a bevy of pamphlets. She grabs a few that look interesting, and slides them quickly into the side of her purse.

"Oh, good," Alice's voice startles Sarah, and makes her jump. "You found the literature table. If you're anything like me, Sarah, you'll be here all the time for classes and treatments, even when you're not working. The good news is that you'll love every minute of it and never want to leave!" Alice laughs out loud and waves her hands around. "I can't get enough of this place and the people. It's just such wonderful energy. Come in here and try the Biomat. It's an amethyst bed that gives off far infrared rays. It's great for circulation and relaxation. You'll love it."

When Sarah arrives home that evening, she's mesmerized by just how relaxed she feels. Even the thought of seeing Jeff and Bethany the next day can't rattle her nerves. The Biomat treatment was a slice of heaven, and Sarah fell asleep almost immediately, as the far infrared waves penetrated her muscles. The negative ions, which emanate from it, refreshed the air that she breathed. Sitting with Reverend Beth was also very soothing. The priest was kind, and the love that radiated from her energy field was palpable. While sitting in the silence, Sarah had an overwhelming feeling of peace and a brief glimpse of oneness: a sudden awareness that everything actually is one. Almost as quickly as she could focus on it, it was gone, and she felt bereft. Ironically, the dharma talk that followed the meditation spoke of the unity of all and the universal mind that we all share.

In the morning, Sarah nearly trips over Click as she runs for her ringing cell phone. She hesitates for a moment when she sees that it is Jeff, and then answers in the most casual voice she can muster.

"Hello?"

"Hey, Sarah, it's me. I got your message. Can you be ready to leave by eleven-thirty?" he asks.

"Sure. I'll see you then." Sarah glances at the clock. It is only eight-forty. Sarah wonders if Jeff can't remember how long it takes her to get ready. He used to be so thankful that she could be ready in fifteen minutes, unlike some of their friends' wives. For as much as Sarah is excited to see Bethany, she's twice as anxious about the thirty minute car ride with Jeff. She wonders if she should tell him about the lawyer.

After showering and spending much longer getting ready than she cares to admit, Sarah sits down at her computer. The screen lights up as she logs onto Facebook. There's a message in her inbox, and Sarah clicks on the icon to see that it is from Lenny.

"Good luck today with your daughter. I imagine it will all going smoothly, and I hope you feel the same. Remember to stay in the moment as much as possible. In this moment, everything is fine, right? Oh, and Happy Thanksgiving! Think of me…I'll be eating peanut-butter-and-jelly (just kidding). Enjoy! Lenny."

He remembered. Sarah can't help but smile and think about how sweet and funny Lenny is. Hopefully, if everything goes right, she'll visit him on her way up to Stowe to see Joe and write her first travel article. She sends off a quick note in return:

"Hi, Lenny, thank you for thinking of me! I'm definitely freaking out a little bit, but I'll try to take your advice. In this moment, everything is fine (I can't guarantee the next moment, though!). Happy Thanksgiving to you! I'm pretty sure that peanut-butter-and-jelly, plus pumpkin pie, is a recipe for diabetes. Be careful! Hugs, Sarah."

After a long walk with Click, Sarah checks her make-up, grabs her bag, and sits down in the chair on the front porch to wait for Jeff. When he pulls up, her defiant legs turn to lead and refuse to allow her to stand. She is sure she might throw-up, and her upper lip begins to perspire. "In this moment, everything is fine," Sarah chants to herself. Everything doesn't feel fine, though. She loosens her grip on the arms of the chair, and focuses on raising herself to her feet. Lifting her bag off the table, Sarah forces herself to walk to the car and lower herself into the bucket seat. The same seat that she's sat on a million times, except now it belongs to Kate. Jeff is saying something, but Sarah doesn't hear a word.

"I'm sorry, what were you saying?" she asks.

"Wow, where were you just now? I asked how you are doing. How was your trip?"

"How did you know about my trip?" she asks.

"Don't worry, I'm not stalking you. I was driving past your mom's on my route, and I saw Sal walking Click. He told me that you went on vacation with Carol."

Sal is so awesome! Only he would leave out the details so that Jeff would think Sarah was off on some leisurely vacation. Louise would have spilled everything in a heartbeat. It's not that she isn't loyal, but she just doesn't know when to stop talking. Sal likes to call it diarrhea of the mouth.

"Oh, yes, it was nice. Thanks for asking. How've you been?" she asks.

"I've been okay, I guess. I got a message yesterday from some lawyer's office. I haven't called them back yet, though. Do you know anything about this?"

Sarah's stomach drops. How could this be happening so quickly? She just talked to the lawyer the other day. The woman did say that she was good. Sarah had no idea she would be this good.

"If it was Lauren Zator, from Feinstein and Feinstein, then it was my lawyer."

"Seriously, Sarah, why would you do this? Lawyers are going to cost a fortune. We could have handled this all ourselves and saved a shitload of money. This is just great. With paying for college and now this, don't you ever use your brain?"

Sarah feels as if Jeff has punched her. Anger flares up inside, and she looks at him in disbelief. "Don't I ever use my brain? I'm not the lying cheat who had an affair and left you with a thousand dollars to your name. God knows, was it even your intention to leave me with that much, or did you just forget to clean out the account?"

"I told you that I would take care of you!" Jeff yells back.

"I know what you said, Jeff, but I also know that I'm not going to be some kept woman, living in exile while my husband lives out his mid-life crisis. There's no way that I'm going to beg you for every nickel and dime, while you're out lavishing Kate with dinners and dancing. Forget it."

"Is that what you think? I am living in a one bedroom apartment, for God's sake. I don't have a yard, and I don't have any privacy. We're all making sacrifices here, and the way I see it, you lucked out with the house and Click." Jeff is furious. Sarah doesn't seem to appreciate anything he is doing to make this easier for her.

"Excuse me if I don't feel bad that you don't have a yard. You poor thing, living holed up with your sex toy, it must be so hard. Might I remind you that you had a house, a yard, privacy, your dog, and me? You chose to abandon those things, so don't expect me to feel sorry for you for a second. As much as I want to trust you, I would be a fool, wouldn't I? This isn't a game, or some trivial little thing. We need experts for this."

"How are you going to pay for your expert? Did you think of that? Don't expect me to do it, that's for damn sure." Jeff shook his head in disgust. "You must think I'm made of money, and I'm not."

"I paid the bills for our whole marriage, Jeff. I know just what you are made of, and it's certainly not money. Realistically, you can't even afford to pay for the house and that apartment. Had you consulted me first, I could have told you that. So, don't worry yourself about my lawyer. The time for you to worry about me has passed. And, you should call her back. It's my understanding that she's going to try to work everything out amicably first, without having to go to court. If you decide to agree to what she says, you might not even need a lawyer."

"Yeah, and then I get screwed!" he glares at Sarah.

"You know what? I'm not the one trying to screw anybody. Do what you want, I don't care anymore. We're going to be at the train station in five minutes, and I don't want Bethany to see us like this. Just so you know, we'll go back to the house, tell her, and then she and I are going to my mother's at five."

"That's not fair! Why do you get her?"

"Are you kidding me? If she's even speaking to you after this, I'm sure she's not going to want to spend Thanksgiving with Kate. If you want to see more of her, you can pick her up tomorrow, if she agrees." Sarah is shaking, but she's proud of the way she handles the situation. Jeff is out of his mind if he thinks they are spending the rest of this evening together. She can't believe how angry he is, and she wonders briefly if everything is going downhill with Kate, although she doesn't dare to ask.

Bethany is coming down the platform steps as they arrive at the station. She looks so happy, and it kills Sarah to know what they are about to do to her world.

"Hi, honey! I missed you!" Sarah and Bethany cling on to each other, and tears spring to Sarah's eyes.

"I missed you, too, Mom! Hey, don't cry! I'm going to be here for four days. We're going to have a great time. Hi, Dad," Bethany releases Sarah and hugs Jeff.

"Hi Baby Girl, you look great."

"Thanks, how've you been? Every time I call, you're never home. I feel like I haven't talked to you in forever!"

"It's been a while, hasn't it? You really look great, though. Are you happy there?" he asks.

"I love it. As excited as I am to come home, I was just as sad to leave everyone. You look like you gained a little weight, Dad. Has Mom not figured out how to cook for two, yet?"

"You think?" Jeff looks down and places his hands on his stomach. "I think I look the same. My clothes still fit."

It must be all that eating out, thinks Sarah, although she doesn't say it. Kate never did like to cook. Bethany chatters on for the entire car ride, and Sarah feels relief wash over her as they pull into the driveway. Telling Bethany may be horrible, but living behind this façade of happiness is torture. The end is in sight, and instead of the anxiety that Sarah once had concerning this conversation, she is unexpectedly calm.

———•ooo‑}◉{‑ooo•———

Once they're all inside, Bethany rolls all over the floor with Click, while Sarah carries her bag to her room. Jeff disappears into the sunroom, and when Sarah returns, she and Bethany join him there. It's a little chilly, so Sarah turns on the space heater.

"Honey," Sarah begins, "there's something that your dad and I need to tell you." Jeff shoots her a look, which according to Sarah's interpretation implies that she's moving too quickly. Sarah doesn't care. She's determined to get this over with, as soon as possible. Bethany looks up from her place on the floor with Click. "You see, after you went to school, your Dad told me that he didn't want to be married anymore."

"What," Bethany looks at Jeff in confusion, "why?"

"Well, it's not that easy to explain, Bethany," Jeff replies. He looks uncomfortable and nervous, which brings Sarah a small amount of satisfaction.

"You have to try, Dad. You can't just tell me something like this and not give me anything else. I'll be forced to make up my own reasons," Bethany shoots back.

"No, there's no need for that. It's just that I felt trapped, like I couldn't be myself, or do the things that I've wanted to do. Your mother and I, we love you. We stayed together for you, but now you're grown, and we shouldn't have to pretend anymore." Bethany swings around to look at Sarah.

"Is this true?" she asks, her eyes glazed with betrayal.

Sarah looks down at her hands. She doesn't want to throw Jeff under the bus, but why does she have to take any fault for this? "It's true that your father no longer wants to be married. It came as a surprise to me, Bethany. I swear to you that I had no idea. I was never pretending to love him."

"So, now what happens? Are you going to move out? Are you getting a divorce?" Bethany asks.

"I already moved out, honey. And yes, eventually, we will get divorced," Jeff replies.

"You already moved out? Where do you live? Why don't I know any of this?" Bethany turns to Sarah again.

"Your mother and I wanted to tell you together, in person, in case you had any questions. I rented an apartment over by the grocery store. It's not far from here at all."

"This is so weird. I feel like I'm dreaming and any minute now someone is going to wake me up," says Bethany.

"Yeah, welcome to my world." Sarah gives her daughter a half smile. "Do you have anything else you want to ask your father? You and I are going to go to Grandma's for dinner tonight. Sal's making a feast, so I'm going to get ready." Rising from the couch, she looks at Jeff and says, "Happy Thanksgiving," and leaves the room.

Sarah closes the bathroom door behind her and sinks to the floor. On her way down she grabs the hand towel and covers her face so that Bethany and Jeff won't hear her sobs. Tears flow, and she cries so hard that no sound can emerge from her clenched vocal cords. Her whole body feels strangled, as if some invisible force is attempting to squeeze the last cell memory of Jeff from her body. Sarah isn't even sure why she's crying. Eventually, understanding flows through her like a river washing her clean. Now that Bethany knows, it's official. She and Jeff are finished, and there's no turning back.

When Sarah finally walks back into the sun room, Jeff stands, helps his daughter off of the floor, and holds her in an embrace. "I'm sorry honey, I never meant to hurt you," he says.

"I know, Dad. I'll be okay. See you."

"I love you, Beth," he mumbles. Sarah can't be sure, but she thinks Jeff is tearing up just a bit.

"I love you, too, Dad. What are you going to do for Thanksgiving?" Bethany looks at Sarah. "Can't he come to Grandma's?" Caught off guard, Sarah just stands there stunned, but Jeff comes to her rescue.

"No, honey, I'm going over to Donny and Amy's. Don't worry about me, I'll be fine." Jeff glances toward Sarah, but quickly looks away. Sarah notes how he conveniently left Kate out of the conversation, and she wonders if he has told Bethany about their relationship while she was in the bathroom. Somehow, she doubts that he has.

As Bethany closes the door behind her father, Sarah lets herself relax into the comfort of the sofa. "Come sit by me," she says, and pats the cushion to her left. Bethany crosses the room, curls up against her mother and lays her head on Sarah's shoulder. "I'm so sorry, honey," Sarah says, as she runs her hand through her daughters hair. "I never wanted this for you."

"Mom, don't be sorry. This is totally not your fault! I can't believe Dad did this to you. I can't believe you're so calm!"

"It's been a few months now, so I guess I've had some time to adjust. I wasn't nearly this calm when it happened. Although, I was in such a state of shock that maybe I *was* calm. I really can't remember."

"When did this happen? I don't understand how you could keep this from me."

"I know, baby, but I didn't want to ruin your first semester at college. I didn't know how you would react, either. I wanted to tell you, trust me, but your father was determined that we tell you together. I couldn't bring myself to go up to Boston with him, and this is the first time that you're home. It was so difficult to speak with you. I just kept myself really busy between the convent and the mission. It helped, a lot."

"Now it all makes sense," concludes Bethany.

"What's that?" asks Sarah.

"I couldn't imagine what possessed you to go to the convent for so long, or on a mission trip no less. I mean, come on, Mom, you have to agree that the whole thing is so out of character for you." Bethany scrunches up her face at Sarah, which makes Sarah laugh.

"I guess it is. It's what I was guided to do, though. Just when I thought I couldn't do it by myself anymore, God just stepped in and said, 'I've got this.' I don't know how else to explain it."

"That's awesome, Mom. And weird. You're pretty cool, you know that? I'm proud of you." Bethany hugs her mother, and Sarah's eyes fill with tears, again.

"Thank you, honey. Thank you for not hating me." Sarah chokes back her tears and squeezes her daughter as hard as she can.

"Duh, Mom, I could never hate you. You rock."

"I'm trying, kid. I'm really trying."

Dinner is nothing less than exceptional, and Sal and Louise are exactly what Sarah needs after this afternoon with Jeff. In the relaxed atmosphere of her mother's Tuscan kitchen, everyone is playful and joyous. Theresa is home from the convent with Sister Ginnie, who's thrilled to have the opportunity to spend the holiday with Sarah. The bond that the two women forged at the convent is still strong, even though Sarah neglected to keep in contact as she had promised. Around seven, while Bethany fills in her grandparents about the joys of independent living, Sarah and Sister Ginnie head outside for a walk with Click.

"How are you really doing?" asks Sister Ginnie. Sarah takes her time piecing together the answer for her friend. She knows that Sister Ginnie doesn't want the cordial answer, but a true assessment of her well-being.

"I am better than I thought I would be at this point." Sarah looks at Sister Ginnie and smiles. "You were right about Bethany's reaction to all of this. I tried not to allow myself to project into the future too much. I met someone at the mission who really encouraged me to stay in the moment, and it helped me with the anxiety of my situation. I talk to God so much that I feel like I know him personally. I'm sure that must sound ridiculous to you. You obviously have a much better relationship with him than I do." Sister Ginnie laughs at this.

"Sarah, God has the same love for you that he has for me. We are all equally important, and he is as present for you as he is for any priest, or pope. The only difference is that the religious are constantly living with God on our mind. We are present for God, Sarah, and you are now present for him, as well. The more you talk to God, the more he will know that you're willing to do his work here. When you are open to that, God always shows you the way. In Jeremiah 29, God says, 'you will seek me and find me, when you seek me with all your heart.' And in Proverbs 8, it says, 'I love them that love me; and those who seek me diligently shall find me.' Keep seeking Sarah, for when you seek, you shall find. Never doubt that God is present for you, and that you have access to his wisdom."

"Oh, Ginnie, this is why I miss you! Nobody else talks to me like this. Never in a million years would I have imagined that I'd enjoy it when someone spews bible verses at me, but you make God seem so real, and wonderful. I used to wonder if any of it were true. Seriously, I thought of the Bible as an archaic novel written by men, for men. Now, though, I see that there is wisdom in those pages, and I want to know more. I like the version of God that I've come to know. I'm so grateful for the peace and guidance that he brings me that I no longer care if he's real or not. Does that make sense?"

"I think it makes perfect sense," replies Sister Ginnie. "These days, science has trumped spirituality, so that many people turn away because God has been changed into a fairy tale. People are no longer taught to quiet themselves, or to go inside their hearts and listen for the voice of God. I'm sure this is why so many people are feeling lost and hurting. They're struggling from the separation."

"I saw a cute bumper sticker on the way over here this afternoon. It said, "If you don't feel close to God, guess who moved?" It rings so true for me. I was far away from God for so long, that I had no idea what was missing."

"Now you know, so what do you plan to do about that?" Sister Ginnie asks.

"What do you mean?"

"I mean how do you plan to do God's work here on Earth?"

"Are you saying that I should become a nun? I don't know if I could do that. I mean, locking myself up-" Sister Ginnie cuts her off.

"I'm not saying that you should become a nun, Sarah. I just suggest that you think about how you can incorporate God's will for you into your work, that's all."

"I'm not sure that I know what God's will for me is. I think I'm supposed to be a writer. It's what comes naturally to me. I like to travel, so being a travel writer sounds like a dream job. I'm not sure how realistic it is, though."

"Why do you say that? Anything is possible with God's help, Sarah. You just need to spend some time in prayer about this. Have a conversation with God about his plan for you and see what happens," suggests Ginnie. "And remember, Sarah, God and the angels can't interfere with your free will. If you want to be a travel writer, you need to ask them to help you. Your job is to determine what you want, not how you will get it. Once you put it out there as your desire, they'll find a way!"

Sarah nods her head in affirmation. "I'll do that. Thank you. Sometimes things are so simple and obvious, and yet I can't see them. Why is that?"

"Sometimes, we just think too much for our own good. Speak to God with your heart, Sarah. Even more than with your lips, you should speak to him with your heart."

———∞◦❦◦∞———

On Sunday, Jeff wants to drive Bethany back to the train station. Since he hasn't seen her all weekend, Sarah is happy to give them time together. Having Bethany home is fantastic, but Sarah must admit she's starting to grow accustomed to her alone time and is content with the empty house. She straightens up a little, throws in a load of laundry, and writes a text to Des in response to her earlier phone message, inquiring about the weekend.

After some leftover turkey and a cup of tea, Sarah sits down to meditate. She asks God about his plans for her, but nothing seems to happen. Somewhat frustrated, she ends by adding whatever it is that he expects of her, Sarah is willing to try, if he'll just give her some direction. She washes her face, writes in her gratitude journal, and falls asleep.

At some point around three o'clock in the morning, Sarah awakens from a dream. The same small boy that came to her once before has appeared again. "It's all in the records, Sarah. Look in the records." He hands her a scroll and runs away. Sarah turns on the light and writes down the boy's words. They don't make any sense, but she read recently that you should write down your dreams in a journal. Afterward, she promptly returns to sleep.

In the morning, Sarah showers and heads to the Metaphysical Shoppe. She and Alice have agreed that she'll come in this week from ten until two o'clock, which will give Sarah plenty of time to write in the afternoons. At the shop, Sarah meets a number of regular clients and customers, as well as a few of the practitioners who see clients there on Mondays. One of the women is Lori, and her personality precedes her into the shop. She has the face of a cherub, with eyes that seem to look right into Sarah's soul. The Italian in her pops right out, as she grabs Sarah by both arms and raises her boisterous voice, "Who is this beautiful soul? My God, I feel like I know you! Do I know you?" Lori tilts her head back and forth, looking at Sarah on one side, and then the other. "I don't know! You don't look familiar, but I feel like we must have known each other before. We'll have to figure that out. I'm Lori, by the way," and she sticks out her hand and Sarah shakes it.

"It's nice to meet you," Sarah says.

"Oh, yeah, yup...there's no doubt about it. I know you!" cries Lori.

"You do?" asks Sarah.

"Yes! Well, no, not technically. Not now. But man, your energy, it's so familiar to me!" Sarah isn't sure how to respond.

"You should open her records, Lori," suggests Alice.

"My records?" inquires Sarah, remembering clearly the message from the boy in her dream.

"Lori reads the akashic records. She's amazing, a true healer. You should read her, Lori. After all, how's she going to be able to sell your services if she has never experienced them?" asks Alice.

"I will. I have two clients this morning, but after that we'll open your records. Wow. I can't wait to get in there!"

The front door opens with a jingle, and Lori yells, "Gloria! How are you, beautiful?" and pulls the woman into an embrace where they rock back and forth like long lost friends. Lori leads the woman upstairs, and Sarah turns to look at Alice, a stunned expression still pinned on her face.

"You're never going to believe this! It must be a coincidence," Sarah stutters, and she proceeds to tell Alice her dream.

"Oh, honey, that's not a coincidence! That's synchronicity! Everything happens in divine order, so don't think for a second that it doesn't. Clearly, this is a sign that you are going to have an amazing reading. How exciting this must be for you!"

"What is an akashic records reading?" asks Sarah, feeling more than a little ignorant.

"Well, Lori can explain it better, I'm sure. Basically, the records are the recorded experiences of a soul through all of its' past lives, up until the present. In a reading, Lori can clear any fears, resentments, or guilt that you have that is holding you back from moving forward.

Sarah is getting excited, and nervous. "I'm scared," she tells Alice.

"Oh, Sarah, you don't have to be afraid. The records only tell you things that'll help you. You're going to love it. It's a very healing and soothing experience, and exactly what you need right now, or none of this would be happening. Go with it, honey. Follow the experiences, and embrace them. It's why you are here on this planet." Alice leads Sarah into the kitchen, and pours her a cup of raspberry kombucha. "Besides, Lori is simply fantastic at what she does. I promise that this will make you want to get closer to spirit, and that is never a bad thing. Have some questions ready for her, though, because while she is very intuitive, she is not psychic. In order to get the most from a reading, it should be as interactive as possible. When the records are open, she'll have access to your spirit guides, so be sure and ask her everything that you want to know."

"What should I ask? I have no idea, and now I'm even more nervous!"

"Look, why don't you head back into the meditation room around 11:30. That will give you a half-hour to meditate about what you should ask. Everything you need is inside of you, Sarah, you just need to remember to take the time to listen," Alice reminds her.

"You're right, and I thank you, but it's so easy to forget about that. How do you remember?"

"It's simply a practice. Check in with your intuition about everything. For example, when you decide to have a cup of tea, choose a couple of types, and then ask yourself which one will best serve you. Empty your mind, and listen. Then, see how the thought of each tea makes you feel. Use that process for everything in your life, and it'll become a habit. This practice does away with so much regret. How many times have you made a decision even though something was telling you not to do it? How many times have you thought to yourself that you wish you had listened to your gut feeling? Always listen, Sarah. You just have to trust that your angels and guides can see the big picture much more clearly than you can."

At eleven-thirty, Sarah enters the meditation room. She chooses a purple cushion and a spot on the floor in front of the statue of Buddha. A small fountain is flowing to the right of the Buddha, and Sarah focuses on the sound of the water dripping into the pool at the bottom. She asks herself what questions she needs to ask Lori during her reading. Immediately, in her mind, she hears that she needs to ask how to forgive Jeff. Sarah is surprised by this, for she expected to hear that she should ask about her career, or her future. There's something about forgiving Jeff that resonates, though. She doesn't think she'll ever be able to forgive him completely, but a comfortable, dull feeling surrounds her thoughts of him lately, so she imagines that she must be making progress. Sarah focuses on her breathing and waits, but nothing else comes to her.

The soft click of the meditation room door causes Sarah to open her eyes. "I'm sorry," says Lori in a soft voice, "are you ready?"

"I am," replies Sarah, and she forces herself off of the cushion.

Lori leads her into the smallest room upstairs, and they sit across from each other in wicker chairs with thick floral cushions. "So," begins Lori, "let me just tell you a little about what will happen here. Have you heard of the akashic records?" Sarah shakes her head from side to side.

"I only know what Alice told me this morning," Sarah admits.

"Okay, so you know that the records are like an ethereal library of every soul's journey, through all of its past lives, up until the present moment. When I open your records, which I will do by reading a short prayer, I won't be able to know everything about you at once. The integrity of the records is protected by spiritual beings, who will only pass on information which will help you to move forward in your life. They pass this information to your masters, teachers, and loved ones in the spiritual realm, who then pass the information down to me, in a way that you'll best receive it. Do you have any questions before we start?"

"No, I don't think so," says Sarah.

"Great. I just need your full name as it is on your legal documents."

"Sarah Marie Jackson," Sarah replies.

"Fabulous. Now, as I read the prayer, there is a part that I need to repeat to myself, and you are going to wonder what I am doing, but now you know. Okay?" Sarah shakes her head in understanding.

After the prayer, Lori announces, "The records are now open." She opens her own eyes, looks up at Sarah, and smiles broadly. "Beautiful. Let's begin. So, Miss Sarah, tell me your story. What's going on?"

"My story?" asks Sarah. "Let's see. Well, my daughter started college in August. She's my only child, and my best friend. I mean, I have a best friend, but I'm closer to my daughter. My husband left me for his friend's wife, and now, well, I don't know…I just feel lost, like I don't have any direction."

"I'm sorry that you are experiencing such pain. It must be very difficult for you," offers Lori.

"It is," Sarah's eyes fill with tears. "Everything that I thought was true about my relationship and my future is all a lie now. I feel as if my compass is just spinning out of control, and I can't find my way. What should I do?"

"First," begins Lori, "I want you to know that your angels are all around you, and you are not alone. They're telling me that you're closer to the true path of your soul than you've ever been in your life, so don't worry. They're showing me you listening, and showing me your ears. Have you been listening to spirit lately, Sarah?" Now, the tears fall over Sarah's lashes and roll down her cheeks, leaving dark splash marks on her jeans.

"I've been listening. My friend thinks I'm crazy, but I feel like God has been telling me what to do, and when I do it, everything seems to happen so perfectly. Am I crazy? Sometimes I feel like I'm losing my mind. I spent my whole life being rational and now I'm some lunatic with my head in the clouds, who thinks that maybe God has some master plan for me. That's nuts, right?" Lori smiles, and pauses before she finally speaks.

"Sarah, God does have a master plan for you, but that plan was created by you. You see, Sarah, you are an extension of God. God cannot experience things, God can only be. We come to this earth to experience, to love, and to create, and when we go back to God at the end of our lives, we bring all of our experiences and creations back into the collective mind of God. Have you heard the expression that we are created in his image? Have you ever wondered how that is possible if none of us look the same? It's because our soul is a part of God, Sarah. In spirit, we're not separate from God, we just forget who we really are and that causes us great pain and suffering. Once we remember our perfection, self-doubt and fear tend to fall away. You are perfect, Sarah. Spirit is telling me that you're dealing with abandonment in this lifetime. I can feel your fear in my heart. Who left you besides your husband?"

"My father," Sarah barely whispers.

"Yes, your father. You came to this lifetime to experience abandonment. After your experience with your father, that underlying fear manifested what happened with your husband. We will clear that for you later. Do you have any other questions?"

"I just don't understand why I would come here to experience abandonment? Who does that? Why didn't I come here to experience love?" asks Sarah.

"Well, it's sometimes more complicated than that. Let me ask." Lori looks down toward the left and closes her eyes. After a few moments, she says, "In a past life, you were a landlord in Asia. You had multiple wives and concubines, spread throughout your territory. All of them cried for your time and attention, but it was impossible for you to be attentive to so many women and children. This lifetime is a matter of karmic healing for you."

"So, I am being punished," says Sarah.

"I wouldn't say that, exactly. You see, Sarah, our society has a common misconception about God's desire to punish us. God loves us, and punishing us is not part of his agenda. We're constantly striving to become better souls, who are compassionate, and more understanding. By coming here to experience abandonment, you're able to understand exactly how it felt, when you left all those women and children on their own. You're now more compassionate and understanding about abandonment, and that's a wonderful thing. Experiencing abandonment is no longer serving you, though. If you're willing to embrace this lesson and truly feel the feelings of abandonment without pushing them away, then we can end this karmic cycle now."

"I would like that. I am tired of feeling this way."

"Okay, give me your hands, and close your eyes. Now imagine a beautiful white beam of light shining down upon you. This is God's love, Sarah. In this light, you are perfect, just the way you are. There is nothing that you can do to offend God, and nothing more you need to do to impress him. He has created you perfectly. Feel his love flowing over you and into you, filling your body from your toes all the way up to the top of your head, and then overflowing. Now in the four corners of the room, imagine four more pillars of light, and I want you to fill each one of these with an Archangel. Big and beautiful, imagine them sending their unconditional love toward you, and bask in the comfort of that love. Behind you, with their hand on your shoulder, is your guardian angel. Sent here with the sole purpose of serving you, your guardian angel can be your best friend. Your guardian angel's name is Agnes. In front of you is your spirit guide. Your spirit guide has been with you through all of your lifetimes and knows exactly why you chose to incarnate into this lifetime. You can come to this place in your mind at any time and ask your spirit guide anything. Your spirit guide's name is Saul. To the left of your spirit guide, in a line stretching back to infinity are all of your masters, teachers, and loved ones. All of the knowledge that you could need is here inside of you, Sarah. Come here to have your questions answered, or to sit in the love and remember that you are not alone. Archangel Gabriel is stepping forward to let you know that he is always with you. He is willing to help you in all that you do. Gabriel is the messenger angel, so if you need to send a message, or you have a message for the world, Gabriel can help you. Are you a writer? You could be an amazing writer with Gabriel on your side.

Right now, Archangel Raphael is placing his hands on your head. Feel his healing green energy flowing through you. Clearing any blockages, and cleansing all negativity and fear of abandonment, feel the energy healing your emotional and physical wounds. Let it clear away any unknown emotional ties and soul contracts, which no longer serve the highest and best version of you."

Sarah is amazed by the peace she is feeling. Transported to another place, she feels as though her body and mind are being cleansed of all the thoughts that have always haunted her. In this place, there is no fear. Why did she ever wonder what other people thought about her thoughts and actions? In this moment, Sarah feels perfect. It's as if she's being seen as the soul that she really is, but it's even better than that. Her soul is enough. She is enough!

Just then, Lori says, "Imagine that there is a giant sphere floating next to your body. On the surface of the sphere is a door, with a latch. I want you to open that door, Sarah. As Raphael is cleansing all of the negative thoughts and feelings, I want you to acknowledge them and place them in the sphere. All of your fears of abandonment, place them in the sphere. All of the hurt that your husband has caused, just toss it in there. The woman, who you thought was a friend, put any negative thoughts of her in there, as well. When you feel as if everything is gone, close the door, and tell me."

They sit for a few moments as Sarah processes her thoughts. She puts everything that comes to her into that sphere, from Jeff's infidelity, to Des' lack of understanding for her new found spirituality. She puts her self-doubt in there, and prays that it won't pop back out. She tosses in her fear of being alone and her feelings of inadequacy as a wife.

"Okay, I'm done," says Sarah.

"Wonderful. Now I want you to imagine that there is a golden cord that connects from the bottom of that sphere to your heart. Pick up an imaginary scissors, and I want you to cut that cord. When you are finished, put the scissors down and push the sphere away with both of your hands, and watch it float all the way out to the horizon, until it disappears. Tell me when it is gone."

Sarah watches as her fears and pain float away. *Good riddance.* As they float over the horizon, she says, "It's gone."

"Good. Now Archangel Metatron is here to clear your energy field. Just sit and enjoy the feeling as he filters out any negative energy that is lingering in your aura. Relax and bask in the purity that is you." After a few minutes, Lori continues, "Now, I want to thank the archangels, and your guardian angel, your spirit guide, your masters, teachers and loved ones, and God, for all of their love, and healing. May you continue to feel their blessing and support. Amen." Lori waits for Sarah to open her eyes, and then asks if there are any other questions that she wants to ask.

"They told me to ask you how to forgive my husband, Jeff. I thought I did forgive him as much as possible, but maybe they know something that I don't?"

"What they know, Sarah, is that there aren't degrees of forgiveness. You either forgive him, or you don't. It's like being a little bit pregnant...you either are, or you're not, am I right? If you are still feeling animosity toward Jeff, the best way to turn that around is to send him love. Morning and night, right from your heart space, just imagine love pouring out toward him."

"How can I do that? He doesn't deserve my love!" Sarah can't believe what she is hearing. Her days of loving Jeff are over. He will just have to get Kate to love him now.

"Sarah, this is not about Jeff. This is about you. You want to be happy, right? Happiness is not something that you can catch and store in a box. Joy is a frequency, or state of being. It's a high frequency, Sarah, even higher than that of love. In order to attain joy, you have to raise your frequency. Emotions like jealousy and fear are low frequency emotions and will bring you down. The best way to clear them is to focus on being thankful and loving. Gratitude has amazing effects on frequency levels; you can't be thankful at the same time that you are sad or angry. If you focus on all that you appreciate, and send love out to everyone, you act as a beacon and attract those same frequencies back to you. As you do this, your life will improve, and you will experience even more love and joy. Beyond love and joy is the frequency of enlightenment. This is the goal, Sarah. When enlightened, you'll be able to truly experience the oneness of the universe and realize that you and your husband are not separate. Hurting him only hurts you. Does that make sense?"

"Yes, I think it does, actually," replies Sarah.

"Good. So, send him love morning and night. Send it to the woman, too. No one needs enemies. On that same note, you don't need to be best friends with these people. Just wish them good will. That's all."

"Okay, I will. Thank you."

"You're welcome! Let's close your records now." Lori reads the closing prayer, stands up and puts out her arms toward Sarah. "Give me a smooch!" She wraps Sarah in a bear hug, and kisses the air next to her cheek. "Aw, baby doll, you are going to be fabulous. I know this about you! You have no idea what you're capable of, but when you figure it out, oh my goodness. Watch out world, here comes Sarah!"

Sarah hugs Lori tighter. "Thank you. Thank you so much. I feel so much lighter, it feels so good!"

"Isn't it great? Everyone says that. It's just such a relief, as you start to remember who you really are. Finally everything begins to make sense."

"I know. The synchronicities, it's just amazing how everything has fallen into place," says Sarah.

"Well, it's like your angels said, you're on the right path, so just keep doing whatever you're doing. Actually, here's a flyer for a class that might interest you." Lori hands the paper to Sarah and looks thoughtfully into her eyes. "I think you would be great at reading for others. Come on, let's get you back downstairs."

While walking Click after dinner, Sarah remembers the flyer, and pulls it out of her pocket. Looking it over, she wonders if what Lori said is true. Could Sarah really read the akashic records for other people? She has no idea, but her interest is piqued. The price on the flyer is the only thing holding her back. It isn't a huge amount of money, but three hundred and fifty dollars is almost fifty percent of what remains in her checking account. An inner voice is screaming for her to sign up, because there's something about this class that feels very important. As she lay in bed that night, Sarah asks God to find a way for her to take the class, if it's what she's meant to do. She visualizes writing the check to Lori, and sitting in the class in the back room of the shop, just as she drifts off to sleep and into a dream. In the dream, the small boy with the scroll is back. He's excited and smiling as he shouts *I told you, Sarah! I told you that it is all in the records. You are an amazing writer. Keep going,*

Sarah, keep going! Sarah wonders where she's supposed to go, but before she can ask, the boy vanishes.

In the morning, Des calls and suggests that they meet for lunch at Grille 3501. Sarah cringes at the thought of spending that kind of money. "My mouth wants to shout yes, but my wallet says that I shouldn't," she explains.

"Oh for God's sake, it's my treat. I want to go to 3501, and I want you to come with me, okay?" Des asks. "And don't tell me no, either. You're going to be back on your feet before you know it. There's no reason for you to give up living while you are waiting for that to happen."

"Fine, then can I at least pick you up?" asks Sarah.

"Sure, that would be great. I'll see you at noon, then." Des hangs up, and Sarah wonders how long she'll be able to keep up with Des' lifestyle. Their relationship consists mainly of shopping, eating in fine restaurants, and drinking ten dollar martinis. She tries to talk about it at lunch, but Des doesn't want to hear any of it.

"You're being ridiculous. It's only a matter of time before there's a settlement on your divorce. Even if you have to run up your credit card until then, Sarah, you just pay it off when you get the money! Why are you stressing about this? In the meantime, just ask Jeff for money if you need it so badly. He said he would take care of you, didn't he?"

"It's not that easy," says Sarah. "I used to pay the bills, so I know how much money he has. Now that Bethany is in school, we can't just live like there is no tomorrow."

"So then change tomorrow! Do something today that will make tomorrow more lucrative for you," suggests Des.

"Like what," asks Sarah, "start stripping?" Des stares at her for a few long moments before she speaks.

"Again, who are you?" she asks. "What happened to the smart and sassy Sarah that I love? This attitude is bullshit, Sarah. Of course I don't expect you to be a stripper, I expect you do something amazing with yourself! You're intelligent and talented, and you're not even trying to put yourself out there."

"That's because I don't know what to do, Des! I'm not an entrepreneur like you, okay? I can't just create something out of nothing! You love buying and selling accessories, and you love running bus tours, but I wouldn't know the first thing about that stuff."

"Sarah, I'm not asking you to be me! Do you think I knew anything about buying and selling, or running bus trips when I started? Hell no! People always loved my stuff and asked me where I bought it, so it inspired me to learn. I love going into New York City, and the bus trips give me the opportunity to do that, and make some money at the same time. What is it that you love, Sarah? What do you want to do so badly, that you would be willing to pay money for the experience?" Des asks.

"I was thinking that I could be a travel writer. Does that sound crazy, though? I don't really know anything about travelling, but I'd love to go to Peru and Istanbul. I'd really love to take a cruise down the Danube and see Vienna. Can you imagine? How would I ever get that job, though?"

"Oh, honey, you don't get it, do you? If you want to be a travel writer, you just need to decide that you're a travel writer. Start telling people that you're a travel writer and do the things that travel writers do -I'm not sure what those things are- maybe you would interview hotel owners or read travel magazines, and then the opportunities will start to happen."

"You're right!" Sarah shouts in a moment of clarity. "I could write an article on traveling as a single woman! I could even start locally and write about Allentown from a single woman's perspective."

"You could," offered Des, "but I think there's a difference between being single, and being newly divorced, don't you think?"

"You're probably right. Who wants to hear some divorced woman's point-of-view?" Sarah is crushed. She doesn't like thinking of herself as used goods, but that's how her pending divorce makes her feel.

"Don't go there, Sarah. There are plenty of women in your position who are looking for an opinion that validates their feelings. You could be that voice. Pulling all of your attributes together is what is going to make you unique in the field, right? Don't apologize for who you are, just own it! You could be the Divorced Diva, the new voice in the Valley. That sounds interesting to me, and I'm not even divorced!"

Sarah listens to Des go on and on about possible career options. She hears all of the suggestions, and she agrees with many of them, but they have to be fantasies. How can she become the voice of the Valley about anything? She is just Sarah Jackson. Her divorce papers aren't even final, so how can she propose to be an expert on divorce? Besides, it doesn't feel like she's doing anything right, so guiding other women would be impossible. By the end of the lunch, Sarah feels even more disheartened than before. Des has the best intentions, but Sarah needs space to heal, and all of this thinking is just making her head pound. She steers the conversation toward Des and her latest karaoke adventures. Riding out the rest of the lunch, Des seems unaware of her discontent. Sarah drops her off at her house, with a kiss on the cheek and a promise that they'll get together soon.

Sarah spends her days at the shop and her evenings on the internet. She's searching for travel stories and websites, and she finds a few that would be willing to pay for her articles. Some are looking for specific places, while others are open to submissions. She fills out a few forms here and there, and at night she asks God to present her with clues and guidance, so that she can find a way to write and travel. On Thursday afternoon when she returns from the shop, she pulls the stack of mail from her mailbox and heads back inside. Closing the door with her foot while she flips through the junk, she comes across an envelope from her insurance company. Afraid of the bill that is likely enclosed, she slowly tears open the envelope and extracts the contents. Facing her is a check in the amount of three-hundred and fifty dollars, the exact amount she needs for Lori's akashic records class. The check is a dividend that usually arrives this time of year, but there's nothing usual about the amount; it's at least one-hundred dollars more than they've received in previous years. Sarah's eyes fill with tears, and she watches in amazement as the numbers and words on the check blur in her vision. "Thank you, God. Thank you!" Sarah whispers. She's overwhelmed by the feeling that she's experiencing a miracle. If she could manifest the money for this class by asking and visualizing, what else is possible? Sarah isn't sure, but she's anxious to experiment with this new found tool.

As she walks into the Metaphysical Shoppe for her first class on Friday evening, Sarah is both excited and nervous. The smell of frankincense is strong, and she prays to be successful. When she enters the back room, she finds a seat in the exact spot where she visualized herself sitting, just a week before. The lights are dim, the candles are burning, and Lori sits like a queen in the front of the room. Wearing a beautiful silk turquoise shirt, her sparkling brown eyes light up when she smiles at Sarah. The eleven other women in the class range in age from twenty-three to seventy. They spend the evening telling their stories, laughing, and getting to know each other. Lori explains exactly what will happen over the course of the weekend. In the morning they'll learn to open their own records and by the afternoon they'll begin working with each other. Class ends with a beautiful meditation involving archangels that raises their vibrations and Sarah can feel her body become lighter. After the class is over, Anna, a soft spoken and stunning Cuban woman, makes her way over to Sarah.

"I feel as if I know you, but I am sure that I don't. I hope we have the opportunity to work together this weekend," says Anna.

Sarah is surprised by the comment. The woman doesn't look familiar, but there's something about her eyes that's friendly and comforting to Sarah. After class they all hug goodbye, and Sarah heads out to her Prius, content that the evening was a success. At home, she takes a long bath and writes some things for which she is thankful in her journal. Courage ranks up at the top of her list. Sarah was never one to step outside of her comfort zone. Failure lurks there, and as a perfectionist, there's too much opportunity for things to go wrong. But, since the convent and the mission trip, Sarah is becoming convinced that it's only in this realm of discomfort where all of the magic happens. She's actually more excited than fearful now, which creates a complete shift in her thinking and influences her behavior.

On Saturday, everyone is smiling and ready to begin. Lori starts the morning with a brief meditation, and they dive right in to learn how to open the records. In order to teach the difference between using intuition and being in the records, Lori asks the class to write down what it is that they believe to be their life purpose. Sarah sits there stumped. Assuming that she will use her writing skills in the future, she writes that her purpose is to write articles that will inspire people to travel more. Then, using their names and a short prayer, Lori has the whole class open their records together. Once again, she asks about their purpose.

Sarah closes her eyes and listens. Almost immediately, she hears a voice in her head that sounds just like her own. It says, "Your purpose is to teach self-love and extend grace." Sarah opens her eyes and writes down the sentence in her notebook. *Extend grace- what does that even mean?* Grace always seems so intangible to her. "It means to recognize the divine in others and bring it to their awareness." Quickly, Sarah writes the response, so that she won't forget. How can this be her purpose? Sarah isn't even sure that she loves herself. She can't imagine how she can possibly teach others. As if on cue, Sarah suddenly feels as if she is swimming in a sea of God's love, and its comfort and peace fill her to her core. She knows that self-love will no longer be a problem for her, for in this instant she can see herself as the extension of God that she has always been. Truly created in his image and likeness, she knows herself to be perfectly divine. Sarah hears Lori's voice guiding them in the background, but she is too wrapped up in bliss to pay her any attention.

After they close the records, Lori asks if anyone wants to share. Sarah feels so humbled by her purpose that she can barely bring herself to speak it out loud. Tears flow freely down her cheeks as she reveals her experience. When she finishes, the other women are silent, and Sarah looks up at Lori.

"Wow," Lori exclaims, "isn't it great? I love the work that we do! Woo hoo! That is amazing! That's beautiful! Who's next?" The rest of the women take turns sharing their stories. Some are truly revelatory, while others are less so, but everyone can feel the divine energy of being in the records. They break off into pairs, and Sarah is sent off to the front room to exchange readings with a woman named Donna. A grandmother of five, Donna is feeling trapped. The two women sit across from each other next to the angel figurines, and Donna suggests that Sarah read first.

Sarah is so nervous! *What if this doesn't work?* Her hands shake as she holds the paper with the prayer printed on it. In the spiral notebook that rests on her lap, she writes Donna's full legal name. The moment arrives when she can no longer delay the inevitable, and she begins to read the prayer. There is a section that needs to be repeated silently, and as soon as Sarah reads the words in her mind, a physical tightening of her scalp occurs, and she imagines a pillar of light extending from the top of her head, which connects her to Source. A slight vibrational feeling convinces her that she is in Donna's records, and she looks up at her face. Where before there was a tired sixty-three year old grandmother, Sarah now sees the most beautiful soul seated before her. She marvels at the glow of Donna's skin, and the shining salt-and-pepper strands of her hair. Even more impressive than her glowing appearance, is the feeling of love that Sarah suddenly feels toward this woman whom she barely knows.

"You look so beautiful," Sarah blurts, grinning from ear to ear.

"Why, thank you," replies Donna who bashfully turns her eyes toward her lap and then back up to Sarah's face.

"So," Sarah begins, "Tell me your story. What's going on in your life?"

"Let's see. I suppose that the major thing is that I am taking care of my mother right now. Mother lives with me, and while I truly adore her, I think this has really taken a toll on me mentally. My husband died of a heart attack twelve years ago, so I am used to being on my own. When my father passed about six years back, I was renting an apartment, so that I no longer had to take care of a house. I moved in to his house because Mother couldn't be alone. It was the logical thing, since I didn't have any other responsibilities besides work. Now though, I'm tired. I would like to retire and move away from here, but it's not even an option because of my mother. She won't consider leaving her home."

Suddenly, Sarah's head is full of voices, as Donna's many spirit guides vie for her attention. "She has siblings. Tell her that she needs to have a conversation with her siblings! She needs to set a date for retirement and then tell them that she is moving to North Carolina. They will agree to take Mother." Sarah opens her eyes and looks up at Donna, afraid to say the wrong thing, and unsure if she is making it all up.

"Do you have brothers and sisters?" Sarah asks.

"Yes," replies Donna, "one brother, and two sisters."

"Okay," feeling more confident, Sarah continues, "you have done your duty for six years, and it's time for someone else to take a turn. You need to have a conversation with them, and tell them that you're retiring in March, for example, and that they will need to work it out amongst themselves, as to who will take care of your mother, because you'll be moving to North Carolina."

"My God! That's where I want to go! I have friends in North Carolina, but my mother hates the heat. I'm going to die if I have to put up with many more of these New Jersey winters. My arthritis is killing me. The thing is, my siblings are all married, and they can't just go and live with Mother."

Sarah listens, and a sudden knowing comes over her. "There comes a time in the parent-child relationship when the roles reverse. Children start to make appointments, pay bills, and do the driving, shopping, and cooking for their parents. Your mother may want to live in her own home, but when her child has been doing all of these things for the past six years, she no longer has the authority to make the final decision about that. She may not be happy about your choice, but she will have to accept it."

"But what if my brother and sisters won't take her in?" Donna asks.

"Then it would be time to discuss how you all are going to pay for assisted living, because you are moving to North Carolina."

Donna stares at Sarah, and while Sarah is tempted to speak, something tells her to hold the silence. She watches as Donna slowly registers her own power, and then begins to giggle, until she is laughing out loud.

"I'm not trapped!" she manages to squeak out between her laughter. "I'm moving to North Carolina!"

So many miracles occur in front of her eyes. The readings take her breath away in their ability to instantly comfort and heal. A woman named Carlotta opens Sarah's records, and after Sarah tells her about her irrational fear of the telephone, Carlotta immediately covers her ears and pulls away. "You were a warrior," Carlotta explains, "and there were explosions. They were so very loud." Tears are suddenly streaming down Sarah's cheeks. *Finally, someone understands me.* But, it flows even deeper than that, because finally, after years of self-condemnation, Sarah understands herself. This unexplainable fear suddenly makes complete sense to her. *I have been afraid that I wouldn't be able to hear the person on the phone!* Immediately, Sarah feels healed. To prove the truth of it, she orders lunch for all the attendees of the class, from two different restaurants, using the telephone. There is no anxiety, and no fear. Sarah experiences her own miraculous event.

During the very last pairing on Sunday, Lori assigns Sarah and Anna to work together. The reaction of joy from both women when they hear their names is palpable. Sarah doesn't know what it is, but she's certainly drawn to Anna. They choose to go upstairs in the small room with the wicker chairs where Sarah experienced her first reading. The sun is going down on that side of the building and the room is illuminated with a beautiful glow. Sarah opens Anna's records, and for the first time, instead of hearing something, she sees a small girl with dark hair and braids, crying on a brass bed. Sarah tells Anna what she sees, and Anna asks, "Why is she crying?"

Sarah asks the girl why she is crying, and an intense sadness grips Sarah's heart. Tears spring to her eyes, because the feelings are so real, and she instantly knows what is happening. "She is sad because she thinks that her mother doesn't love her. But your spirits want you to know that it's not true, Anna. Your mother was raised in a house where children were to be seen and not heard. She never received any affection, and as a result, she has no idea how to be affectionate. But you're not like that. This cycle ends with you." Immediately, Anna starts to cry.

"That's the reason I don't want kids!" she tells Sarah. "I was always so afraid that I wouldn't be able to love them. I can't believe this. I don't know how to love. I don't even know what it is!" She blows her nose and tries to get herself back together. When she finally opens Sarah's records, Anna says, "Oh! Someone is here with us! It's a man, with a mustache and a square face." Anna makes the motions around her chin with her hands, trying to paint a picture for Sarah of the man only she can see in her mind. "He is right here," she says, holding her hand above the front, right side of her head, "and he is so nice."

"Is it my Poppy?" Sarah asks. Her maternal grandfather died when she was only nine, but they were close, and his German face fits Anna's description perfectly.

"Yes!" exclaims Anna. "He is so happy to see you! He is smiling."

In her mind, Sarah speaks to him, *I love you, Poppy. Give her some love.* Just then Anna lifts her hand to her own cheek and brushes it with her knuckles, twice. "He's doing this," she says with her eyes closed, "It feels nice."

Sarah smiles. "I told him to give you some love."

Anna's eyes fly open, "I feel it! Oh my God, I really feel it." She closes her eyes again and basks in the shower of love. "It's amazing." Watching this experience fills Sarah with such wonder for this work. It's so humbling to see what spirit can do when it is allowed to enter.

After they finish, Lori comes in to ask how everything is going. When they give her a brief synopsis, Lori says, "You girls should open your records together and see what happens." Lori remains, and the two women go through the process of opening their records at the same time.

Immediately, Sarah sees the view out of the window, of what she knows is her house in a past life. There are children outside playing, and some of them are hers, while the others live next door. Just then, a woman comes around the front of the next house with a laundry basket on her hip. She doesn't look like Anna, but Sarah knows that it is her soul. Just then, Anna says, "We were neighbors!"

"Yes," says Sarah, "I see it! You had kids, Anna!"

"I did? Oh my God, I had kids!" Anna is so happy. The two women hold hands, and Lori suggests that they ask why they are together in this lifetime.

"To help Sarah," says Anna.

At the same time, Sarah says, "Because I have a hole in my heart." Sarah knows that her old friend has returned to fill that emptiness, so that Sarah will never feel alone again. The two women embrace, and Sarah says, "This is so strange! I feel as though I have known you forever!"

"I know," answers Anna, still wrapped in Sarah's arms, "it seems that we have! Whatever is happening here, I'm just so glad that we have found each other."

That night in bed, Sarah's mind will not stop spinning. Deciding that sleep is futile, she crawls out of bed and returns with the records prayer. Opening her own records, she lays in the silence and imagines her angels and spirit guides surrounding her. It feels so peaceful and relaxing, and just as she thinks she might drift off to sleep, she hears very clearly, "Book the trip to Machu Picchu." *What? What trip?* "Book the trip to Machu Picchu." After that, she hears only the sound of her breathing. Giving up, she closes her records, writes the statement in her red notebook, and falls asleep.

Even though Sarah loves her job at the Metaphysical Shoppe, Monday morning still feels like a Monday. Dragging herself from a sweet sleep, she shuts the alarm, throws her feet over the edge of the bed, and slides into her old fuzzy slippers. Sarah feeds Click, lets him outside, and then carries her steaming cup of jasmine tea to the computer to check her email while it cools. Jeff has installed a spam filter on her laptop, but now and then a stray email will come through promoting male enhancement drugs or other nonsense. She hesitates a moment before she clicks on the email from Travel Systems, but decides to go for it, since it contains the word travel. It must be one of the companies whose form she's completed, for it claims to be looking for female travel writers who are willing to contribute information pertaining to food, lodging, spirituality, or eco-tourism in Machu Picchu.

"What?" Sarah shouts. "No flipping way!" Jumping from her chair, she spins around with her hands on her head. She reads the email again, just to be sure. "You are not kidding me! Machu Picchu! This is insane." Her mind is racing. How can she get the money? She can charge it. She will charge it. Somehow, she is going to Machu Picchu. Clearly, she believes, this is supposed to happen.

At work that morning, Sarah tells Alice about Machu Picchu, from her message in the records to the email and its details. "I'm going, Alice. When I get home, I'm going to start investigating flights and hotels. Should I write about food or spirituality? Both seem so exciting to me."

"Why don't you wait until you get there and see what moves you? You can write about both, and maybe they'll pay you more!" she suggests as she walks toward the door to leave.

"What a good idea!" All day, Sarah seems to be floating. She dusts and sweeps, while the sounds of the wind chimes and harp music fill her with peace. Her new sense of direction and adventure sparks a renewed interest in life, and in turn, she finds herself more interested in every customer that walks through the door of the shop. A few of the regulars are beginning to recognize her, and she's beginning to get a feel for the products and the routine. Everything seems to be falling into place. When the door opens at one-fifteen, she turns from straightening the essential oils, and with sincere interest and joy says, "Hi! How are you today?" Then, she stops dead in her tracks.

"Hey, I know you!" The man responds to her initial happiness with a joy of his own. "I am just fantastic, how are you?"

Sarah can't believe it's him! She's so nervous that she can barely speak. This is the same man that she had bumped into a few weeks ago on the way to her dinner with Des. He looks incredibly hot in his jeans and loafers, with a navy sport jacket and crisp white shirt. It's unbuttoned at the top, and his hair is slightly ruffled from the wind, unless he styles it like that on purpose. Either way, it's a good look. She wonders what might bring him into the Metaphysical Shoppe. "I'm great, thanks for asking. Can I help you find something?"

"Maybe," he replies. "How is your arm?"

"My arm?" she asks.

"Yes, the one I almost knocked off when we passed on the street." Sarah looks down at her left arm.

"Oh, it's fine," she smiles. "No worries."

"I'm glad." His grin shows his beautiful, straight, white teeth. "What's your name?"

"Sarah," she manages to say. Again, he flashes that smile.

"Sarah, it's nice to meet you. I'm Trent Alexander. Do you mind if I take a minute of your time?"

"No, I'm here until two." *You can take as many minutes as you would like!* Sarah walks behind the jewelry counter and leans on it, facing Trent. He places a portfolio that he's carrying on the counter and pulls out a sheet of paper, placing it between them.

"I am wondering if you might be willing to hang a flyer in here?" he asks. Sarah looks down at the paper. She doesn't know what it says, but two words at the top stand out in bold print. *Machu Picchu.*

"What is this?" she asks. Her eyes scan the page as quickly as possible. *Is this really happening? How can this possibly be happening like this?* Sarah's whole body is buzzing with energy, and she strains to focus as Trent begins to explain.

"It's a trip to Machu Picchu next month. I'm a travel guide, and I run tours like this all over the world. There are still a few spaces open on this one, and well, since it has a spiritual bend to it, I thought that some of your clientele might be interested. We'll be meeting with a local shaman there and experiencing a few ayahuasca ceremonies. I've never run it before, but people seem very interested."

"I'll go," Sarah blurts out. "I'm in."

"Are you serious? That's fantastic!"

"I know!" Sarah claps her hands together. "You have no idea how fantastic this is!"

"So, tell me, please." Trent stares at her with such kind eyes. She wants to tell him everything, but he'll certainly think she's crazy.

"I don't even know where to start. This is such synchronicity!"

"How about the beginning," he suggests.

"I'm afraid that might take a while," she laughs. He watches her with an amused expression on his face. Years of trying to meet women in bars have him feeling impressed by her gentle kindness and natural look. She's so unassuming, and he wants to know more.

"I've got plenty of time, and you've got until two. So, please, go ahead and tell me about this synchronicity."

Sarah evaluates his request. He seems sincere, so she decides to go for it. She tells him everything; Jeff, the bet with Des, her trips to the convent and the mission, her struggle to find a career niche, all the way through to her opportunity to write about Machu Picchu.

Trent listens to every word, and he likes her all the more for it. She's brave, and she trusts her gut. He admires that.

"Well then, I guess you're in! I can't wait. I think this is going to be an important trip, for both of us."

"I know, I'm feeling very blessed today," says Sarah, as she stares into his beautiful eyes.

"I look forward to seeing you again," his voice is smooth, and rich. He reaches across the counter to shake her hand, and when Sarah places her hand in his, he doesn't let go. Her energy is just what he needs, and he wants to hold on to it.

"Me, too," Sarah whispers, not wanting to let go. They stand there like that for a few moments longer, and when he releases her hand it pulls at something deep in her heart.

At two o'clock, Alice flies in through the kitchen door. "I'm so sorry I'm late, Sarah, the traffic on Tilghman Street is a mess. Are you okay? I'm not keeping you from something, am I?"

"No, Alice, it's fine! It's only just two o'clock now. You know I don't have anywhere to go. Oh, Alice, you are never going to believe what happened today! I still can't believe it myself. I'm going to Machu Picchu in three weeks, isn't it a miracle?" Sarah is talking so fast that Alice just stands there staring at her, bags dangling on her arms and her mouth hanging open.

"What? When did this happen? I've only been gone for a couple of hours..." Alice looks behind her at the door, clearly confused.

"Look!" Sarah picks up the flyer and thrusts it at her friend. Alice reads the page and looks up at Sarah.

"I don't understand. Where did you get this?" she asks.

"It came to me!" exclaims Sarah. "Isn't it incredible?"

Alice places her bags on the table. She pours some iced-tea for the both of them, takes a long drink and waves her hand to indicate that Sarah should take the seat across from her. "Okay, I see that you're excited. Now, can you please slow down for one minute, and tell me exactly where you found this flyer?"

Sarah laughs. Of course Alice is confused. Sarah is confused herself, and she had seen the whole thing happen! Slowly, starting with the day on the sidewalk, Sarah relays the scenario to Alice. Lucidity floods the older woman's face, and she brings her hands up to her heart. No matter how many times Alice has seen synchronicity at work, it never ceases to amaze her. When you lay out your plan to the universe, it will get to work to make it happen for you. Alice knows this. Through the death of her husband and all of the loss that she's experienced in her life, Alice has discovered the secret. Tell God that you are willing to do his work here on earth, and ask him to guide you. Do those things that appeal to you and avoid the things that don't. Help, love, and forgive others. Be grateful for all that you have been blessed with, and place your efforts into learning those things that you enjoy. Flow past the obstacles like a leaf on a river. Be flexible and willing to change directions if you must. Opportunity will present itself at every turn, and happiness will be yours all the days of your life.

The drive home is a blur. Sarah's mind races, and the fear of using her credit card to fund this trip begins to build inside of her. Her mother may be crazy, but she taught Sarah good money management skills. For years, Louise had to work two jobs to dig herself out of credit card debt after raising Sarah on her own. She always stressed to Sarah that credit cards are only for emergencies, and Sarah can hear her words playing over and over in her mind. Sarah knows that she must go on this trip, though, and the credit card is the only viable option. She justifies it by reminding herself that eventually she'll be paid for her articles, and in turn, will pay off the debt. Sarah parks the car in the garage and walks out to the mailbox. Inside, is a large white envelope from the office of Feinstein and Feinstein. Cautiously, Sarah slides her thumb under the flap at the top of the envelope, pulls out the contents and begins to read the cover letter:

Dear Ms. Jackson,

Enclosed, please find a copy of your divorce settlement, signed by Mr. Jackson. You will find that the settlement terms exceed our initial expectations, as we did not take into account your half of Mr. Jackson's accrued retirement fund.

Please read the document carefully, and call our office if you have any questions. Otherwise, please sign the highlighted areas, and return the entire document in the enclosed envelope. Upon receipt, a copy will be mailed to you for official use.

Thank you for choosing Feinstein and Feinstein. If I can be of further assistance, please do not hesitate to contact me.

Sincerely,

Lauren Zator, Esq.

Sarah hugs the envelope to her chest. Right there, in the middle of Mapleshade Drive, she spins around in circles clasping the envelope, her head tilted back, her eyes marveling at the beautiful blue sky, dotted with fluffy, white, cumulus clouds. With tears on her cheeks, a smile on her face, and a love in her heart that rivals any she has yet to experience, Sarah whispers, "Thank you, God."

Acknowledgments

THIS NOVEL HAS BEEN AN incredible journey. Sarah Starts Living began as a 50,000 word challenge during National Novel Writing Month, in November of 2013. The fact that it has turned into a real book, is nothing short of a miracle to me. I extend my sincere thanks to the people of NaNoWriMo.org for the inspiration and motivation. Winner!

I wish to thank the School Sisters of Notre Dame for the incredible family that they provided for my Aunt Doretta during her years in Baltimore and Wilton. I sincerely apologize if, in fictionalizing convent life, I have offended in any way. I have nothing but the deepest love, respect, and gratitude for all of you.

I need to thank the following people, without whom I could not have written this book: My cousin Maria Curlej for her insight into mission life; Denise Martindell and Barbara Berger, for their editing assistance and support; Gail Ginda, my mother, and the only person I trusted to read this as it was being written; my cheerleading squad, including Liz, Sister, Sharon, Louise, Tara, Beth, Carrie, Lori and Anna; and my wonderful family, Paul, Morgan, and Josh, who lived without a wife and mother so that Sarah could start living.

I offer my utmost gratitude to Archangels Gabriel and Raphael, who promised to help me write this book. Most of all, I thank God for my clarity of purpose; to teach self-love and extend grace. I see the divinity in all of you, and I hope that this book helps bring it to your awareness. I extend my deepest love and thanks to all of you. My wish for every one of you is that you may experience God for yourself. Bless you all, and please join the discussion on Facebook at Sarah Starts Living.

Book Club Questions

1. Do you believe in signs from God or Angels? Have you ever received one?
2. Who was your favorite character and why?
3. How much compassion, if any, do you have for Jeff?
4. Do you think Des is a good friend? Why? How do you feel about Sarah's reaction to Des' lack of support? Do you think Sarah and Des will remain friends?
5. Staying at the convent and going on the mission were outside of Sarah's comfort zone. What would you like to do that makes you uncomfortable?
6. Did Sarah do the right thing speaking up about Joseph's behavior? Would you have done it?
7. Aggie Ritter's mother would ask her if she has loved enough. In your own life, what are some ways that you could love more?

8. By the end of the book, Sarah absolutely believes that the messages about Machu Picchu are meant for her. Has she become better at picking up the signs? Do you believe this is something that can improve with practice?

9. Would you be willing to listen to God and do what he tells you, even if it makes you uncomfortable?

10. Do you think it's possible to have your own experience of God in this day and age, or are those things reserved for stories in holy texts?

22977243R00244

Made in the USA
Middletown, DE
13 August 2015